"Who's after you, Bella?"

Her breath caught tightly in her chest as she stared into his midnight-dark eyes. This was ridiculous. She had every right to be scared—but not to be attracted to this man called Malone. Why did he have to be so damn appealing? "I don't know," she maintained. "And even if I did, it wouldn't be any of your business."

Reaching out, he caressed her cheek with his fingertips, sending shivers through her. "Oh, but it is," he said softly, gazing into her eyes. "Either you tell me the truth here and now, or I'll take you back to the people who kidnapped you."

He wouldn't, she thought, then looked at him again and sighed. He would. Malone was not a man to make idle threats. "Oh, all right. I'll tell you the truth. I'm not a hardened criminal. I just have a problem with the first nine years of my life."

An uncomprehending ridge formed between Malone's black eyebrows. "What kind of problem?"

She looked him straight in the eye. "I don't remember them."

Dear Reader,

When a woman's alone, who can she trust, where can she run...? Straight into the arms of HER PROTECTOR. Because when danger lurks around every corner, there's only one place you're safe—in the strong, sheltering arms of the man who loves you.

In this exciting promotion, you'll meet women in jeopardy and in love—with the only person who can keep them safe.

Jenna Ryan brings you the story of Bella Conlan, a woman with a past that she can't remember but that is coming back to haunt her. After careers in modeling and the travel industry, Jenna is now a full-time novelist who makes her home in British Columbia.

Look for all the books in the HER PROTECTOR series!

Regards,

Debra Matteucci
Senior Editor & Editorial Coordinator
Harlequin Books
300 East 42nd Street
New York, NY 10017

Belladonna

Jenna Ryan

Harlequin Books

TORONTO • NEW YORK • LONDON
AMSTERDAM • PARIS • SYDNEY • HAMBURG
STOCKHOLM • ATHENS • TOKYO • MILAN
MADRID • WARSAW • BUDAPEST • AUCKLAND

To Kathy for putting up with me.
To Mom and Dad for putting up with us.
To Shauna for thirteen years of being an atypical cat.

ISBN 0-373-22364-1

BELLADONNA

Copyright © 1996 by Jacqueline Goff

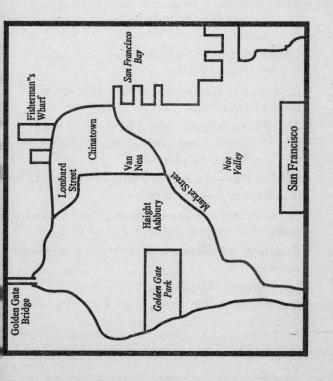

CAST OF CHARACTERS

Belladonna Conlan—Childhood amnesia has rendered the first nine years of her life a blank.

Sean Andrew Malone—A finder of missing persons, he finds Belladonna—for money—then rescues her.

Larsen Rudge—A bounty hunter who values money above all else.

Mick Tock—A hired henchman with more brawn than brains.

Charmaine—Cool, calm and elegant; she is one of the notorious Birds of San Francisco—and she knows Belladonna.

Madame X—The mystery Bird whose main goal is to destroy Belladonna.

Hobson Crowe—The enigmatic third Bird who seems well acquainted with Belladonna.

Ronnie MacMalkin—Malone's quirky Scottish cousin.

Lona Conlan—Posing as Belladonna's grandmother, she knows more than she is telling.

Prologue

"Lona, please, you have to help me."

The woman's voice on the Alaska phone line crackled. Yet even accounting for that, Lona Conlan was certain she didn't recognize the caller. "Who is this?" she demanded. Clamping one sturdy hand over the end of her long gray plait, she tightened the other on the receiver. "Do you realize that it's the middle of the night?"

"Yes, yes, I know." The woman's tone verged on desperation. "I've been driving forever, all the way from Seattle in a malfunctioning Subaru. Before that it was buses, trains and planes, even a boat. We sailed from Dover to—" The line snapped, causing Lona to pull the earpiece away. "I had to escape somehow, some way. Any way. Please, Lona, there's no one else I can turn to."

"Who are you?" Lona repeated, unmoved.

"Amanda." The woman had to shout above the rising static. "I'm Geraldine Johnson's daughter. You must remember Geraldine."

Geraldine Johnson. Of course. Amanda was her only child. Why, Lona hadn't seen Geraldine for thirty years or more, about ten years before she'd died. But she did remember her, and fondly so. Lona's manner softened instantly. "What is it, my dear? What has you so frightened?"

"I can hardly hear you," Amanda shouted. "Oh, Lona, please, you have to help me help my little girl. There was trouble.... I couldn't get ... out. I'm sure we were seen....

They'll be after us by now. But I have to try, have to be smart.... It's too important. I can't leave—"

Confused, Lona interrupted her. "Can't leave what? Who'll be after you? Amanda? Amanda!"

"Knows I ran...took Bella... Couldn't get... No time...completely single-minded, Lona...and evil."

Although she strained to hear, Lona caught only snatches of Amanda's sentences. Something about her child and someone pursuing them—a husband, perhaps.

Wind whipped December snowflakes around the window, the Christmas window that Lona lit day and night for the twelve days of Christmas, a tradition started by her Norwegian grandmother. "Can you come to me?" she asked in her soft Nordic accent. "Can you get here from where you are?"

"I think so." Amanda's voice faded. "I'll come tonight, or try... Have to get Bella to safety, before I..."

"Before you what?"

But Amanda's answer, if indeed she offered one, was swallowed up in a loud burst of static.

Wind rattled the panes of Lona's large home, as if mocking the circumstances under which she had chosen to live.

"I burned our papers." Amanda was yelling now. "No identification...too dangerous...hope you'll recognize me. I've no proof."

"I'm sure I'll recognize you well enough," Lona answered. Running a capable hand around the back of her neck, she massaged a rheumatic kink. "You and young Bella come to me. We'll talk then."

Amanda protested, "No time...so powerful.... Please take care of Bella."

"Who is this person after you?" Lona demanded.

A sob reached her ears, surprisingly clear over the crackling line. "Not a person anymore, Lona, a monster... wants to control everyone. Gave a poisoned nickname to my ba... Like Romaine, only worse. Deadly nightshade, a deadly poisonous flower. I should have seen it, should have realized the truth behind Romaine. Deadly nightshade. Oh God, it is, it's just like Romaine...."

A series of pops came on the line. Just like Romaine? Deadly nightshade? What did she mean? Lona compressed her lips. She would wait for Amanda to arrive with her daughter, Bella. Then the story would come out.

"I'll be here, Amanda," she promised. "You'll need chains for the roads and a good four-wheel-drive vehicle. Do you have these things? Amanda? Can you hear me?"

But although she repeated herself three times, she heard nothing except the brittle sound of static on the line and the taunting howl of winter wind about the windowpanes.

Resting the phone against her shoulder, Lona moved her eyes to the frosted glass. Snowflakes bobbed like Russian dancers about the Christmas lights, then swirled off into the darkness. A treacherous winter darkness through which a distraught young woman and her daughter would soon be traveling. With what tale to tell? Lona wondered, and what form of danger following in their wake?

A chill feathered along her spine as the old woman settled herself on the pink-and-black-flowered sofa. Pulling her rose-patterned shawl tight, she watched the snow with wary eyes and waited.

"YOUR GRANDDAUGHTER? Hell on wheels, you sure about that, Lona?" The sheriff scratched his grizzled head. "You ain't even seen the girl yet. Or the accident scene, either, for that matter. Come to think of it, how'd you hear about this mess? Power's out all over town." When she didn't reply, he grunted. "She's cute, you know. Pretty and quiet. Maybe eight, nine years old. Hasn't said two words since Daly found her huddled next to that snowdrift. Old Polly reckons she has amnesia." He pronounced the last two letters separately. "Don't know how she got out of the car before it went over, but it's a good thing she did. Can you imagine anyone stupid enough to drive a junker Subaru with bald tires on these roads? It was her mother driving, you say? Well, so far we can't find hide nor hair of her. Saw a dead raven, of all things, near the cliff, but so far no mother."

Lona held tight to her composure. "May I please see Bella, Win?"

"That her name? What is she, Italian?"

"She's my granddaughter," Lona lied again. "Bella's father died when she was born. My daughter, A—" She started to say Amanda, checked herself and substituted firmly, "My daughter was bringing her to live with me."

"Is that so?" The sheriff nodded. "Funny you never mentioned having a daughter before."

Lona forced a smile, gathering her cabbage-rose shawl tighter. "I haven't mentioned many things, Win. May I see the girl now? Alone," she added, when he would have accompanied her to the back room.

"Well . . ."

"Please." She laid a beseeching hand on his arm. "If it's as you say, she'll be terribly frightened."

The sheriff hesitated, then nodded in agreement. Lona gave a nod of her own and started for the rear of the jail, where apparently the little girl had spent the night with old Polly, the retired nurse who'd spotted her next to that snowdrift. With the roads so bad she hadn't been able to make it home.

Giving the door a firm thrust, Lona entered the room. It smelled faintly of wood smoke and was lit with four fat red candles that had been placed in a green bowl. The girl sat in a stuffed chair between wood stove and bowl. Old Polly was gone; the girl was alone. Alone and staring unblinking at Lona.

She was pretty indeed, Lona acknowledged, summoning an encouraging smile. Quite beautiful, really. Fine featured and delicate looking, but no doubt as wiry as a Gumby doll. Her eyes were very large, very dark and highly mistrustful. Her small chin was thrust out at a determined angle. Lona would have called it a defiant angle had it not been for the telltale quiver of her lower lip.

She greeted the girl with a blend of compassion and brisk efficiency. "Hello, Bella. I'm your grandmother, Lona. Your mother was bringing you to me. Do you remember that?"

The girl stared intently for several seconds, then slowly shook her head.

Relief coursed through Lona's body. She stepped closer, one sturdy hand extended, palm up. "You must trust me, Bella," she said. "You must let me help you, yes?"

It might have been her face—she'd been told she resembled an old-style European grandmother—or merely the absolute conviction in her tone. Whatever the case, the child responded. Tentatively at first, she inched slowly forward in her seat.

"Come to me, Bella," Lona coaxed. "I will tell you the story of your life as only I know it."

An ironic statement, given the circumstances, but Lona didn't think that was what made the little girl suddenly stop moving. Her dark eyes lit up, looked away, then returned to Lona's face. "Bella," she said carefully. She had a slight English accent. "Bella—donna. Belladonna!"

Amanda's words roared back into Lona's mind. "A poisoned nickname," she'd said. "Deadly nightshade—just like Romaine."

At the little girl's uncomprehending look, Lona gave an emphatic nod. "Belladonna Conlan, that's your name. But I will call you Bella. There will be no poison in your life, child, as long as I am a part of it."

Chapter One

"G'night, Bella. Happy New Year." Irish Max, the theater prop man, nudged open the rear door and treated her to a toothy smile. "Accept an old codger's advice, my girl, and take a stab at acting. You'd make a dandy Nancy."

He was talking about the Market Street Playhouse's current production of *Oliver*, a musical based on the Dickens classic.

Hoisting her leather backpack over one shoulder, Bella grinned at the podgy, white-haired man she'd known for more than fifteen of her thirty years. "I can't sing, Max. Besides, my knees turn to rubber in front of a live audience."

"That is a problem, all right," he agreed. "So you do makeup for bad actors instead."

"I consider it an art."

Irish Max gave a disbelieving snort. "Temporary art," he said in his heavy brogue. "All your hard work gets washed into the bay at the end of every performance."

"I can handle that." Bella propped the door open with her foot. "Happy New Year, Max. And no trying to sell fake stocks to that nice Nob Hill lady who praised your props tonight, okay?"

He chuckled. "You shoulda been a cop, Bella girl. Or better yet, a crook. You can pick a pocket better than anyone I'm acquainted with. And we both know you didn't learn that little trick from Lona."

"Hah, you make me sound like a professional thief."
Bella poked his stout chest with one finger. "I only did it
once, Max, and then only to save your slippery hide. Next
time you decide to pass counterfeit bills, don't do it to the
theater's prime investor." Grinning, she gave him a peck on
the cheek. "I have to go. I'm spending my week off in Bodega Bay. I'll say hi to Lona for you." She arched a wry
brow. "I'll tell her you've gone straight."

"You do that, and she'll laugh in your face. We go way
back, your grandma and me. With a few gaps, of course."

Just like herself, Bella reflected. Except that her "gap"
embraced the first nine years of her life. That, however, was
a problem she preferred not to dwell on. "I'll tell her you
went half-straight. Night, Max. See you after the New
Year."

"Watch out for Hitchcock's Birds," he warned in parting.

Bella surveyed the alley as the door clicked shut behind
her. A blanket of fog from the bay enfolded her like mummy
cloth. She shivered, though not with fear so much as antic-
ipation, because as far back as she could remember, she'd
loved being frightened. Lona called it a quirk; Bella called
it a fascination. She considered Alfred Hitchcock, Edgar
Allan Poe and Mary Shelley to be geniuses. What a talent
they had possessed, to inspire fear in a seamless and spell-
binding fashion. Violence of the mind was Bella's prefer-
ence. Only the reality of the streets had the power to unnerve
her... and sometimes late at night, the blank pages of her
past.

Freeing her long dark hair from the collar of her gray-
green raincoat, she turned in the direction of her car. Theatre Lane ran between the Playhouse and Straw Hat the-
aters. Usually a well-lit alley, tonight it had all the earmarks
of the *Twilight Zone,* right down to the indistinct murmur
of voices ahead of her.

Bella listened. Probably a couple of actors, she decided.

Probing the fog with her eyes, she located the source of
the muted voices—two men. A stocky blonde was handing
an envelope to his taller, dark-haired companion.

Whatever the exchange entailed, Bella knew better than to interrupt it. With a stealth she credited to Irish Max, she slipped past the fog-shrouded men to continue on her way.

She'd almost made it to Market Street when the sound of measured footsteps reached her ears. Squishy steps, like sneakers on wet pavement.

Were they coming toward her? With all the murkiness and fog in the alley, Bella couldn't tell.

One thing was certain, though. Lona would sharpen her tongue on her for walking alone in San Francisco after dark.

Bella glanced into the gloom. A chill feathered along her spine, but she ignored it in favor of pinpointing the direction of the sound. Behind her, definitely.

Her heart knocked against her ribs. It must be one of the men she'd glimpsed earlier. Had she witnessed an illicit deal in the works? If so, had the men spotted her?

The shadow materialized before Bella could turn her head again. She saw a gloved hand, a handkerchief, then smelled an odor so potent it made her senses spin. Although she struggled to overcome it, the drug flowed into her mind and lungs as surely as if she'd been pricked by a needle.

"That's it, sweetheart," a gravelly voice said in her ear. The speaker sounded smug. Bella hated smugness. His tone, more than his actions, impelled her to fight harder. But only for a moment and only to the point where she was able to wrench her mouth free and twist her head around far enough to glimpse her attacker's face.

He had short blond hair and strong, broad features. He looked tough and unrelenting despite the smirk that lingered on his lips. "Relax, baby," he crooned. "Make it easy on yourself."

"No..." Bella's protest echoed along the alley. She knew her elbow made contact with the man's ribs when she heard his surprised "Oomph" of pain. However, all that her struggles earned her was a none-too-gentle sideways jerk and a gruff, "Toss her in the back and let's get the hell out of here."

Her body drooped, then seemed to float upward. A large hand caught her hair, yanking it until her eyelids fluttered.

The blonde's broad, wolflike features swam into fuzzy focus.

"Beauty and the beast, my ass. This beauty's a bitch on the outside. The beast's the beauty that pays. You're gonna net me a bundle, baby."

Although she wanted to scream, Bella's throat muscles refused to cooperate, just like the time when she'd been . . . She searched her mind. When she'd been what?

An image started to form, but dissolved before she could grasp it. She was falling through an void, like Alice toppling into the looking glass. She landed with a thump on a hard surface. She sensed motion and heard indefinite noises. Then her eyes closed. . .and the world and the night and the fog went black.

"No . . ."

The feeble protest filtered through the fog, causing Sean Andrew Malone's head to come up as he made his way toward his car. His expression characteristically somber, he glanced down the narrow alley. From the bay, a foghorn moaned. Above that rose the sound of late-night traffic on Market Street. The air smelled of Chinese take-out food and seawater. Must have been a bird, he decided.

He was turning for his car again when a familiar sound reached his ears—Larson Rudge muttering. Malone frowned. That bloodsucker had better not be harming the woman that Malone had so diligently tracked down for him.

"Find her," Rudge had said bluntly three weeks ago, tossing a photograph across the table in the Fisherman's Wharf Café.

"She's pretty," Malone had noted. It made no difference to him, but truth was truth, and the woman was a beauty— a fair-skinned Gypsy, by the look of her.

Rudge's teeth had flashed. "Yeah, real pretty." At Malone's narrowed eyes, he'd grunted. "Knock if off, will you? You're no saint. You're in this for the money. No one's gonna hurt her. I do what I'm paid to do, but I draw the line at murder."

"So what's the deal then?"

"No deal. Just find her, Malone. That's your line of work these days—tracking down missing persons. Healthier than making book in London, I suppose, but nowhere near as profitable, right?"

Although Malone had been tempted to knock a few yellowed teeth down Rudge's German throat, he'd merely returned the man's cocksure gaze with a steady one of his own. "What do you want with her?" he'd demanded.

Rudge's expression had turned insolent. Leaning across the table, he'd drawled, "She's my sister, okay?" At Malone's unamused expression, he'd backed off. "Look, she won't be hurt. That's what I was told, and it's what I'm telling you."

Malone had thought about it. "Is it a family problem?"

"That'd be my guess. I don't get told squat." Rudge had then dipped his hand into the right side of his jacket. "Find her, call me and I'll deal you another one of these. Double the amount on exchange." An envelope had landed with a plop beside the catsup.

Malone hadn't counted the bills. He knew Rudge's type. Bounty hunters wanted no quarrel with anyone. Get In, Get Paid, Get Out was their motto.

So what the hell was Rudge doing if not roughing up his prey? Malone wondered now in irritation. Never trust a greedy bounty hunter.

Cursing his stupidity, he flipped up the collar of his raincoat, pocketed his keys and started silently down the lane. The muffled "Oomph" that reached him had to have come from Rudge's throat—which must mean that the woman, Bella, was a fighter. Well, he'd figured she might be, given her colorful collection of friends.

Pickpockets, counterfeiters, poets, painters and privateers—the people Bella Conlan knew ran a wide gamut. She had an intriguing grandmother, too. Straight as an arrow on the surface, she'd been married to an Irish hooligan named Casey Conlan, who'd fled to Alaska after blowing a plan to con a trio of big-business baddies into purchasing an innovative—and totally useless—computer system.

"Bitch," he heard Rudge grunt. The fog parted slightly. Through the wisps and whorls, Malone's sharp eyes picked out another person, a short bald man with a paunch and a chain-link earring. When the man pushed Bella Conlan into Rudge's dirty green Chevrolet, Malone's muscles tensed.

"Tie her up?" the fat man inquired. He sounded Greek.

Rudge took a few considering puffs on his cigar. "Yeah, let's be safe. She's worth a bundle, and I don't intend to lose her because she has a high tolerance for chloroform."

Malone paused, telling himself he shouldn't care. He'd found the woman and been paid for his efforts. Rudge wasn't likely to kill her. The man might be many things, but a murderer didn't number among them. His bounties were invariably delivered alive.

On the other hand, "near dead" was technically alive. So were "badly bruised" and "manhandled." *Damn*, Malone thought with a resigned sigh. He should have followed his instincts and tossed this job back in Rudge's smirking face.

Malone surveyed the alley. It wound down to a dead end. Rudge and his fat friend would have to pass him in order to get out. Which meant that he could leave ahead of them, wait in his own car and follow them—wherever.

Closing his eyes, he massaged his temples with the thumb and middle finger of his right hand. He really didn't need to get involved in Rudge's affairs. Bella Conlan was a name to him, nothing more. A name and a face in a fuzzy photograph. And Rudge had coughed up the full price for Malone's services.

"Ankles, too?" the fat man asked.

"Yeah, and gag her while you're at it."

Malone opened his eyes. Why couldn't his mother have been born half-English like his father? True Irish meant a person had too many scruples intertwined with too many passionate emotions and far too little control over the resulting hodgepodge.

Tempering his annoyance at Rudge's duplicity, Malone let his hand drop and turned for Market Street, wondering as he did if passion and temper were qualities that could be exorcised.

BELLA AWOKE SLOWLY, as if she were swimming upward out of a muddy black pool. "Mother," she heard herself mumble. "Where are you, Mother? Mo—" Something in her mind snapped and she shot to a sitting position. "Where am I?"

But she wasn't entirely alert, and she couldn't see a thing.... Well, nothing except a tiny point—no, two, three points of light. What was that?

Pressing the fingers of both hands to her temples, Bella stared until the flickering points resolved themselves into a meager fire.

Conscious of her throbbing head and the fear in her chest, she peered into the gloom. Wherever she was, it smelled stale and musty, unused. She supposed it might be a sofa under her, but it felt dangerously close to a mortician's slab.

"Welcome back, sweetheart," a lewd voice drawled. A match flared, and in that illuminated instant Bella spied the blond man from Theatre Lane. Outrage momentarily overrode terror.

"You!" she exclaimed accusingly. "You grabbed me in the alley."

Clamping his teeth around a cigar, the man smiled, a crude, arrogant smile. "That I did."

"Why?"

His smile widened as he rubbed his thumb and finger together.

Whatever response Bella had been anticipating—and she wasn't sure what that might have been—money had no part in it. Oblivious to the icy tendrils of fear gripping her muscles, she ventured confusedly, "But why kidnap me? Lona has no money, and neither do I."

The man laughed. "You're not being held for ransom, baby."

The lump climbed higher in Bella's throat. "What then?"

"Bounty." At her uncomprehending stare, he chuckled. "You heard right. Someone wanted you, and I found you. Well—" he blew a fat smoke ring "—truth be told, I didn't actually do the finding. I paid Malone to do it."

Into Bella's mind flashed a picture of a lean man with dark, curling hair and vaguely attractive features. Better looking than the person seated next to the fire, but obviously just as big a rat.

"Malone's a people finder," the blonde elaborated. He flicked an ash from the end of his cigar with his thumbnail. Something about the carelessness of the gesture sent a chill across Bella's skin. The man's eyes shot up suddenly, his face crinkling in a humorless smile. "Malone used to be a crook," he revealed. "A bookie. Sharp as a tack, they say, but not so sharp that I couldn't outwit him. Oh, he plays the reformed cynic, but five'll get you ten if he'd known about the price on your head, he'd have said, 'Ta-ra, chump,' to me and turned you in for the cash himself."

"Charming." Bella's voice came out vaguely strangled.

Her mind, as it tended to under adverse conditions, resisted the reality of this situation. But it *was* happening; she had to accept it and respond accordingly. Lona had taught her that. Life's problems must be faced, dealt with; then ultimately set aside to make room for more. A gloomy thought, but Bella knew what Lona meant. Excluding the first years of her life, which her stubborn will either could not or would not return to her, she had done her best to follow her grandmother's advice.

"Oh, Malone can be charming, all right," the man was saying now. "Charming like a snake. It's just a good thing I never gave him the chance to welsh on our deal." He tapped his temple. "I kept the upper hand, so to speak. I'm in with Romaine—he only knew Rudge."

As if cued, a fat bald man with a clinking earring shoved open the door. "Hey, Rudge, Parret says shut up and get your butt out here."

The man called Rudge made no move to go. "I'll leave when I get my money," he said around his cigar.

"A wise precaution, but you'll have to come out in order to receive that money," remarked another male voice, a cultured one this time. This third man might hail from England, but he'd left a long time ago.

Bella probed the shadows of the doorway, but saw no one. Only her surroundings registered, stark and Spartanly furnished, like Scrooge's house the night Marley's ghost had visited.

Why was she thinking about that? She squeezed her hands into fists. Because Christmas was over, New Year's Eve was coming and she couldn't seem to control her thoughts, that's why. The fog beyond the windows must be slithering into her brain.

A frightened sob rose inside her, but she pressed her lips together and wouldn't let it escape. Men like Rudge fed on fear. And pain. Oh, God, yes, pain so strong it was creating black spots in front of her eyes. Her head pounded and her neck muscles felt like she'd suffered whiplash. Her captors had untied her, but what good would that do when she couldn't even see straight? Maybe she should take a nap and think about her predicament some more later....

The room spun in increasingly large circles. A sitting room, Lona would call it. They had rooms like this in English houses, didn't they? How did she know that? Silly question. She'd traveled to England several times in her life; three times as a child with Lona, once when she was in college and twice more after that.

Yet something about this particular room struck her as vaguely familiar. Possibly the fireplace. Big hearth, small fire—yes, that rang a bell. But only a distant one and only for a split second. Then Rudge's voice penetrated, sending a tremor of unnamed terror along her spine.

"Yeah, you sleep, baby, sleep your pretty little head off." His chair scraped on the hardwood floor. His tone dropped. "'Cause I'd lay odds that's what's gonna happen to you in the end." Through bleary eyes, Bella saw him draw two fingers across his throat. "Just like that lady Queen of Scots."

"Mary," Bella mumbled sleepily. In her mind she pictured a blade. But not a guillotine blade. The image Bella saw, though fleeting and shrouded with fog, was that of a long, skinny knife. Long, sharp and stained with blood.

"BELLADONNA. Bel-la-don-na." The woman filing her bright red nails enunciated each syllable, then made a disdainful face. "I don't think she's pretty at all."

A man of medium height and fifty-some years entered the darkened room behind her. He glanced at the two-way mirror hanging on one long wall. "I didn't think you would."

Miffed, she demanded, "Where's Charmaine?"

"Gone."

She swung around. "Did she pay the bounty hunter?"

"I did."

"Is he gone, too?"

"I imagine so." The man arched inquiring brows. "Do you require his services further?"

The woman gave a light laugh, flicking her burgundy bangs with the nail file. "You're such a stuffed shirt, Hobby. You have the manner of a perfect English butler. Always polite, always correct, and yet you run the San Francisco branch of the business like a..." Spreading her long white fingers, she searched for the right word.

"Crook ?" Hobby, better known as Hobson Crowe, suggested.

She shrugged. "Actually, I was going to say like an old pro, but have it your way, or rather the way of your lingering conscience."

"Old habits die hard," he quoted without inflection. "What would you have me do with our prisoner?"

The woman's nail file tapped the marble end table, a signal of her rising annoyance. And yet she felt something underneath that emotion, an involuntary fascination that drew her gaze repeatedly back to the glass. How much time had gone by? More than twenty years, and yet this Bella Conlan creature had done nothing, said nothing, spilled the truth to no one of import. Why?

The file tapped harder, faster. "When did Charmaine leave?" she demanded.

"Ten minutes ago."

"Didn't she even want to see her?" The woman stabbed her file at the two-way mirror. "I mean, if for no other reason than curiosity. It isn't every day that an eyewitness who could effectively put us out of business turns up. What am I supposed to do with her? Kill her? Not that I wouldn't love to, mind you.'' A wicked smile curved her red lips. "Oh, yes, I'd love to, all right, and I will, too, just as soon as we find out what she knows.'' Propping her long fingers together in a steeple, she tapped the file contemplatively against her front teeth. "I think she should be tied up for a while. You know, trussed like a turkey. Maybe shave her head as well—her hair's too shiny and dark.''

"That's cruel,'' Hobson Crowe remarked.

"I know.'' She continued to stare. "What do you think, Hobby, should we skin—''

"No.'' Hobby's response was no less emphatic for being so quietly offered.

She moved a negligent shoulder. "Oh, all right. But do me a favor and find that Rudge person, will you? And that bald muscle man of ours, too. Tic-Tac or whatever his name is.''

"Mick Tock,'' Hobby corrected, heading for the outer door.

"Whatever. Tell him to lose the earring, lock our guest in her room and get in here pronto. And switch off that stupid mirror thing. I'm sick of looking at her.''

Hobby inclined his head. "As you wish.''

"As you wish...'' she mimicked in his wake. "God, Hobby, but you are a drudge. How you got started in all of this, I'll never understand.''

She laughed, then dismissed Hobson Crowe from her mind as her gaze lighted on Bella Conlan once again. *Belladonna,* she thought with a stab of malice. Maybe poison *would* be best. A sprinkle of deadly nightshade in a cup of cocoa and it would be bye-bye Bella. Yes, that's what she would do, poison her. But slowly, very slowly.

Feeling smug, the woman tipped back her head and laughed again. To hell with Charmaine, if she couldn't even hang around long enough to discuss the matter. She, not Charmaine, was in control these days; she'd deal with the situation herself.

Reaching into her sleeve, she slid out a long, slender weapon, savoring the feel of its pink, metallic edges. But, no, poison was better—slower, more painful. Tic-Tac would scrounge it up, Hobby would administer it and she would watch it all. That would be an end to it. No more threat to their lucrative business. No more long-lost eyewitness wandering about. And best of all, no more Belladonna.

Chapter Two

"I thought you'd left, Mr. Rudge."

"Yeah?" A match flared as Rudge relit his cigar. "I guess you thought wrong, Hobson."

Concealed in the shadows of the old house off Castro Street, Malone watched a medium-sized man with gray-brown hair and placid features emerge from the front door. He looked and sounded like the quintessential British butler.

Smiling as if at some private joke, Rudge gazed at the row of tall, dark Victorian houses, set so close together that scarcely a foot of air space separated them. "I thought you called the shots in the Bay area," the bounty hunter remarked, still smiling.

The man, Hobson, gave no outward reaction. "I do."

"So it was your decision to switch off the two-way mirror and pull the guard on Bella Conlan's door?"

"I see you number eavesdropping among your many talents, Mr. Rudge."

"It has its advantages," Rudge murmured with a cryptic expression that Malone didn't trust for a minute. Larson Rudge was up to something, and he had a fair idea what it was. "So the big cheese has a job for Tock, huh? Nothing too complicated, I hope. Mick Tock has as much between his ears as he has on his head."

"I'm sure the big cheese, as you put it, is aware of that."

Rudge pushed off from the creaking porch railing. "Heading home, Hobson?"

The man slanted him a level look, but said nothing.

Chuckling, Rudge zipped up his black leather jacket. "Me, too. My job's done for now. Word of advice, though. You shouldn't lock your prisoners in a room so close to the trellis. Be a piece of cake for them to smash the window and climb down."

"Climb down three floors on a rotten trellis after smashing a bolted window? I think not, Mr. Rudge. The breaking glass alone would alert too many people."

"I didn't notice any crowds tonight."

"Tock will suffice in this case." Hobson made a polite gesture. "After you."

Rudge grinned and, chomping his cigar, stuffed his big hands in his pockets. He descended the eight steps to the walk, humming an old swing tune.

Malone followed their departure with his eyes, but didn't dwell on his mounting dislike for Rudge. Once the men were out of sight, his gaze traveled upward. No guard, interior surveillance off, third floor near the trellis. He'd scouted out the sturdy old house well enough to know that the only trellis stood at the head of the so-called garden. Assuming Rudge was right about there being few people inside, he shouldn't have too much trouble relocating the woman he'd been foolish enough to locate in the first place.

Damn, he thought in self-directed annoyance. From the moment he'd seen Bella Conlan—the woman, not the photograph—he'd felt something. It wasn't an emotion he could identify, but whatever it was drew him to her as surely as a magnet. The question was, if he gave in to the pull of the magnet now, would he be able to free himself from its effects later?

SHE WOULDN'T SCREAM, Bella promised herself. Not that she could have, since her throat was almost too dry to swallow. But in this case, screaming would only make an already bad situation worse.

She tried wedging the window open, to no avail. Leaning on the wall, she ordered her muscles to stop trembling. That didn't work much better than tugging on the sash.

She fought back a sob of futility. Dear God, how was she going to get out of this horrible place? It was cold, dusty and damp. The fire had gone out, and the people holding her had to be maniacs. On top of that, there was no light except for the fire and the unearthly blend of fog and street lamps that shone through the pane.

Determined despite her fear, Bella forced her legs to carry her to the door. She'd tried this escape route five times already, but what else was there to do except get panicky? She was close enough to that state already.

Knife blades kept flashing in her mind. Thin, blood-stained blades. She saw nothing else. No people, no identifying surroundings, nothing except blackness—and a presentiment of death that made her stomach twist into an icy knot.

Closing the fingers of both hands around the doorknob, she gave it a hard yank.

Bella hadn't actually expected to succeed. However, when she landed with a thump on the floor, she knew she had. Either that or she'd pulled the knob off.

But no, a weak beam of light now spilled in from the corridor.

From the floor, staring shocked into the gauzy light, Bella perceived an outline: male, about six feet tall, wearing black pants and a long black raincoat. She heard something that could have been swearing, though not in a tongue she understood.

The man moved with pantherlike speed. Before Bella could scramble backward, he'd slipped across the threshold and eased the door closed with one black-booted foot.

"Not a word," he warned, as Bella, too startled to utter a sound, stared up at him. Again he moved too swiftly for her. Sinking to his haunches beside her, he grasped her arm. "Are you hurt? No? Then come on."

Come where? her frightened brain demanded. If only her vocal cords would cooperate.

"Who—uh..." she stammered while discreetly resisting his hold.

He shot her an impatient look. "Not Rudge, be thankful for that."

A thousand thoughts raced through Bella's mind. She recognized him. He'd been in the alley with Rudge. Malone, Rudge had called him. Of English descent, ex-crook, now a people finder. He'd found her for Rudge. He'd actually turned her in to a bounty hunter.

She blinked as another thought registered. He was good-looking—not exceptional, but he had what Lona would call a good face. His dark hair was long and curled becomingly over his forehead and neck. His even-darker eyes were large and intense, either Latin or Black Irish. He had a nice mouth, not too thin or too full, a strong nose and a lean, athletic build. His expression, as if from long custom, revealed nothing.

And that was only the beginning.

Sex appeal...

The phrase popped into Bella's head, and it was apt. Too apt. She didn't dare acknowledge it. She couldn't possibly trust him, let alone go anywhere with him.

When she resisted his hold, he knit his brow. "What's wrong? Are your legs broken? Move it, lady, unless you enjoy being spied on."

Bella stilled her struggles. "Spied?" she repeated, then remembered her situation and began twisting her arm again. For all his pantherlike grace, he had the strength of a bear.

He nodded at a long, dusty mirror behind them. "It's a two-way."

Bella's mistrust rose. How did he know that? Keeping her gaze on his face, she gave a final wrench and broke free. "Who are you?" she demanded. "What do you want with me?"

"Name's Malone, and I'm trying to help you. Now, let's get the hell out of here before Tock shows up and decides I'd look good with a bullet in my brain."

"Tock?"

"Fat, bald, earring," he returned and, with his gaze still darting about, recaptured her arm.

The man—Malone—came from England, Bella decided. Probably from the northern part, if her ear for accents was accurate.

He hauled her unceremoniously to her feet. Should she kick, scream, scratch? Or should she wait and do it after they reached the front door?

He shot her an impatient look as he propelled her, still half resisting, through the doorway and into a drab corridor. "Stop fighting me, will you, lady?"

"Go to..." She paused, then reconsidered. "Why?"

"I told you why." He sounded cranky. "Now shut up and move."

She started to pull away, but stopped when his hands suddenly spanned her waist. Without warning, he pushed her into a room on their left. From behind, he kept one arm wrapped around her. "Don't move," he murmured, his mouth disturbingly close to her ear.

Wisely, Bella swallowed her objections. Very close by she heard the click of a door, followed by the plodding of heavy feet.

"Tock," Malone murmured. Seconds later the bald man lumbered past. He stopped for a moment, scratched his throat, then moved on.

The instant he turned the corner, Malone shoved Bella forward. "Stay on the left side of the hall." At her uncomprehending look, he added in an exasperated tone, "The right side squeaks."

Did that knowledge come from habit or from climbing those stairs tonight? Did it matter? He was her way out. She should seize the opportunity, not fight it.

She wished she could fight Malone's sensuality as well, or at least not be quite so aware of it. Of all the times to notice a man, this had to be the worst.

"Go," he said in her ear.

Bella glanced at him, then obeyed.

It could indeed have been a replica of Scrooge's house, she noted distractedly. Everything about it felt black and white. Shadows fell at sharp angles across the floor and walls, and although there was scarcely a stick of furniture to be seen, what few pieces Bella's eyes could discern were scarred and drab.

"Hey," a voice shouted unexpectedly from the third floor. "Hey, where'd she go?"

Malone swore again, in Gaelic, Bella presumed. Taking her hand, he said, "If you want to live, lady, you'd better run."

Lights flared in their wake. A bright yellow beam shone out of a second-story window directly onto them. "There!" Tock shouted. "That's her."

Malone ducked low, dragging a breathless Bella with him. Through the fog, he led her down a hill into a narrow alley and over to a classic black sports car.

He didn't tell her to get in, merely tore open the driver's-side door and thrust her inside. She had to hoist herself over the stick shift to avoid being crushed by him when he followed.

"Hold on," he said, starting the engine with a firm flick of his wrist. It roared, banged, coughed twice and banged again. Bella thought it would die for sure when he slammed it into gear, but, miraculously, it kept running.

Over her shoulder, she made out the bulky form of Tock at the top of the alley, both hands raised. A second later she heard the *thwack* of something hitting metal.

Malone ground his teeth. "You'll pay for that one, Tock."

Bella looked over the back of her seat, but saw nothing. "Pay for what? He missed."

"He bloody well did not. He shot my car. A '69 Jaguar, and that bastard put a hole in it."

Too tired, confused and frightened to argue, Bella dropped back into her seat. This was a nightmare; it had to be. Who on earth would want to shoot her? Even through her involvement with Irish Max and his friends she'd never done anything worth getting shot over.

"It's a mistake," she decided. "That's all. They want someone else."

The Jaguar zoomed out of the alley, but not before Tock planted another bullet in the fender. It wasn't until they'd reached the relative safety of the street that Malone answered her. "Trust me, Bella, there's no mistake."

"It's Belladonna, and there must be. I haven't done anything."

He smiled, a polite little smile that held no trace of humor. "We've all done things, we just don't necessarily realize it. You've never seen Tock before?"

She shook her head.

"What about Rudge?"

Arms folded across her chest, eyes staring at foggy Castro Street, she said flatly, "No." She couldn't resist adding an ungrateful, "I've never seen you before, either."

His lips twitched. "You're not supposed to see me."

Her fear had subsided sufficiently to allow her aggravation through. "Are you a bounty hunter, too?"

He glanced at the red light ahead of them. "No."

"Why did you help me escape then?" He'd rescued her, actually, but it was a minor point.

"I don't like Rudge."

Anger made her brash. "You liked him well enough to find me for him."

"He gave me a picture and an assignment." Malone's tone was benign. "I did my job."

"Then you came and got me out. Why?"

"God, but you're persistent. Can't you just be grateful and leave it at that?"

"Should I be grateful?"

"Of course you bloody well should." He sounded offended. She'd gone too far.

"I'm sorry—" she began, but he cut her off irritably.

"Like hell you are, lady."

"I am!" she retorted, stung.

"Bull." He fixed his dark, somber eyes on her. They were incredibly beautiful and sensual. "You think I got you out so that I could turn around and sell you again."

There, he'd said it, and now that he'd said it Bella felt obliged, albeit reluctantly, to take it all the way. "Will you?'' she challenged with far more bravery than she possessed.

He stared evenly at her. "Yes."

"What?"

"Isn't that what you wanted to hear?"

"No." She clamped her mouth shut.

"Then don't ask stupid questions."

"I'm not—" The look Malone slanted her should have been a warning, but Bella disliked having her intelligence questioned and so set her jaw before adding defiantly, "—stupid."

Not surprisingly, he said nothing to that; he just continued to drive.

The San Francisco streets flew by in a blur. Holiday lights glowed red, green and gold in the fog, which continued to creep inland from the bay. Bella's active mind, which usually conjured up images of the Barbary Coast, cable cars and the neon splendor of Chinatown, tonight seemed fixed on blood, and now on the man beside her. Rescuer or not, she had to get away from him.

When Malone didn't speak, Bella gathered her courage and calmly asked, "Where are you taking me?"

He turned off Market Street onto Van Ness. No cable cars clanged; in fact, there was very little traffic to hinder them.

"I know a safe place," he answered shortly.

His eyes darted back and forth from the road to the rearview mirror. They were heading for the marina, or so she thought until he swerved off Van Ness onto Vallejo. Here the close-set houses rose up in colorful Victorian rows.

Three turns later, however, Bella lost her bearings in the fog. They might be on Telegraph Hill, but it was hard for her to be sure of anything with her head throbbing and her nerves stretched well past the breaking point.

She was still endeavoring to get her bearings when Malone turned one last time, braking his Jaguar to a halt on a steep hill behind what at first glance appeared to be a stone tower. Anyway it was round, and the base loomed several imposing feet above them.

Given the fog and all the ghostly shadows of night, Bella realized that she might never get a better opportunity. Before Malone could react, she kicked open the stiff door, jumped out and ran.

But where should she go? Down; yes, get off the hill. The fog would be even thicker at a lower elevation.

She heard him close behind her. The word *idiot* registered, along with a few less-flattering terms. But whether he was directing them at her or at himself she had no way of knowing. She simply ran through the dampness and the tendrils of white and prayed the fog would conceal her flight. If only she hadn't worn leather boots...

Under normal circumstances Bella knew he wouldn't have caught her. Irish Max had taught her well—but in sneakers, not in designer boots. And there was another, less-tangible obstacle. For all her desire to get away, she was having to battle feelings of fear the likes of which she'd never experienced in her conscious life. It was as if she'd undertaken such an escape before, or something terrifyingly close to it.

But Bella refused to let her fear, no matter how deep-rooted, win out. That would be suicide. She fought it with images of Myrna Loy and William Powell, the Li-Chi Club and gangsters named Dancer, Lum and Fingers. The sound of the big bands, Irish Max's favorite music, rang in her ears, followed by her own favorite, Gilbert and Sullivan.

When those thoughts faltered, she summoned up pictures of Lona and Bodega Bay, of Alfred Hitchcock and Tippi Hedren.

The Birds, she recalled. Yes, she loved that movie. Something about it struck an oddly familiar chord in the darkened recesses of her mind.

"Yeaahh!"

He caught her off guard, tackling her with no more warning than that muffled sound and hauling her into a patch of shrubbery outside someone's darkened house. Bella landed hard, but on Malone, not on the ground. Although she came down kicking and squirming, he held her fast, offsetting the knee that would have connected with his groin. Instead, he shifted their positions until, on his knees, he towered over her.

"Let me go," she panted, working at the wrists he'd trapped on either side of her head.

"You are an idiot," he stated, shaking her. "You could run into Tock down here, or worse, Larson Rudge."

She made a sound of frustration in her throat. "How do I know you're any better than they are? Maybe you really do want to collect a second bounty on me."

"And maybe—" he lowered his head until his mouth hovered tantalizing inches from hers "—I just want to help you."

She had enough defiance left to glare up at him, even if there was an unfamiliar ball of heat spiraling downward from her stomach. "I don't believe you."

"Fine, I'll turn you back over to Rudge then. He's out there, and probably not far away."

Suspicion crowded in. "How do you know?" she challenged recklessly. "Are you working together?"

He regarded her with half-lidded eyes, cursed softly and said, "Rudge set this whole thing up, Bella."

Suspicion gave way to confusion. "You mean Rudge wanted me to get away?"

"Something like that." To her relief, Malone moved so he was no longer straddling her. Maintaining his hold on her wrists, he stood, bringing her effortlessly with him. "He wanted me to get you out. He knew I was outside listening."

"But that doesn't... Ah. He wants to collect a second bounty for himself."

"Yes, well, he's devious."

"He's sleazy. And greedy."

"And good enough at his job to be on our trail already." Malone darted a look into the fog. "He doesn't need any help from us."

As they started back, Bella's eyes slid upward. Through her lashes she studied Malone's features. They weren't delicate or remotely feminine, and they certainly weren't pretty, but there was an arresting quality to his face, a sort of somber beauty that made her shiver deep inside. If she couldn't identify the source, she could at least acknowledge a dark, vaguely dangerous aspect of his character. Part of her was tempted to take her chances with Rudge.

They returned to the stone tower, which was really a house that had been divided into four apartments. Via an outer staircase, they climbed to the second floor. Once there, Malone removed a file from his inner coat pocket and began plying the lock.

"I take it you don't live here," Bella observed, cold down to her bones.

He made a snarling sound when the lock refused to give. "My place'll be one of the first Rudge checks out. I doubt if he'll be able to trace me here in a hurry.... Damn." He rattled the knob. "It's rusty."

Or he was. "Let me try," Bella offered. "I'm good with locks."

"Yes, I've heard that." He made a subtle head motion. "Take your best shot."

Sinking to her knees, Bella probed the old lock. "Exactly how much do you know about me, Mr. Malone?"

"Just Malone, and only the basics. You were raised in Alaska by your grandmother from the age of nine until you turned eighteen, at which time you moved to Northern California. You went to Berkeley, took philosophy, history and art and eventually landed a job with the Playhouse Theater. Your grandmother moved to Bodega Bay while you stayed on in San Francisco. You got your *Irish—*" he said the word as if it were distasteful to him "—friend, Max McCrimmon, a job at the theater, but neglected to mention that he had a police record. You know how to pick pockets, lie and cheat at poker. You love cats, Chinatown, horror movies and old detective stories."

The lock clicked and Bella stood. "I also mind my own business, hate snoops and pick locks better than pockets." She stuck the file between his belt and waistband. "And I don't have a lot of faith in men who make their living turning people over to bounty hunters."

Malone's eyes narrowed—a bad sign, Bella suspected, but frankly, she was too tired to care.

When he flipped on the interior lights, she'd stepped wordlessly inside. To her surprise, the apartment was charming, comfortable, cluttered and disorganized, much like Lona's house in Alaska. The furniture was upholstered in a buttery-soft, dark brown leather; the bookshelves overflowed with detective novels, murder-mystery videos and old audiotaped radio programs: *The Shadow, Suspense* and *Sherlock Holmes.* Even Dashiel Hammett's *Thin Man* series was there. Bella loved it instantly.

"Who lives here?" she asked, looking around.

"No one. A friend." Switching off the overhead light, Malone glanced through the curtain. "I think we lost him."

Bella stared at him for a long time. When he didn't elaborate, she marched over to where he stood. "Look, Malone, I don't understand any of this. What is it that whoever hired Rudge wants from me?" Another thought struck her and she eyed Malone in suspicion. "Why did Rudge hire you to find me? I'm in the book."

He scanned the sidewalk and street as far as the fog would permit. "Keep your voice down. He didn't know your name."

"Then how...?"

"A picture."

"He had a picture of me?"

The muslin curtain dropped back into place. "Yes, he did. And, no, I don't know how he got it." Opening his black raincoat, he removed a photo from the inside pocket.

Beneath his coat he wore a black jersey with the top three buttons undone. Bella felt an immediate tug of sexual desire and had to shake herself in order to tear her gaze away. She focused instead on the picture he held, which, though a trifle fuzzy, was definitely of her. Unfortunately, the background objects were too blurry for her to distinguish them.

She studied it closely. "Who took this?"

"Don't you know?"

She should have been paying closer attention. Malone had come up on her from behind. She could feel the heat from his body warming her spine as he regarded the photo over her shoulder.

Bella drew in a deep breath. "I don't even know where it was taken."

"It looks like San Francisco to me," he said mildly.

Something snapped in Bella's mind. She rounded on him angrily. "Doesn't it ever bother you what you do?" she demanded, stepping wisely out of range as she spoke. "You sold me to a bounty hunter, Malone. For all you know he could have been hired to kill me."

His bland expression didn't alter. "Rudge has a reputation," he said calmly. "He's a hunter, not a killer."

"People change, and reputations aren't worth sh—" She started to swear as Irish Max had taught her, then caught herself as Lona had taught her. "They change with the people who possess them," she finished. "I'm going to Bod—" Again she checked herself, but not quickly enough, it seemed.

Malone's dark eyes glittered in the pool of light from the single floor lamp. "Bodega Bay, Bella?" he challenged in a vaguely intimidating tone. "Where Lona lives?"

"Don't you dare brin—" she began, but forgot what she meant to say when he started advancing on her.

"I know all about Lona," he said in that same deceptively even tone. "What I don't know about is you. Who's after you, Bella Conlan? You know the answer—you must. People don't put out high-stakes bounties for the hell of it."

Bella's breath caught tightly in her chest. This was ridiculous. She had every right to be scared—but not to be attracted to this man called Malone. "I don't know anything about it," she maintained mutinously. "And even if I did, it wouldn't be any of your business."

He stopped less than a foot in front of her. "Oh, but it is," he said bitingly. "Either you tell me the truth here and now, or I'll take you back to that house and a very annoyed Mick Tock."

He wouldn't, she thought. Then she looked at him again and sighed. He would. Malone was not a man to make idle threats.

"Oh, all right. I'll tell you the truth. But it won't change anything. I'm not a hardened criminal. I just have a problem with the first nine years of my life."

A ridge formed between his brows as he frowned uncomprehendingly. "What kind of problem?"

She looked him straight in the eye. "I don't remember them."

Chapter Three

"My mother's name was Amanda." Bella finished her story over coffee in the wood-and-tile kitchen. "I don't remember her, and Lona doesn't have any pictures, but she told me that my mother and I were coming to live with her in Alaska."

Eyes focused on the table, Malone digested her story. He'd glanced at her several times in the past hour, but always with the controlled expression for which he was famous. The last thing he needed was for Bella Conlan to think, even for a minute, that he might care about her in a personal way.

Because he didn't, he told himself flatly. He wouldn't allow himself to get involved. He'd been through hell and back with his parents' marriage. Involvement on a personal level was definitely not for him.

Raising a flowered mug to his lips, he slanted Bella a skeptical look. "Your grandmother didn't have pictures of her own daughter?"

Bella moved a shoulder dismissively, as if that were the least of her worries. "She and my grandfather left California in a hurry. They had time to pack only the bare necessities."

Malone fought the smile that threatened to play on his mouth. "Yes, I did a little research on your grandfather. He was quite a character."

"I know." Her steady gaze offered no apology for the old man's behavior. "I'm told my grandfather was an artist. What were you in your heyday, Mr. Malone?"

"Just Malone." He contained a sigh. "And nothing that would interest you."

"Rudge said you were a crook."

One dark brow rose, exaggeratedly polite. "You believed him?"

"Why would he lie?"

"To make himself look good, maybe?"

"Hah, next to him, Professor Moriarty would look good."

"I think we're losing the thread of this conversation." Malone swirled the dregs of his now-tepid coffee. "Are you sure you don't remember anything about the first nine years of your life?"

She opened her mouth, then seemed to think better of it and shook her head. "Nothing."

His eyes narrowed. In the background, Glenn Miller's "Chattanooga Choo-Choo" played on the radio. Fog continued to swirl outside the windows. "Spill it, Bella," he told her. "I can't help you if I don't have all the facts."

Setting her own mug down, she leaned forward on her elbows. "Fine. I saw a knife. But only in my mind, and only recently."

Frowning, he asked. "When?"

"Tonight. It's the first time I've seen it. The blade was ultrathin and covered with blood. I don't know if it's connected with my past or not. I work in the theater. We deal with props."

"Did it seem like a prop?"

"I don't know." She cupped her chin in her hand. "Look, Malone, I'm tired, and my head really hurts. I'm not even sure if I trust you yet. For all I know you could be part of some elaborate setup."

"And you could be lying about having amnesia."

"So it appears we've reached an impasse."

He'd warmed his coffee from the floral pot. Now, tasting it, he burned his tongue and swore. Damn thermal carafes—and Bella Conlan as well. After all he'd done, she didn't trust him an inch. He should walk out and leave her to fend for herself.

He should—but he wouldn't. Couldn't, because for all their flaws and fights, and all the impassioned threats they'd leveled at each other, his mother and father had done a decent job of raising their only son. Fine, so he'd made a little illegal book under tutelage from his father, and yes, his mother dealt a mean game of blackjack from the bottom of a deck, but they'd managed to instill a sense of fair play in him even so.

Through the veil of his lashes, Malone surveyed the woman across from him. *Beautiful* seemed an inadequate description, somehow. She had an unusual vibrancy about her, a glow that translated to a strong lust for life. She had energy, as well, and a spark inside her like nothing he'd ever encountered before. Frightened she might be, but she intended to survive.

She was tall and slender and long limbed, with dark hair that tumbled in thick, silky waves past her shoulders. Her skin was clear and golden; her eyes hovered somewhere between brown and amber.

"Are you going to call Rudge now?"

Her question broke into Malone's thoughts and set his teeth on edge. Careful to show her nothing more than a polite mask, he arched his brows. "Is that what you want me to do?"

She stared at him for a long moment before finally making a tiny negative motion with her head. "Not really."

Malone kept his gaze steady. "What do you want then?"

She set her hands on the table, as if weighing her options. "I want this to be a nightmare, but I don't think it is. And yet, if it isn't, where do I start?"

"You remember a knife covered with blood."

"Which might or might not be pertinent."

"Are you always this stubborn?" he asked, then held up a conciliatory hand. "Yes, all right. What about your grandmother, Lona?"

Bella bit her quite-delicious lower lip. "I'm not sure. She might know some little detail that would help."

"Like where your father is, maybe?"

"She told me he was dead."

"What about his name?"

"She doesn't know. He and Amanda—my mother— eloped. Lona never met him."

Sighing, Malone massaged a sore temple. God, he was tired. It had to be after five a.m. by now. "Is that all she told you?"

"It's all she knew. I'm sure Amanda would have related the whole story, but she died before we reached Lona's place."

Lona . . . It came back to that woman every time, back to a grandmother who currently resided some sixty miles north of San Francisco in Bodega Bay.

"That's it then." Malone said decisively. "We start in the obvious place."

She raised her eyes to his implacable face. "Lona?" she asked, and he nodded.

"Lona."

"PLEASE, LONA," Bella entreated her grandmother on the phone. "Meet me—us—at the Excelsior Hotel on the coast. You know it—it's that English-style resort twenty miles south of Bodega Bay."

Oh, yes, Lona knew the Excelsior, a very posh British-style hotel, with tea and meeting rooms, charming lounges, an elegant dining area and suites fit for a queen. She warmed to the idea instantly—until Bella elaborated.

"Someone's after me. I don't know who, but so far I've been kidnapped by a bounty hunter, locked in a room, rescued by—well, anyway, his name's Malone. I've been chased, shot at and followed in the fog. All I can think of is that it must be connected to my past. . . ."

Lona sat dead still for several minutes after the phone call. It was ten a.m., chilly near the bay and overcast. In a few days it would be New Year's Eve. She had planned to spend it with Bella, dressed to the nines watching Gilbert and Sullivan's *HMS Pinafore* at the Opera House. But that was before, when the charade had been alive and Bella had been her granddaughter. Now reality had intruded and she was faced with an impossible decision.

Heaven help her, she had knowledge of Bella's past. She knew unpleasant truths about Amanda Johnson's life twenty years ago in London, though little about the people with whom she had associated. If only she could have learned the whole truth. Unfortunately, her connections had gotten her only so far. Now the question presented itself: how much of what she knew should she disclose to Bella?

After eighty-five years of hard living, Lona's hands were gnarled and tough. They caressed the three-inch oval picture case she'd received from the police in Alaska two days after Amanda's death. It wasn't until four days after that that she'd received a letter, mailed by Amanda from the East Coast.

Lona's fingers stilled on the silver case. She'd done a reckless thing, tossing that letter on the fire. Yet she recalled most of Amanda's hastily scrawled words—her confession, as it were.

Oh, how nice if honesty really were the best policy. But in Bella's case who knew what nasty memories might have been triggered had Lona divulged the contents of the letter.

"Just like Romaine," Amanda had said on the phone, and while the meaning still eluded her, Lona understood enough to realize that Amanda had feared not only for her own life, but also for Bella's.

"Belladonna," she'd called the girl, a synonym for deadly nightshade. "Just like Romaine...." But what had she meant?

Rubbing her cheeks with her palms, Lona made her decision. Bella must be told. Perhaps through partial knowledge she could offset the poison that sought to infect her from the past.

The elderly woman regarded her hollow, rawboned cheeks in the living-room mirror. She'd lost weight in recent months, more still these past few weeks. Bella had been understandably alarmed at Christmastime.

"It's nothing, child," Lona had lied calmly during her visit. "Just old age and a finicky appetite."

Now, staring at her own gaunt reflection, with its sagging skin beneath a cap of plaited gray hair, Lona saw a haunted old woman, in pain both physically and emotionally. Allowing her eyelids to close, she moved her pale lips. "Please God," she prayed. "Let what little I know help her to survive. Give me that much strength—and that much time."

THE EXCELSIOR HOTEL had long been one of Bella's favorites. It possessed a strong air of England—of Cornwall, to be precise. Designed in the Tudor style, it stood like a sentinel above the rugged Northern California coastline, timeless in its grace and charm, an elegant yet comfortable retreat from the anthill pace of the Golden Gate City some forty miles to the south.

Malone had rented a car for the Coast Road drive. Bella in turn had borrowed an outfit from his unnamed "friend," a female, she'd discovered. Whoever the woman was, she had excellent taste in clothing as well as in decoration.

"Borrow anything you want," Malone had said, waving an unconcerned hand at the bedroom closet. "Annie won't mind."

Yet even when Bella had asked him point-blank, he'd refused to explain who Annie was or what their friendship entailed.

Bella had made her choice carefully, selecting a matching garnet-colored skirt and top of pure Oriental silk. The skirt was long and full, the top of a clingier design. The throat dipped into a semi-alluring V that could be closed with two long ties or left open. Bella opted for open. She pushed the sleeves halfway up her forearms, donned her Italian-leather boots and dusted off her gray-green raincoat. Leaving her hair loose to tumble about her shoulders, she set her unwarranted pangs of jealousy aside and prepared to meet the day head-on.

Now, though, stepping from the car outside the Excelsior after a sleepless night and a silent drive up the coast in

the company of the somber yet alarmingly sensual Sean
Andrew Malone, her resolve wavered. Did she really want
to involve Lona in this mess? Moreover, could she trust
Malone to help her?

To his credit, it had been Malone who'd suggested meeting away from Lona's house. "If they know about you,
they'll know about Lona by now," he'd explained with aggravating logic. "They're probably watching her place."

Watching Lona? What if that watching turned into
something more dangerous? Like kidnapping?

Her concern must have shown, because Malone shook his
head as he joined her on the sidewalk. "That isn't Rudge's
style, Bella. For one thing, he'd make less money bringing
Lona in than you. Trust me, it's you he wants, and for the
moment I'd guess that he's their leg man."

Trust me. . . .

Bella glanced sideways. Sexy he might be, but trustworthy had yet to be established.

They entered the hotel through the main lobby doors.
There must have been a convention, because the front desk
was swamped. Bellmen in red jackets and caps heaped their
trolleys with suitcases and dragged them toward an ornate
bank of elevators.

"Is that the lounge?" At Bella's nod, Malone cupped a
hand around her elbow, and headed toward a cluster of
marble pillars and chintz chairs. For all its opulence, the
place had a comfortable atmosphere. She felt right at home,
as always.

The mirrored tea lounge lay behind a set of wooden
doors. The tables were formally set with Irish-linen clothes,
white china and polished silverware. In the center of each
table stood a red carnation in a delicately carved bud vase.
Gauzy white curtains held back with sashes graced the tall
windows. Clouds loomed outside, but within the hotel walls
all was warm and cozy.

"Hey-o, Malone." A cheerful male voice with a Scottish
accent hailed them from the right. "What brings you here?"

A man approached them, grinning like the Cheshire Cat.
Dressed in chef's clothes, he wore a small floppy hat on his

head and a white jacket over baggy corduroy pants. He was taller than Malone by about two inches and weighed, Bella estimated, on the high side of two hundred and fifty pounds. He had a massive red beard, long, curly red hair and twinkling blue eyes that surveyed her even as he grabbed Malone's hand and shook it vigorously. "You're looking good. I see you've got a pretty lass with you."

Malone maintained a politely stoic expression, extricating his hand with difficulty from the paw that held it. "Yes. Bella, this is Ronald MacMalkin. Ronnie, Bella Conlan. Yes, fine, all right," he amended at a quick look from her, "Belladonna."

Satisfied, she smiled. "Hello, Ronnie."

The man pumped her hand. "Hello right back at you." He motioned from Malone to Bella. "Are you two social or business?"

Malone gave him a smile so quick that it came and went before Bella was sure she'd even seen it. "None of your business. Have you seen an old woman hiding among the ferns recently?"

"Oh, aye, plenty. How old?"

"Eighty-five," Bella interjected. "But she looks seventy—or did," she added with a pang. "She has a Norwegian accent and her hair will be braided and pinned."

Ronnie chuckled. "By the window, lass. Shore side. Say, Malone, would you be needing any help with your people-finding business?"

Malone seemed surprised, then mildly suspicious. "Why?"

"Oh, I'm thinking of quitting is all. Too hectic here."

While Ronnie chatted, Bella scanned the tearoom. She spotted Lona behind a potted holly tree and felt her heart sink. Her grandmother looked terrible—old and frail, less than two-thirds her normal robust weight. Bella waved, however, and plastering a smile on her face, started toward her.

"I'll bring the tea trolley round, then, shall I?" Ronnie called out.

"Yes, do that," Malone said, so close behind Bella that she jumped.

"Don't you ever make noise?" she demanded, glaring at him. "Why don't you hang out with your friend? I'll talk to Lona."

"Because Ronnie has a soft spot for beautiful brunettes. He's gone off to fetch you a plate of hot raisin scones. Is that her?"

Bella's concern resurfaced. Her grandmother looked so old. "Yes."

"Bella!" Lona exclaimed, spotting her. "Thank heaven you're safe."

Bending, Bella hugged her. She felt bones under the black print dress and had to mask a shiver. In the weird, late-afternoon light pouring through the window, Lona's wrinkles seemed doubly pronounced.

"Oh, my dear, I've been so worried about you." Her gaze rose to Malone. "You must be the man who helped my grand—er, Bella. Malone, isn't it?"

"Yes, it is." His effortless courtesy brought Bella's head around in surprise. He never used that tone with her.

Slipping out of her raincoat and handing it to him, she took a seat across from her grandmother. "Can you help, Lona?" she asked without preface. "Is there anything you haven't told me about my past?"

Lona compressed her lips. "Is it that serious?"

"Yes," Malone answered for her. He shot a somewhat-annoyed look at Bella, placed her coat on an empty seat and pulled out the chair next to hers. "There's a bounty hunter after her. His name is Larson Rudge, and he's as cunning as a fox."

"More like a weasel if you ask me." Bella reached for one of Lona's gnarled hands. "Why would someone want to kidnap me, Lona? *Who* would want to? Did I do something as a child? Did my mother?"

"Here we go, hot tea and scones," Ronnie interrupted cheerfully. "Oh, there, let me draw that other curtain back for you. It's a wicked day out there for sure. Look at those black clouds over the water." He reached around Bella to secure the curtain. "Silly host. He seats you by a window, then blocks half your light. Not that they usually seat people at window tables in the dead of winter, mind," he went on amiably. "Too drafty near the water. I wonder why—"

"Yes, thank you, Ronnie." Malone cut him off with strained civility. "We'll call if we need you."

"What? Oh, sure." Unoffended, Ronnie grinned. "Enjoy your tea."

Bella waited until he'd moved off, then squeezed Lona's hand. "Tell me, please."

The old woman's eyes closed—as if she were in pain—Bella thought. Something flashed briefly in her peripheral vision, but she ignored it in favor of watching her grandmother. "Are you all right?" she asked her.

The old woman pressed one hand to her forehead. "I'm fine. And you have a right to know." She drew a deep breath. "I'm not..." She faltered, then tried again in a gruffer tone. "Child, I'm not really your grandmother."

If the china had sprouted legs and started dancing, Bella couldn't have been more shocked. Fortunately, her reaction was forestalled by Malone's indignant, "What do you mean, she's not your granddaughter? I traced her records to Washington State. She was born in Seattle."

Lona met his gaze. "Those records were false, Mr. Malone, all of them. Credibly forged by friends of my late husband."

"That's impossible!"

"Not for people who know about such things. Difficult, yes, and costly, but not impossible."

Malone rounded on a stunned Bella. "Did you know anything about this?"

Neither the question nor his outraged expression fully registered on her. What did he have to be upset about? She was the one who'd been duped all these years. Deceived by her own grandmother. No, not her grandmother. By... whom?

When the initial shock passed, a sense of numbness set in. Bella stared at Lona as if at a stranger. "Who are you?" she asked of the woman she had thought she'd known for twenty years. She saw the hurt in her eyes, but couldn't bring herself to respond to it.

"Amanda telephoned me," Lona said quietly, "the night of the accident. She was desperate. The connection was bad. She was in trouble—I realized that much—running from someone. She begged me to take care of you."

A group of convention-goers paused outside the window, laughing and pointing at the clouds massing over the ocean. Bella continued to stare at Lona, oblivious to their muted chatter. "Who was she running from?"

"She didn't say, or if she did, the line was too garbled for me to hear. She told me that someone had invented a poisonous nickname. Then she said an odd thing."

"*Then,* she said an odd thing?" Bella echoed.

Lona took her unresisting hand. "She said she realized the truth behind Romaine."

Lost, Bella said, "What are you talking about?"

"I wish I knew. I do know that the poisonous plant deadly nightshade has another name—Belladonna. Romaine?" She spread her fingers. "I'm not sure."

"Are you sure you didn't know any of this?" Malone demanded. He sounded more irritated than surprised. Outside, the conventioners chattered like magpies. Wind buffeted the windows as the storm crept closer.

"She didn't know." Lona's gaze fastened on Bella's pale cheeks. "'Just like Romaine.' That's how she put it to me."

Bella wondered distantly if she was having a nightmare. She certainly felt removed from reality at this point. Even the thunder on the ocean had a surreal sound to it.

"So you were my mother's friend," she said, trying to sort it out. Then she frowned as the old woman set a small, tissue-wrapped packet on the table. "What's that?"

"It's all I have to give you, child."

Bella regarded the package as if it were a snake.

"Please understand, Bella," Lona implored. "I couldn't have loved you more had you really been my grandchild."

In spite of everything, Bella believed that. Nodding, she murmured numbly, "I know. I love you, too. But—"

Lona released her icy fingers. "No buts. Open the package, and I will finish my story."

There was more? But, of course, there must be, mustn't there? Carefully, Bella unwrapped the tissue.

Again something glinted in her peripheral vision. Outside, several of the women raised their voices. Suddenly one of them screamed, and they scattered like birds.

Before Bella could locate the source of the problem, Malone swore and clamped a hand on her neck. "Duck," he shouted, shoving her down. Bella's cheek hit the edge of the table a split second before the shot rang out. It made a neat hole in the window, but wasn't as loud as she would have expected. A volley of other shots followed.

Recovering her wits, Bella raised her head slightly. "Lona!" she exclaimed. She scrambled around the table and reached up to pull the paralyzed woman sideways. "Get down," she whispered, tugging hard.

Lona obliged, but not in the usual way. Her hand fell limply to her side; her head tipped backward; her body stiffened. Her breath, it seemed, came out in a whoosh. At Bella's touch, she turned a fraction in her seat.

That's when Bella spied the entry mark below her left shoulder—and the blood that flowed like a crimson river over her breast.

Chapter Four

"No!" Horrified, Bella shook her grandmother's arm. "Lona!"

The next thing she knew, Malone was gripping her neck, hauling her away. "Stay down," he snapped, but she batted at his hand and, crawling forward, pressed a linen napkin to Lona's chest. Was she breathing?

More shots rang out. Awareness swept through the lounge as the terrace doors burst open and a group of conventioners ran in.

"He's got a gun!" one of them gasped. "It's—it's a man, I think. A big man."

Feet pounded on the carpet. Chairs overturned. Two women screamed. One must have fainted. There were grunts and squeals and the sound of crystal shattering as panicky people shoved tables roughly out of their way.

Bella heard the commotion, but saw only Lona's deathly white face. A big man had shot her. Rudge? Tock?

Malone moved to kneel on Lona's left, directly beneath the window. "Get Bella out of here," he ordered Ronnie tersely.

"No," she murmured.

"Yes!" His head came up, his gaze steady on hers. A moment later a pair of large hands were clamped about her upper arms.

"Come along, lass," Ronnie urged, pulling her to her feet. "Malone'll do the necessary."

"Move, everyone. That's it. Let me through, please," a man said. "I'm a doctor. I'm—" He broke off, spluttering as another stream of bullets was released.

"Go, Bella," Malone growled. "Now. There's nothing you can do." He grabbed the arm of the cowering doctor and yanked him to safety.

"There must be."

"He's still out there," a terrified woman screamed.

"Stay calm, everyone, please," the headwaiter begged.

"Ronnie!" Malone snapped.

"Aye."

Malone's hands were covered with blood—Lona's blood. This time Bella couldn't seem to fight when Ronnie, bent low, drew her away. She just floated upward. Funny how she felt again as if she'd been through this before.

The floor—in fact, the room—began to pulse. In her mind, the hotel lounge dissolved, replaced by a cramped, indistinguishable chamber. A closet, perhaps, or an anteroom?

She felt small, frightened, yet curious. Where was she? Why couldn't she see? She wasn't alone; she knew that instinctively. Someone was nearby. She heard an urgent whisper as the person behind her gave her shoulders a gentle shake.

"We can't stay here, Bella," a woman's voice with a Southern accent whispered fearfully. "You mustn't make a sound, darling. Promise me you won't make a sound...."

The scene unfolded like a foggy dream. Bella felt herself nodding. She remembered thinking that she might never open her mouth again, because if she did she might never stop screaming.

Why? What lay behind the black wall in her mind, the one she couldn't see through or even seem to chip?

Feelings of horror and dread assailed her. Her mind hovered between past and present. The anonymous woman was tugging on her; Ronnie was tugging on her. The black wall wobbled; so did the hotel lounge.

"Come on, we've got to... get out of here." The woman's voice transformed into Ronnie's, and with it, the memory shattered. Bella caught back a startled breath. She was in the Excelsior Hotel, and Malone was endeavoring to staunch the flow of blood from Lona's wound while a frightened doctor crouched beside him.

But it seemed so far away from her now, farther than it should have been.

Shaking the cobwebs from her head, Bella pulled herself together. With a jolt, she realized that Ronnie had dragged her halfway across the lounge.

"No, wait," she objected, but he held her fast.

"The doctor will handle it, lass." He cast a worried look at the shattered window. "It'll be all right."

How could it be all right? Lona was dying—if not already dead. Bella dug in her heels. "No, Ronnie. Is Lona still . . . ?" She twisted her head and, through the stampede, caught a glimpse of the woman she'd called grandmother for the past twenty years. Malone was supporting her head; the doctor was huddled over her chest.

There was too much blood, Bella thought desperately. Lona was bleeding badly. Just like . . .

An image too brief to grasp flickered through her mind. While the doctor administered to the wound in Lona's chest, a ghostly, disembodied hand appeared to remove from the same general area a knife like a stiletto, dripping with blood.

ON HIS KNEES across the room, Malone supported Lona's head while the terrified doctor worked. The shots came in groups of three, three groups of three so far.

"This is bad, very bad," the little, bespectacled man murmured. His head bobbed up. "Were those more shots?"

Malone clenched his teeth and said nothing. Ronnie had taken Bella away; he didn't have to maintain the facade, and yet he really did, because if he let go of his rigid control, who knew what kind of disastrous chain reaction might follow.

As he watched Lona's face go from white to deathly gray, Malone was startled to see her eyelids flutter. "Child," she rasped.

"Quiet," the doctor barked.

Malone gave him a cutting look, then returned his gaze to Lona. People continued to charge by like elephants.

Her fingers clawed at his wrist. "Help her," she pleaded, then gurgled deep in her throat.

"Blood, blood, blood," the doctor groaned. "We need an ambulance." He jumped again. "More shots?"

"Yes," Malone grunted tightly.

Lona's blue eyes impaled his. "She's my granddaughter—in my heart. Tell her that."

"I will," he promised. Would any of these hysterical people have thought to call a bloody ambulance?

"Belladonna." Another gurgle emerged. This one seemed to spring from her chest. "'Just like Romaine...' Must mean something. Shouldn't have burned the letter. Please—" Lona's grip became viselike for an instant "—tell her I love her. Dying anyway. So much pain." She swallowed with difficulty. "Tell her..." Her nails dug into his flesh. "Amanda..."

Malone frowned, bending forward. "What about Amanda?"

Each breath seemed an agony. "I saw..." she gasped. "Amanda's not..."

"Keep her still," the doctor snapped. His teeth chattered with fear. "The blood's bad enough, but the bullet could still shift. Is she awake?"

Lona's mouth moved, though not, Malone suspected, for the doctor's benefit. Her chest heaved and rattled, then slowly the breath flowed out of her.

Her blue eyes, so bright in life, continued to stare at Malone, who could only close his own against a sight he'd hoped never to witness again in his lifetime. Death was not a pretty thing to behold.

For a moment, the doctor forgot about the gunmen outside. "Oh, dear," he said softly.

Oh, damn, Malone thought bleakly. His head fell forward. But only until another round of bullets blasted through the base of the window.

The doctor yelped and jumped up. Malone had to use both hands to drag him back to his knees. As he did, he glanced quickly out the window. There, backed by a mass of brooding black clouds, he spotted two things: a single raven or crow circling the rocks and a large man with a distinctive cap of blond hair. The man had one hand clamped over the barrel of a rifle, and his ice-blue eyes were locked on the hotel.

"Bastard, Rudge." Malone swore, moving to a crouch.

The doctor poked his head up. "Who? I don't see anyone."

"He's gone."

Malone took one final look at Lona's waxen face and sighed. Shoving the doctor ahead of him, he said, "There's nothing more we can do for her. Let's get the hell out of here."

"No!" Bella twisted fiercely in Malone's grip. "I won't leave her." A sob climbed into her throat, but she swallowed it. "I love her."

"She's dead, Bella, and we'll be joining her if we don't keep moving." He was hauling her around the perimeter of the hotel in an effort to avoid the hysterical mob out front.

"That's ridic—" Her eyes widened suddenly. "Wait! Malone, that man by the oak tree. It's Tock, I'm sure of it."

Rudge and now Tock, Malone thought angrily. The terrible twosome. He could credit Tock as a killer, but he'd hoped Rudge would be above that.

He pulled Bella to a halt in the bushes. Thunder rolled ominously over the water. If shots were fired now, no one would hear them.

"We have to get away." His gaze darted about the open landscape. "I don't know who's doing what or why, but I do know Lona's gone and our getting killed won't bring her back. The host must have been tipped to seat us next to the window. Anonymously, no doubt. Rudge is no amateur— Bella, for God's sake, what is it now?"

"The package!" she gasped. "I left it on the table."

"Yes, I took it from the table," Malone responded. Seeing no one nearby, he gave her a small push. "All clear. Go. The car's in the main lot."

And Lona was in the hotel.

But as stricken as Bella was, she understood logic. She nodded and put her hand in Malone's. Eyes alert, they raced across the lawn, through a line of wind-tossed cedars and into the hotel parking lot.

Intent on their destination, Malone failed to notice the shadow that trailed them until, above the roar of wind and thunder, he heard an evil snicker.

Bella discovered the source of the laughter first and clutched at his arm. He followed her transfixed gaze to a gap in the trees where a smirking Mick Tock stood, his rifle aimed at the pair of them.

"I missed you earlier, pretty lady," he said in his heavy Greek accent. For a big man, he had a whiny, high-pitched voice.

Malone tucked Bella discreetly behind him. "Bad pun, Tock."

The fat man shrugged. "I wasn't sent to play the clown." Widening his smile, he raised the rifle higher.

Malone said the first thought that came to mind. "I counted fifteen shots back there, Tock. You're out of bullets."

Tock's chuckle had a vicious edge. "I reloaded. Too bad for you, I can count, too."

Malone felt Bella curl her fingers into his coat and hold on. He glanced first at her, then at Tock, then decided "what the hell" and lunged for the man.

Tock didn't hesitate. He whipped the rifle sight to his eye and squeezed the trigger.

Malone didn't stop, not even when he heard the shot. If Tock's bullet had hit him, he couldn't feel it, and it hadn't hit Bella because she was behind him.

For an instant, parking lot, cars and trees became a blur. He launched himself at Tock—or rather at what he thought was Tock. He certainly slammed full force into someone, landing hard on his stomach in the process.

He rolled over, checking for blood before anything else, then almost had a heart attack when Bella's hands gripped his arm. He jerked his head around. "Get back," he snapped with a blend of fury and disbelief.

"Get back yourself," grunted a muffled voice beneath him.

He'd recognize that accent anywhere. Frowning, Malone looked down. "Ronnie? What are you doing here? Where's Tock?"

"Out cold in front of you." Bella sank to her knees on the grass. "Are you two all right?"

"I will be when this big lug of a cousin gets off my back."

"Cousin!" She stared. "You're related?"

"Unfortunately." Malone stood and dusted himself off. "We like to... Damn!" he swore. "He's gone."

"He can't be!" Bella declared. "Where did he go?"

A bullet whizzed past her ear, answering that question. Malone grabbed her hand. To Ronnie, he shouted, "Get back to the hotel and deal with things. He'll follow us. Go!" He barked the last order at Bella, but needn't have bothered. She was already scrambling for the car.

"Maybe he's dizzy," she panted once they were inside. "He's not—" A bullet blasted through the windshield.

"Hitting his target?" Malone finished with a grimace. "Come on, start, you bas—" He had to duck midword to avoid the shot that turned the windshield into a web of cracked glass.

"Can you see the road?" Bella demanded as he shoved the car into gear.

"I can't see bloody anything," he retorted. "Hang on."

"Thanks. I wouldn't have thought of that." Bracing her foot against the glove box and her hand on the dash, she darted a look over her shoulder.

"Have we lost him?" Malone asked tersely.

"I think so." Two bullets penetrated the rear windshield, impacting in their headrests. She winced. "Obviously not."

Downshifting, Malone floored the vehicle. The little rental car screamed onto the street with a squeal of tires that was audible even above the thunder.

They'd gone two city blocks before he risked a sideways glance. He could see it in her profile: she was thinking about

Lona, the woman who'd raised her and who now lay dead in the lounge of the Excelsior Hotel.

"Ronnie'll handle it," he promised, his compassion uncharacteristic and somewhat unnerving. Beautiful or not, appealing or not, she shouldn't be getting to him emotionally. She shouldn't, but she was, he thought with a heavy, inward sigh. Damn, life was complicated.

Bella stared into the rain, which had started to fall in large drops. "Tock killed her in cold blood."

"Yes, well, one of them did," Malone agreed.

"Was Rudge there, too?"

She didn't seemed surprised. But, dammit, he was. And disappointed. In Rudge, and in himself for misjudging the man so badly.

He located a spot on the shattered windshield through which he could see. More gently than was his custom, he said, "She was dying anyway, Bella. She told me."

"I know."

He frowned. "You did?"

"She never said anything, but I knew. I just wanted more time with her. I don't care if she was my grandmother or not. I loved her, and...well, thank you for saving this package for me."

For some reason her fist clutching the tissue-wrapped parcel caused Malone's stomach to tighten. A knot of resistance, he wondered? Or desire? Possibly both, he thought glumly. Oh, God, he was in deep, deep trouble.

She stared dry-eyed at the package. He heard tissue crinkling. "What is it?" he asked.

She hesitated, obviously puzzled. "It's a—a picture case. And a note. It says 'Bella, the pictures in this case are of you and Amanda. I don't believe they will help you in your quest, but I do feel the time has come for you to have them. Amanda wrote me a letter, but foolishly I burned it. Please forgive my deceit. I have only ever wanted the best for you. I love you, my dear, as I feel certain Amanda must have done. None of us can change the past, Bella. I only hope and pray that you will learn of yours and benefit from that knowledge in the end. Love always.' " Bella's voice broke on a stifled sob. " 'Lona.' "

"MIRROR, MIRROR, on the wall,
Who's the prettiest of us all?
And if you think that I'm so vain,
You've never met our dear Charmaine."

Smiling in what she knew to be a dangerous fashion, the woman turned from one of the many mirrors that hung in her Chinatown office and faced the man she call Tic-Tac. *Idiot man,* she thought. *His brain must be the size of a pea.*

"I told you to watch the old woman," she said in a deceptively pleasant voice. "Watch, Tic-Tac, not kill. I'm also positive I made no mention of you shooting at dear Bella Conlan and that British ninny who's helping her."

"No, ma'am," Tock said, then ruined it by letting a smile creep across his mouth as he glanced at Hobson Crowe in the corner.

She pulled a slender pink weapon from her sleeve. "No, ma'am, what?" she demanded, advancing on him.

The smile vanished. "No, ma'am, you didn't tell me to do those things."

She leaned over him where he sat, a hint of intimidation in her stance, the weapon touching his nose. "Then why, pray tell, did you do that?"

"Because I told him to. Hello, Hobby. Getting drunk, are you?" A tall, slender woman in the shady area between forty and fifty strolled into the room. She wore a sleek, black silk pantsuit with Oriental symbols around the cuffs and collar, and held a cigarette in a silver-and-ebony holder between her long, carefully manicured fingers. Her dark hair fell straight and shiny to her shoulders. Her eyes beneath a thick fringe of bangs were hazel and currently gleamed with satisfaction.

Charmaine Parret, cool, elegant and aggravatingly composed, had the irritating ability to set her counterpart's teeth on edge.

"You interfered?" the woman asked levelly. She didn't clench her fists, because Tic-Tac was watching. However, had he been anywhere else, she surely would have slapped Charmaine's face. Hobby's, too, because he'd probably known what she was up to from the start.

He knew everything, the worm, yet he never did a damned thing with that knowledge. Heaven save her from ever becoming so utterly apathetic. He sipped his sherry calmly, because he was always calm, and watched as Charmaine sauntered across the floor.

"I have every right to 'interfere,' as you so crudely put it," Charmaine replied with a serene smile.

The woman despised serenity—and poise and polish and beauty as well. Charmaine possessed all those qualities in abundance, but not naturally. No, she hadn't been born with them. "You," the woman noted disdainfully, "are a bitch."

Only Charmaine's eyes moved. They slid to her face and held her challenging gaze. "I," she countered with no trace of rancor, "am not subject to your will."

"I run the business, Charmaine."

"Yes, but I am more familiar with this particular aspect of the business."

The woman's voice rose. "Hobby?"

He merely lifted a placid brow. "No comment."

"Wimp," she muttered.

"If you say so." He raised his glass. "Why did you order the old woman killed, Charmaine?"

She drew delicately on her cigarette. "I thought she might know something."

"Hah!" The woman turned back to the mirror. "If she did, she'd have spilled it long ago."

"Possibly. Or perhaps she was waiting for just such a moment as was presented to her when the girl escaped from us."

"You mean when Bella escaped from me, don't you?" the woman challenged.

Charmaine arched her eyebrows. "Well, it does put us in a rather awkward situation. Oh, Mr. Rudge is willing to recapture her, but we'll have to pay for his services all over again. By the way, although I'm sure Mr. Tock hasn't mentioned it, your friend the bounty hunter was also at the Excelsior Hotel today. The interfering fool showed up just as my friend Mr. Tock was about to put an end to our witness problems."

"Good. I told Rudge and I'm telling you again, I want her alive."

"So you can kill her yourself?"

The woman's head came up stiffly. "Have you got a problem with that?"

Charmaine turned away. "Take my advice, go back to your mirror. Pretend you're the fairest in the land and leave me to deal with this matter."

"Or I could," Hobby suggested from the low black-and-red Chinese sofa.

"No," the women said as one. "Wait outside, please," Charmaine added to Tock.

While he obeyed, she fingered one of the colorful, low-burning lanterns that adorned the office, her mouth curving into a pleasurable little smile.

The woman's blood boiled. The office air that normally smelled of sandalwood and Opium perfume was marred now by the smell of Charmaine's signature scent, Poison.

Fine, so Charmaine had status in the business. She always had and always would, but she did not oversee it. . . .

And she wasn't all that pretty, either. No, not pretty at all. She didn't have short burgundy hair, and even if she had, it wouldn't have suited her complexion. Charmaine's background was a combustible blend, unlike her own, which was a more-flattering mixture of nationalities. Charmaine's skin was too fair, her hair these days too black, her eyes too much like a cat's. Robert would have ditched her eventually—if he'd lived to do it, that is.

"Drifting off, are you?" Charmaine inquired in amusement.

Rousing herself from her momentary lapse, the woman glared at her via the smoky bamboo-framed mirror. It was a bold look, but then she needed to be bold where Charmaine was concerned. "I want her alive," she repeated. Her gaze centered mainly on Charmaine. "I want to do this myself. My way. The old woman's gone. If she was a threat, she isn't one anymore. Rudge is good. He'll catch Bella—and that interfering ex-bookie, Malone, to boot. You can have him, Charmaine, but I want her. I want to destroy Belladonna."

Chapter Five

"There's something," Malone muttered, pacing distractedly. "There's always something somewhere." He shot Bella
a hooded look while he paced and she studied the pictures
that Lona had given her. "Are you sure you don't remember any more about the night you were taken?"

She sat, chin cupped in her hands, and stared at the open
case. "No, I'm not." Her gaze fastened on the double pictures—two pictures of herself at seven or eight years of age,
one with pigtails, one without. She was posing in both with
a smiling, blond-haired woman in her mid-to-late twenties.
Her mother had been blond, or so Lona had told her.
Blond, pretty and full of life. Bella examined the photos
more closely. "There's something in the background," she
said. "It looks like a country building of some sort."

"Yes, fine, a building," Malone said testily. "The question is does it trigger any memories?"

She thought for a minute, then said, "Only the one I told
you about in the hotel lounge." She lifted her gaze to the
window. "I have to go back. I have to make arrangements
for...Lona."

"No."

"She was my grandmother, Malone, the only family I've
ever had. She wanted to be cremated, and I'm going to see
that she gets her wish."

Malone stopped pacing to glower at her. "Later, Bella,
when we don't have hit men and bounty hunters chasing us

all over hell and the city." He knit his brows. "What are you doing?"

"Lighting a candle." She struck a match as if to burn away her anger. Lona shouldn't be dead. It was her fault. The bullet must have been meant for her. "We're in Chinatown, in someone's—and you refuse to tell me whose— cluttered apartment, with dozens of fans, bamboo screens and pieces of wicker furniture surrounding us. Candles give the place atmosphere."

He made a disagreeable sound—his way, Bella suspected, of venting frustration. "Stay on topic, will you? Did you see or hear anything last night in the house?"

She suppressed a sigh. Sexy or not, the man was ridiculously single-minded. Her grandmother was dead. Malone should be offering solace, not treating her like a suspect in some dimestore detective novel.

Her eyes followed him as he resumed his preoccupied pacing. She felt awful and wanted to feel that way; she had the right. Malone on the other hand had absolutely no right to look so gorgeous, to be wearing faded black jeans and a white cotton shirt with the sleeves rolled partway up his forearms. He looked so serious and so absorbed that for a moment Bella considered marching up to him and demanding that he put those sexy arms of his around her and hold her. She wanted to be held so close that she could hear his heart beating and feel the warmth that spelled life radiating from him.

She craved an infusion of life. Love, too, but she couldn't see getting that from the hard-nosed Malone. Comfort, possibly, providing she made the first move. But love? No, Malone took care of Malone first and foremost.

"Well?" He looked at her now out of intent eyes. *Beautiful eyes,* Bella thought. Then she collected herself.

"Rudge told me I wasn't being held for ransom. He called me bounty. He called *you* a snake—or maybe I did that. He said you'd been a bookie, but now you find people for a living. He also figured you'd have welshed on your deal with him in a minute if you'd known about the stakes." Something clicked in her brain and she sat up. "He said a name, too, but I can't remember what it was."

"A name?" Malone, who'd been looking somewhat vexed, frowned deeply. "Whose name?"

She concentrated. "He said that you knew him—Rudge, I mean—but that he had an in with Ro...Romaine. Isn't that the name Lona mentioned?"

"Yes, wonderful, but who's Romaine?" Malone came to lean his hands on the glass-and-rattan table in front of her, until his beautiful, somber face was mere inches away.

"I have no..." The sentence tapered off. That blood-stained knife glinted once again in her mind's eye. "We have to run, Bella, get away," a woman's faraway voice insisted. Did she have blond hair? Yes, Bella could see it. Just the ends, but it was golden blond, like the woman in the picture case. Like her mother.

The flashback vanished, leaving her with only the mystery name, Romaine. "I don't know." She moved her head. "Maybe it's familiar. I can't tell."

He stared at her for several long moments. She saw his eyes scanning her face, felt his breath on her cheek, then heard him make a small sound of discomfort as he drew back. "Yes, well, it'll probably come to you eventually." He seemed uneasy somehow. Because of her? "Uh, would you like...dinner?"

"Sure, I'd—" Inwardly pleased, Bella started to answer him, but stopped and sat up sharply. "Parret!"

"What?" He'd placed his thumb to his lower lip. Now he removed it to stare down at her.

"Parret," she repeated, testing the name. "Tock came in and told Rudge to shut up. He said that Parret said to get out of the room. And there was a man."

Malone crouched in front of her. He took her hand and shook it gently, as if to jostle her memory further. "A third man, Bella?"

"Yes. He sounded English, very proper."

"Like a butler?"

"Like that, but it was a different accent, as though he'd been away from England for a long time."

"Hobson," Malone murmured. His head dropped forward. "God, of course. How could I have been so stupid? Hobson Crowe. And Charmaine Parret."

Bella stared. "You know these people?"

"Not personally, but I've heard of them. There are three of them, or so the word on the street goes. Parret, Crowe and one other. Probably a bird name of some sort."

"A what?"

"That's how they're known, Bella. Parret, Crowe and their third partner. They're called the Birds."

"Well, well, well. You must be Lady Parret." Larson Rudge had his feet propped up and crossed on Charmaine's desk when she entered her hazily lit office.

"Mr. Rudge, I presume." She sent him a cursory look as she skirted her lacquered-mahogany desk. "What are you doing here?"

"Looking for answers." The door opened and quietly closed. Without a backward glance, Rudge said, "Evening, Hobson. Were you in on this afternoon's fun and games?"

Charmaine had no time for Rudge's queries. Leaning her elegant body against a delicately papered wall, she said point-blank, "You have no business barging in here. If we'd wanted a face-to-face meeting, we'd have arranged one. What do you want?"

He answered just as candidly. "I like to know who I'm dealing with."

"Then I'm afraid you're out of luck, because you're not dealing with either Hobby or myself anymore."

"Which leaves either a Mr. or a Ms. X."

"Personally, I'd leave well enough alone."

He removed the unlit cigar from his mouth, dropping his feet heavily to the floor. His icy gray eyes flashed. "Don't play coy with me, Lady P. I've figured out the truth."

"I believe he means he's eavesdropped," Hobby interjected.

"Whatever. I know you're the Birds. And you're notorious." He smiled smugly and sat back. "You're also loaded."

"We're also murderers," Charmaine stated coolly. "Doesn't that worry you at all, Mr. Rudge?"

"I can take care of myself."

"So if I were to have Mr. Tock shoot you on the way out, you could take care of that?"

"Tock's not here. Besides, the day he can catch me off guard is the day I retire."

Charmaine was growing bored. "Make your point, Mr. Rudge."

"My *point*," he said, emphasizing the second word, "is that I was hired, by your boss if I'm not mistaken, to locate Bella Conlan and bring her in. Alive. Tell your man Tock to back off. The lady isn't worth squat to me dead."

"My, what high moral standards we have," Charmaine mocked. Her fingers located a Chinese bust on the ledge behind her. "To say nothing of audacity. You're telling me to back off because you need Bella Conlan alive in order to receive a second payoff."

He feigned innocence. "She didn't escape from me."

"True." Charmaine smiled. "And yet somehow, Mr. Rudge, I feel you did have a hand in her escape. Perhaps not directly, but in some small way. What do you think, Hobby?"

"I think it's time I returned to my office."

She laughed. "Poor Hobby. It's so difficult to be a pacifist in this violent business of ours." She glanced down. "Is that your lighter on the floor?"

Hobby looked. So did Rudge—a natural reaction to a subtly played ace. When the big man's eyes dropped, Charmaine's hands came up. She brought the plaster bust up and smashed it against his skull with great force. Rudge sat stock-still for a long moment, then slumped slowly sideways until the chair arm stopped him and he fell facedown to the floor.

Outside, Chinese fireworks paid homage to the festive season.

Hobby didn't bat an eyelash. He simply asked, "Is he dead?"

Charmaine flicked a large piece of plaster away with her toe. "No. The man's an ox. Have Tock take him away and tie him up. I'll let him know what to do after that."

Hobby's brows rose in evident surprise. "You're going to let him live?"

"For the moment. It wouldn't be prudent for me to cross the Queen of Spades upstairs right now. Dead bodies can't be kept on hand, and they can be difficult to dispose of quickly. I wouldn't want him floating to shore in Tiburon or rubbing soggy shoulders with someone's houseboat in Sausalito. He's seen me, Hobby. Insolence aside, I don't like it when someone of his ilk can identify me. *You're* our front man. People see you, not us." She indicated the office above with a barely perceptible movement of her head. "We like our anonymity."

"It's kind of you to want to protect her as well as yourself," Hobby noted.

Charmaine's laughter rang out. Picking up her cigarette and holder, she lit the tip and inhaled deeply. "Protection isn't my plan, Hobby. She can take care of herself. But this situation is another story. A very old story, as you well know. There's a great deal at stake here—more, I think, than you and she can handle."

"Are you going to kill Bella?"

"Oh, yes. Absolutely yes."

He glanced upward. "She'll be upset."

Charmaine blew out a long, contemplative stream of smoke. "I know. But that's her problem. I have my own to contend with. And where mine are concerned, I trust no one to solve them but me. Belladonna is mine, not hers—and, British bookie notwithstanding, as good as dead already."

MALONE AWOKE TO DARKNESS and a bloodcurdling scream that raised the hair on his scalp. He was out of bed and across the floor before he fully understood the reason.

Bella!

Her name shot through his brain. He'd been sleeping on the leather sofa and smashed his foot into an end table en route to the bedroom. The pain barely registered as her scream came again.

She hadn't bolted the door, but it stuck, as doors tended to in the fog-damp climate of San Francisco. He had to put his shoulder to it, and even then it didn't want to budge.

"Pink knife," she was screaming when he finally stumbled across the threshold. "Blood...the mirror. The mirror!"

Her head thrashed on the pillow; her fists were clenched on either side, ready to strike, it seemed to Malone. He ran to the side of the bed. She looked beautiful in sleep, even in nightmarish sleep. Bewitching, red lipped, golden skinned. Damn her for having such a potent effect on him. Damn black lashes, witchy eyes and a mouth just made for kissing.

Despite the circumstances, Malone felt himself getting hard. *Damn that, too,* he thought, setting reluctant hands on her shoulders. The spaghetti straps of her red chemise fell aside, bringing a groan to his throat that only his clenched teeth prevented from slipping out.

"Bella." He shook her gently, trying to ignore the scent of her skin and hair, which reminded him of summer roses.

"Pink knife," she said again, then squirmed and attempted to fight him off. "Coming for me," she panted. "They see me. They must."

They?

Again Malone shook her, and this time he had to duck to avoid her flailing fists.

"Bella, it's me." His soothing tone surprised even him. "You're safe. I won't let them hurt you."

She twisted her body one last time. "Pink knife," she whispered. "Covered with blood. They see me. Why don't they kill me?"

A fair question, but unimportant at the moment. Although she'd quieted enough for him to release her, he didn't do so immediately. Instead, he eased the sheet and blanket up, partly to keep her warm, but mostly to cover her firm breasts, so disturbingly delineated by her skimpy negligee.

A rush of heat and desire swept through him. "Oh, damn." Malone sighed, dropping his head forward in utter defeat. This wasn't supposed to happen.

Stroking the dark hair from her face, he stared at her in sleep. And knew in his soul that he was lost.

"DON'T FIDGET," Malone ordered, trapping her restless right wrist as they walked along the pier. "We'll look conspicuous."

"Like we don't already," Bella grumbled. She gave his arm a none-too-gentle poke. "This isn't going to work, Malone. I don't know the first thing about being a waitress in a place like this."

"Pretend it's a party. You're the hostess, and you don't want anyone to drop food or drinks on your brand-new carpet."

"Thanks a lot." Sighing, Bella adjusted her blond wig. How on earth had she gotten into this mess?

"We have to meet the Birds, or at least see them," Malone had explained reasonably last night. "I called in some favors and found out that they're hosting a charity casino aboard their restaurant yacht, the *Sun Sen.*"

Bella recognized the name. She'd been there once several months ago with a group of people from the Playhouse. The decor was lush, red and gold, and spoke strongly of the days when gambling dens and exotic brothels had been the norm in San Francisco. Atmosphere or no, however, she had major reservations about Malone's plan.

Pose as waiters? It sounded reasonable in theory. After all, his cousin Ronnie had connections and could get them in, no questions asked. They could watch, listen and try to discover which Bird was which. Assuming they showed up, which Malone assured her they would, since this was their party. After all, it looked good to claim that they'd raised a small fortune to benefit no less than three national charities.

Which was disgusting and the height of hypocrisy, considering that they dealt in all sorts of nasty things, from stolen jewels to dynamite to hard porn. As for killing, well, Lona's death proved that life meant less than nothing to them. The fingers of Bella's free hand curled in determination. If it killed her, she was going to bring down the monsters responsible for Lona's death.

She'd had a nightmare about the incident. Of course, Lona had been there, but she'd been stabbed rather than shot. The hand doing the stabbing had been gloved and...something else, something Bella hadn't quite been able to fathom, because the dream had shifted abruptly at that point and the knife had seemed to be floating toward her.

She hadn't been able to run in the dream, only to cower deeper into the shadows under the table. But that hadn't helped, because she could see the knife moving ever closer. She'd looked up and spotted her face in a mirror, then suddenly she'd realized that the blade was poised directly in front of her. Yet, oddly, except in the mirror, she couldn't see it.

She'd screamed long and loudly in the dream. She'd thrashed out at someone, too, but thankfully that person hadn't been wearing gloves, and she'd felt immediately comforted and safe. The way she did now in Malone's company...

She'd woken up that morning shaken but calm and had agreed to Malone's plans. She'd used her talent for theatrical makeup, together with the putty, hair, shadows and tints Malone had purchased in Chinatown, to fashion their disguises.

Malone's had been a piece of cake. A small beard, a little putty and a change of clothes had worked wonders. He hadn't needed a wig; Bella had simply changed the style and added a bit more curl to the ends of his own dark hair.

In an effort now to calm the butterflies in her stomach, she studied his profile. He looked very handsome, like a pirate or a bullfighter in his black pants and vest, white shirt and knee-length boots. Handsome and unbearably appealing.

Her own costume pleased her less. She'd had to don a blond wig, but since the color didn't really suit her complexion, she'd also been obliged to lighten her skin with foundation and a variety of powders. Using pencils and shadows, she'd made her eyes rounder. She'd also added a few body curves, mainly in the bust area, had blotted out her high cheekbones with contour and had finally donned the navy blue dress and white apron required for tonight's performance. She looked like a cross between Brigitte Bardot and Shirley Temple. *Très sexy,* she thought, resisting an urge to giggle.

At the end of the pier they boarded the cruiser that would transport them out to the *Sun Sen.* With the fog twining around the rails and seawater slapping against the hull, Bella felt as if they were sailing to a ghost ship, back through time to the days of saloon girls, bordellos and gambling houses.

A group of the other employees stood close by on deck, chatting about the money that would flow like wine that evening.

"Try to look professional, will you?" Malone said about halfway out.

"I am," Bella retorted. She released a pent-up breath. "Look, Malone, I'm simply not good at balancing trays. What if I drop something?"

He rolled his eyes. "For God's sake, Bella, it's an act. Use your imagination. I can't believe you don't have one. You've spent enough time around Irish Max and company."

She pulled her raincoat, the one he'd thankfully remembered to bring from the hotel, tighter. "You make them sound like hoods. They're not dangerous or threatening. In fact, they aren't much of anything anymore. They've gone straight—well, mostly."

He slid her a dubious look. *Why, oh why,* she murmured inwardly, *did he have to look so dark and dangerous, especially tonight?* She masked the shiver that started deep in her belly.

"What about you?" he asked.

The shiver stopped. "What about me?"

"Have you gone straight?"

Insulted, she glared at him. "I've never *not* been straight. I did a favor for a friend. If you want to get technical, I undid a crime for him. The only pockets I've really picked belong to Max and his friends, and I was only after candy and... Hey, wait a minute. Back off, Malone," she warned when he reached a hand toward her.

"Your cheek's smudged," he said, rubbing a spot with his gloved thumb.

Even through the leather, Bella felt the contact. She already knew his hands very well. They were warm, slightly callused and long fingered.

He'd admitted to being born in Durham, in the north of England as she'd suspected. Durham was a county of farms, mines and fishing ports. People there did manual labor, the kind of work that created calluses both physical and mental. Oh, Malone was tough all right; the question was, could he love?

It surprised Bella a little to discover that she wanted to know. Surprised and, strangely, pleased her, too. The shiver she'd staved off earlier rippled through her again.

"We're here," the cruiser pilot called down from the cabin house. "The *Sun Sen*."

Malone looked up at the lighted ship. "Moment of truth, Bella. Get your climbing shoes on." He cupped her elbow in his hand. "We're about to meet the Birds of San Francisco." Lesser-known than Alfred Hitchcock's, but far, far, deadlier.

Chapter Six

"You're tipping your tray, Bella."

Malone made the stoic observation as he passed her in the dining room. *You'd think he'd been born in service,* she reflected resentfully. *That and to give orders to those beneath him. Must be a British thing,* she decided.

The main dining room was located just below the casino, which was situated on the ship's upper deck. The vessel was huge, Oriental in design and plush inside and out. Red velvet curtains adorned portholes and entryways. The floor was polished planking, the tables covered with white linen and draped with a smaller square of red cloth. Candles burned in dozens of wall sconces. The air, delicately scented, smelled of holly berries, spiced wax and smoldering incense. Unlike the staff, the Birds' guests were, as Lona would have described them, dressed to kill. If they were friends of the Birds, who knew, maybe killing *was* their job.

Bella drifted from a group of business people to a circle of men and women talking politics. She was fighting a yawn and attempting to catch a glimpse of Malone when a sultry voice behind her said, "Chablis, please."

Turning, Bella spied a tall woman of indeterminate age with black hair and bangs, wearing a long, red silk gown and carrying an unlit cigarette in a holder. She had an odd, British-American accent. Only her delicate jawline and painted mouth were visible. The rest of her face was covered with a pair of large, round sunglasses and a mesh veil attached to a broad-brimmed hat. Like Greta Garbo, she apparently wanted to maintain her anonymity.

"I . . ." Bella forgot her role for a moment, then recovered. "This is champagne, ma'am," she said politely.

The woman treated her to a practiced smile. "Yes, but I want Chablis."

"I'll see if I can find some."

"Wait." A slender hand, the skin fractionally older looking than that of her jaw and throat, waylaid her. The contact even through her uniform caused Bella's skin to prickle. "Do I know you?"

Confident in her disguise, though still uncertain about her reaction to the woman's touch, Bella replied, "I don't think so, ma'am."

"Hmm." Through dark glasses that reminded Bella of enormous bug eyes, the woman studied her. "I admit the light's bad, but I swear I've seen you before. In Los Angeles, perhaps?"

The light was bad only because of her sunglasses. Bella forced a smile. "I don't think so. I'm from Cincinnati."

"Ah, well, I'm from Vicksburg myself. What's in Cincinnati?"

WKRP sprang to mind, but Bella settled for a less flippant response. "Not a great deal, I'm afraid."

"Hobby, come here." The woman beckoned to a middle-aged man with a thickish body, brown hair and nondescript features.

"Yes, Charmaine?"

Bella's heart jammed into her ribs. Charmaine? As in Charmaine Parret?

"Does this woman look familiar to you?"

Between her shock and the man's inspection of her, Bella experienced a moment of panic. What if her makeup had smudged again?

"I . . ." He screwed up his face. "No," he said at length. "But she reminds me of someone."

"Who?"

"Amanda."

Charmaine Parret's reaction and Bella's couldn't have been farther apart. Charmaine's mouth compressed to a grim bronze line. From behind her glasses, she shot Hobby—Hobson Crowe, perhaps—what could only have been termed a cutting look.

Bella, on the other hand, couldn't seem to control her expression. Her mother had known the Birds.

"Excuse me, Ms. Parret, Mr. Crowe." A familiar hand grasped her arm. Numb inside and out, Bella continued to stare. Malone smiled a totally false smile. "Selma's only been with us for a few weeks. Can I get you anything?"

Charmaine's composure reasserted itself so swiftly that the slip might never have occurred. "Chablis," she said, her tone as pleasant as her smile—her perfect smile, which Bella suddenly realized *she* had seen somewhere before. Where, though? And when? Recently? In the past? The answers danced tantalizingly out of reach.

"I'll have it sent over at once," Malone promised. Nodding politely, he drew Bella through the crowd to a quiet corner near the bandstand.

It surprised her that he didn't snap her head off. Instead, he trapped her chin with his long fingers and brought it up until her eyes met his. "Are you all right?" he asked.

Not with him so close, she wasn't. "Of course. I just didn't realize who she was."

"Yes, but she might have guessed who you were."

"I doubt it. Though Mr. Crowe said I reminded him of Amanda."

Malone's brow furrowed. "He knew your mother?"

"Apparently. So did Charmaine. I don't think she liked her, however—Charmaine, that is." She paused. "I got a funny feeling from her, Malone."

"Funny how?"

"I can't describe it. It was prickly, like sparks on my skin."

"Threatening ones?"

"Not exactly."

"What then?" He was losing patience. In spite of everything, Bella had to hide her amusement. He was very sexy

this way, short-tempered and reluctant to get involved.
There was a great deal more to this man than he let on. But
that was for another time.

"Like Frankenstein," she answered him.

His steady stare and level "What?" told her plainly what
he thought of that response.

She gave his chest a quick poke. "Like a static charge,
Malone. Or maybe fireflies."

A smile that really wasn't a smile curved his lips. "Have
you been sampling that champagne, by any chance?"

"I told you I couldn't describe it."

"I can see that." His eyes darted around circumspectly.
He caught her arm. "Come on, let's see what other intriguing tidbits the Birds' yacht has to offer, shall we?"

"Chablis," she reminded him. She glanced at Charmaine Parret, who was deep in conversation with another
woman. Bella couldn't see the second woman's face, but she
was tall and slender and had short burgundy hair. Like
Charmaine, she wore a hat, in her case a pillbox with a veil
and tinted glasses. God, what a spooky pair they were.
Spooky but fascinating.

Absorbed, Bella dragged her feet until Malone, irritated
at their lack of progress, sighed and paused. "What is it,
Bella?"

"A woman."

"Yes?"

"She's talking to Charmaine Parret. They're both wearing hats and dark glasses. Another Bird?"

"Very likely," Malone agreed. He looked over, considered, then made a sound in his throat and pushed her forward with a hand pressed to the small of her back. "Let's
go."

Bella lost sight of the mysterious Bird women and
couldn't find them again even when Malone stopped to give
Charmaine's drink order to another waiter. "So it's a Ms.
Bird to round out the trio." Aware of his erotic touch on her
back, she started down a set of narrow, winding stairs.
"Why do they want to be anonymous? Why doesn't Hobson Crowe?"

"They're in a dangerous business. Anonymity's safe, especially at a party like this. But they need a front man, someone who looks respectable. Evidently Crowe fits the bill."

"He doesn't say much. I don't trust people like that. They could be planning to pat you on the back or knife you in it. You wouldn't know which one until they did it." She could feel the warmth of his hand through her uniform. Sending him a speculative look, she mused, "You're sort of like that yourself, Malone."

"Thanks," he murmured dryly, then nodded to the right. "The offices are that way."

Bella made a face, but turned obediently. "Who'd you pay off to get that information?"

Again he flashed that quick non-smile. "I charmed one of the waitresses."

"Naturally... Malone?" Bella halted in a corridor lit only by a handful of electric candles and tipped her head sideways. "Why don't you ever charm me?"

Her candid question took him by surprise. Momentarily flustered, he searched the corridor as if for an answer. Either that or a way out. But then his defenses kicked in and he said simply, "I didn't think you'd fall for it."

Was that a compliment or merely a convenient out? Bella's suspicious eyes remained on his face as they started off again, but hard as she tried, she couldn't penetrate his impassive mask.

Wooden doors came into view ahead of them. *"C.,"* Bella read from one.

"For Crowe," Malone remarked. At her skeptical look, he nodded to a second door. *"P.,"* he said. "For Parret."

Bella peered at the third. *"S.* For Seagull, Sparrow, Starling?"

"Stork?"

"We should look in there first," Bella decided. "Wait!" She spun around, darting a glance along the shadowy passageway. "I heard something."

"That was me." Malone tested the knob. "Keep your voice down. Damn."

"What's wrong?"

"It's locked with a dead bolt. Apparently Ms. S. values her privacy."

"So does Ms. P.," Bella noted, trying the handle. "Ah, here's something. Crowe's is locked, but it's not the same as the others. Do you have your file?"

He hesitated, then released a long-suffering breath and brought it out for her. "You're a good little B-and-E artist," he observed in a richly ironic tone. "Courtesy of Irish Max?"

"Nope—Lona."

Disbelief showed through his even expression. "What?"

Bella waited until she heard a click, then climbed to her feet. "I used to lock myself in the bathroom when I was little. I locked us out of the house a couple times, too. That's not a smart thing to do in Alaska in the dead of winter, and Lona had a phobia about spare keys outside. So she taught me how to break in—or out, as the case may be." Her eyes clouded, but she refused to let the tears come. "Do you think Ronnie took care of her body?"

Malone started to lift a hand to her cheek. Halfway there, however, he checked himself and let his arm drop back to his side. He looked at her steadily as he said, "I'm sure he's taken care of everything, Bella. Ronnie's like that."

Yes, but what was Malone like under that guarded surface? Bella wished she dared find out for herself. Was he trustworthy? Troubled? Kind? Cranky? Gentle? Nasty? What?

Out of nowhere, she had an overwhelming and completely uninhibited urge to kiss him, to stop in her tracks, wrap her arms around his neck and set her mouth on his. The idea brought a rush of heat to her cheeks and had him frowning at her.

"What is it? Are you all right?"

Bella gathered her composure, wrapping it around herself like a steel cloak. "I'm fine," she lied. "Shall we go in?"

They entered a meticulously clean office. Not a paper was on the desk, not a book or jade figurine out of place.

"Try the drawers," Malone suggested. "I'll see if there's a safe."

Unfortunately, every drawer Bella searched was either locked or contained nothing more exciting than paper clips. The storage closet was the same.

"There's a connecting door," she noted, crossing to it. "Maybe I can pick the lock between..." The rest of the sentence died in her throat. When she pushed on the brass knob, the door opened so easily that she literally toppled into the next office.

"Klutz, " Malone muttered. But he was at her side instantly, helping her up. "Did you hurt anything?"

"Only my dignity." Fixing her wig, Bella stepped out of range and allowed her eyes to comb the room. Office P., for Parret.

A strange sensation stole over her, like an Arctic breeze blowing across her skin. She stood absolutely still for a moment, trying to determine the source of the sensation. What was it she felt?

Hot and bothered, but that was Malone's fault. Scared, but who wouldn't be under the circumstances? Every groan sounded like a footstep, every creak a voice.

Another chill feathered along her spine. It moved outward to engulf her whole body. What were her senses trying to tell her?

In the dim light of the portal, Bella noticed several things, but first and foremost she noticed the lacquered letter opener on the desk. It had the carved figure of a parrot on top, and she stared at it for the longest time before shaking herself out of her trance and moving on. Even then her gaze kept returning to it....

There was an In basket and a bigger Out basket, both brass, both empty, and a selection of classical compact discs with Strauss at the top and *The Mikado* lying open on the stereo. She was about to see what other Gilbert and Sullivan titles there were when she spied a movement in the mirrors that dotted the tiny cabin. Grabbing a stapler from the desk, she whirled.

"What?" Malone appeared at the door.

Had she spoken? "Nothing." She rested her hand on the desk. "It's my reflection. I didn't recognize myself. Did you find a safe?"

"No, but there was a stack of invoices in the wastebasket, heading for the shredder, I'd guess. Have a look at this."

Bella held it up to the light, squinting. "It doesn't say what's being shipped."

Ever wary, Malone kept his eyes moving while he tapped the upper left corner.

"'London,'" she read. "So they're international. I figured they would be. I'm sure they're into stolen jewels and—"

"The merchandise isn't important, Bella," he said with a trace of his customary impatience. "Look lower."

"There's a *C* attached to a scribbled line. Crowe's signature, I presume."

"Lower," Malone said through his teeth.

"Ro—" She stopped, unbelieving. "Romaine!" Forgetting the effect of Malone's proximity on her, Bella brought her head sharply up and around. "Lona said that name—or my mother did. Something was 'just like Romaine.' But she didn't... What was that?" she demanded. Her fingernails bit into his wrist. "Malone, there's someone coming."

"You're imagining things."

"I'm not. I heard a noise."

"So do I, and you're making it."

"I heard a noise, Malone, a squeak. Like stairs squeaking, maybe?" Her tone, despite the apprehension that underscored it, challenged him.

"Yes, fine, I'll look." He headed back across the threshold to Hobson Crowe's office door.

Bella stayed close on his heels, pressing herself into his shoulder as he checked the corridor.

"Nothing," he said. "Ships creak, Bella. It's their nature."

Possibly—but it wasn't her nature to imagine things. Nevertheless, Bella forced herself to shrug in agreement. After all, it wasn't as though she wanted to be right.

After locking the door, and with the invoice safely tucked inside Malone's vest pocket, they started back along the passageway. The air was still, the entire deck bathed in silence. A groan of timber from deep in the hold attested to the age of the vessel—close to a hundred years old, Bella would guess.

Tapping Malone on the shoulder, she whispered, "Why aren't we going back the way we came?"

He pulled her up disturbingly close behind him. "Curiosity."

She almost laughed. "I didn't know you had it in you."

"Very funny." He pointed to a hatchway. "That looks promising."

His hair smelled nice. So did his skin. In the dim passageway, his eyes glinted with a dangerous light. What a pirate he'd have made. Bella shook herself. "It looks like the back of the ship to me."

"It's called the stern, Bella." Malone glanced back, a frown grazing his mouth. "What are you doing?"

She drew swiftly away. "Nothing. You had some office dust in your hair." She caught his arm. "Wait. I heard it again."

"It's the boat shifting, Bella," he said tolerantly. "Will you please stop panicking?"

"I am not panicking. I'm edgy. You try being kidnapped, Malone. Try having your grandmother murdered right in front of you. I want to cry and feel bad, not creep down hallways with little bits of memory dancing like faceless puppets in my head. I don't know anything about the first nine years of my life, except that my mother's name was Amanda and that Lona wasn't my real grandmother.... Why do you have that look on your face?"

"I don't have any look," he began, then broke off and yanked her sideways so fast that her neck snapped.

She looked around, mystified. "What?"

"Keep quiet."

"But—"

His hand clamped over her mouth, cutting off her protest and most of her oxygen as well. She squirmed, but he wouldn't loosen his grip. So she did the only reasonable thing. She stopped squirming. All it accomplished anyway was to make her more aware of the fiery area in the small of her back where his body was molded to hers.

They stood like statues in the shadows, while around them the patterns created by the electric candles altered by increments. It was probably just the movement of the ship, Bella decided, wishing she dared try to wriggle away again.

She worked her mouth free, mostly because she needed air. "I don't hear anything now, Malone."

"Neither do I." He released her slowly. She would have said reluctantly, but no doubt that would have been her imagination. "All right, let's get out of here."

Bella tugged irritably on her blond wig. A thousand unnamed emotions collided inside her. She hated it when that happened. Lona had done everything in her power to teach her granddaughter self-control. Why did it always desert her when she needed it most?

The air below deck had a claustrophobic quality about it, another sensation Bella disliked. She must have gotten stuck in a closet as a child.

"I'll go first," Malone said when they reached the ladder.

He was setting his foot on the bottom rung when Bella heard the sound, a telltale click that could only mean one thing.

"Malone..." Catching his sleeve with her fingers, she gave an urgent tug. "Did you...?"

"Yes."

"How perceptive," a smug masculine voice remarked.

Rudge. Bella closed her eyes. The bounty hunter strolled closer. "You have good ears. I barely heard that myself, and I'm holding the gun. Now turn around all the way. Slowly. That's right. No tricks, Malone. I've no quarrel with you." Rudge smiled like a wolf. "All I want is Bella."

So much for their disguises.

Malone eased Bella nearer to him. "How did you know?" he asked, stalling.

"I followed you," Rudge replied. He had an unlit cigar in his mouth and a white bandage wrapped around his head. A glint of spiteful amusement danced in his eyes. "I'll give you credit, Malone, you've got balls. I didn't expect you to show up here tonight. Didn't know if I'd make it myself, but as I was able to, I thought, he's a cunning bastard, he just might try it. So I snuck on board and hid. Then I watched and listened. Picked out your voice right off, angel," he said to Bella. "You should've used an accent. Uh-uh, don't even think about it, Malone," he warned in the same pleasant tone. "For what this pretty lady's worth to me, I'd plug you in a second. Not that you'd understand my reasons, but I'm in a plugging sort of mood tonight."

As usual, Malone's face was an implacable mask. "The same mood you were in when you plugged Bella's grandmother?"

Rudge made a dismissive gesture. "You know I didn't do that. Showed up, sure, but the damage had been done by then. Tock, for all the fluff between his ears, swings a mean rifle butt. I was out for twenty minutes."

Bella heard a tiny creak, but was too riveted by the gun in Rudge's hand to investigate the source. "What were they going to do to me?" she asked in a fear-choked voice. "Who are the Birds? Why do they want me?"

Rudge shrugged. "Ask them. They don't confide diddly to bounty hunters. Word of advice, though, put your questions to Crowe. Tock may swing a mean rifle, but that's nothing to the wallop Lady Parret's classical busts can dish out."

A shadow falling across the carpet behind Rudge caused Bella to freeze. She knew Malone saw it, too, but apparently Rudge didn't. Hobson Crowe detached himself smoothly from the wall, his movements silent, his countenance benign.

"I see you escaped, Mr. Rudge," he said, so unexpectedly that Rudge gave a start and whipped his head around.

Everything happened swiftly after that, so swiftly that Bella doubted she would ever get it all straight. Crowe laid a hand on Rudge's arm, that much she did see. He also said something, but if Rudge heard it, he was the only one.

At the first glimpse of Crowe, Malone's muscles tensed. The instant Rudge's head turned, he grabbed Bella and literally flung her onto the ladder.

"Go," he hissed, and she must have obeyed because suddenly the hatchway loomed above her head and she was shoving at it with her palms, breathing hard and thinking that they were both going to die any second now, because either Rudge or Crowe was bound to shoot.

Miraculously, neither did, at least not immediately. Malone's hands appeared beside hers, and together they were able to dislodge the sticky hatch. It swung back on stiff hinges, allowing Bella to scramble through to the safety of the upper deck.

She peered downward as Malone hoisted himself up, and saw Rudge taking aim. Hobson Crowe stood several feet behind him. Bella couldn't see the male Bird's expression, only Rudge's bared teeth biting into his soggy cigar.

The shot came, hushed but certain. It embedded itself in the ladder just as Malone's foot left the last rung.

Using both hands, Bella slammed the hatch closed. He couldn't shoot through metal, surely.

Malone gave the iron wheel several hard twists. "It's locked," he said, then motioned behind her with his head. "That way, Bella. Go."

She was on her feet in an instant. She'd lost her wig somewhere and most of the bobby pins that held her hair. It fell now in a silky, tangled mass over her face.

Ignoring it, she started to run. She was pushing the impeding strands from her cheeks when something came into view on the carpet before her.

She spied feet—huge, wide, booted feet. Malone's feet weren't big, and besides, he was behind her.

She skidded to a halt, but not quickly enough to prevent herself from colliding full force with the person in her path. Off guard, Malone crashed hard into her.

It wasn't until the pain and black spots cleared and Bella could breathe again that she was able to identify the human wall she'd hit. Shocked, she found herself staring straight into the face of Lona's murderer—the evil, smiling face of the Birds' psychotic hit man, Mick Tock.

Chapter Seven

This was absurd, Malone thought, getting angry. *Did everyone in the Birds' employ carry guns and wear stupid grins on their faces?*

"Smile, suckers," Tock said. Idiot that he was, he lowered his gun a notch to taunt them.

Pouncing on the mistake, Malone pushed down on Bella's head, brought his arm back and shoved his fist into Tock's startled face. If there was one thing he'd learned in his native Durham, it was how to throw a punch. Tock staggered backward three paces, dropped his gun and hit the wall with a thud. Malone followed up with a punch to his protruding belly, then grabbed Bella's hand.

"Run," he ordered, and astonished though she was, she complied.

But, Tock didn't go down easily or stay down for more than few seconds. Grunting and swearing, he righted himself and began lurching after them.

"He's gaining on us," Bella panted, racing through the first door she came to.

"He's more agile than he looks," Malone muttered. "Keep going."

"Where?" They'd reached a three-way fork.

"Uh, straight," Malone decided. "And through the door at the end."

She knew how to run, he'd give her that. Her stride was long and smooth, like a gazelle's, he supposed, though he'd never actually seen one. Under less-harrowing circumstances, he would have enjoyed the sight of her.

It wasn't the only thing he could have enjoyed where Bella was concerned, but this was hardly the time for fantasies. Tock burst through the door behind them with a snarl and a squeeze of his trigger-happy forefinger.

"Get down!" Malone shouted to Bella, who, luckily, had the reflexes of a cat, because she ducked and shoved the second door open in the same motion. "Go. Go!" he whispered tersely, then swore as Tock fired another bullet.

Bella's vengeful exclamation, "I wish that stupid gun would blow up in his face," brought a reluctant smile to Malone's lips; unfortunately, he couldn't afford to be amused. They'd entered the ship's pantry. That left only one option: the kitchen, dead ahead. Thank God they still looked like part of the staff.

"Quiet," he said in her ear. Keeping her pressed to his side, he added in a low voice, "Act nonchalant."

He felt the tremor that rippled through her. In a terse undertone, she whispered, "There must be twenty chefs in here, Malone. They're going to notice us."

"Yes, well, just so long as Tock doesn't. Try to blend in."

"With what? The busboys?"

He didn't answer, merely smiled briefly at one of the junior chefs as he propelled Bella through a sea of staff and equipment.

Dinner was about to be served. The kitchen was in chaos, with white-coated cooks and chefs rushing to and fro from stove, sink and fridge. The air was redolent with the scents of chicken, garlic, clams, curried beans and onions.

"Soup starter," one of the chefs demanded above the clatter of china and metal. "Nuke those chicken strips and drain the pasta.... Hey, wait a minute, what are you doing here?"

The question was fired at Malone, who, after setting Bella aside, proceeded to shoo her forward with a subtle motion of his hand.

"Ms. Parret sent me to deliver a message," he lied.

"Oh, yeah? What's that?"

"No cream sauce on her chicken."

The man snorted. "What are you, a joker? Lady Parret packs it away like a horse." He stuck his florid face in Malone's. "And it just so happens that my white-wine sauce is her favorite."

"Mine, too," Bella said unexpectedly from behind. She smoothed her hair with a nervous hand and summoned a smile. "It's true, though, what he said. No sauce for Lady Parret tonight."

The charade screeched to a halt when the kitchen door flew open and Tock rushed in, stabbing a dirty finger at her. "Stop that woman! Stop them both!"

The chef had been softening, dammit. Another few seconds and he'd have been putty in Bella's hands. They could have walked out and taken the hourly cruiser back to shore.

Of the kitchen staff, only two responded to Tock's order, and then only to scurry across the floor and out of his way.

"Come on!" Malone grabbed Bella's hand and ran. He had to shove the flushed sauce chef aside, as well as a taller one who didn't seem to know where to go. Bella banged her elbow on one of the soup pots, twisted out of harm's way, then suddenly froze. Eyes wide, she pointed at Tock, who was charging down the narrow aisle between stove and countertop, knocking over pots, pans and skillets as he went.

Malone spotted the danger as she did. "Don't, Tock!" he shouted, but his warning came too late. The hit man thrust aside one of the chefs, and in doing so, knocked himself off-balance. He collided with a fryer full of hot oil, tipped it onto the burner, then jumped sideways with a dumbfounded expression as flames burst out beside him.

Bella stared. "My God!" she exclaimed softly.

"Fire!" the head chef screamed. "Salt, baking soda, hurry!"

Malone was amazed at the furor that erupted around them. The flames appeared to sprout legs and leap across every gap in the kitchen. Within seconds, the entire room was consumed. The fire extinguishers did nothing, and no one ever did locate the salt.

"Malone!" Bella tugged on his arm. "Tock's still coming."

"What?"

Incredible though it seemed, she was right. Like a creature possessed, Tock was barreling through the wall of flames toward them.

"Abandon ship!" someone shouted.

Malone suddenly couldn't see, so thick had the smoke grown in the past minute. He squinted through it. "Where's Tock?"

"I don't know—" Bella choked, broke off, then, to Malone's horror, pulled away from him.

He caught her by the apron strings. "Where are you going?" he demanded. "Tock's still got his gun, you know."

A strident ringing filled the air. "Fire alarm," Bella answered, coughing. "Which way do we go?"

"Wherever Tock isn't."

She waved at the smoke. "I don't see him."

"You won't until his gun's in your face. Are you claustrophobic?"

"No—yes. I'm not sure. Why?"

He yanked open a small door. "Get in."

"What?" She backed off in horror. "No way, Malone. You're crazy. I'm finding a regular door."

"They're blocked, Bella. This is a dumbwaiter. We can hoist ourselves to an upper deck."

"We'll suffocate in there."

"Maybe, but we'll die in here. Now get in."

"But I—"

He abandoned reason and, snatching her up by the waist, plunked her inside. "Legs," he ordered.

She glared at him through the smoke and confusion. "You're a maniac, Malone. I hate maniacs."

"Yes, but do you hate hit men, too? Tock'll be on us in a minute."

With a final, resentful look, she pulled her legs inside. Just in time.

Tock's round, scowling face appeared through the smoke like a thundercloud. "Gotcha, bastard," he growled, flashing a broad, toothy smile.

Why did psychotics always love their work?

Malone was sizing up his chances of kicking the burly thug in the chest when a pair of chefs jostled Tock's arm as they ran past, distracting him long enough for Malone to haul himself through the dumbwaiter door and for Bella to yank it closed. She made a tiny sound of fright but swallowed it and, at Malone's instructions, tugged on the wires that ran in two taut lines beside her.

"Keep it level," he ordered, pulling on his own side.

She let out a tight breath, but said nothing.

Through the wooden walls, he heard the boisterous sound of cancan music and laughter. The guests were having a great time, it seemed.

The fire alarm wasn't ringing up here, he noticed. That would be Rudge's doing if, as he'd said, he'd had to sneak on board. Why sneak? Malone wondered distantly.

The billowing smoke reached the dining room moments before he and Bella did. The music stopped, instruments clattered, feet began to thunder on the polished plank floors. Women screamed, men shouted, then several men began screaming, too.

Teeth gritted, Bella said, "You know, just once I'd like to go somewhere and not wind up in the middle of a stampede."

"Pull," Malone responded unrelentingly.

"Aren't we there yet?"

"Just pull, Bella."

"I am. Look, why don't we just get out and use the stairs?"

"You obviously don't understand grease fires. They spread faster than any other kind, and they're spasmodic. The kitchen will be an inferno by now."

"So it's better that we suffocate in here?"

Malone glared at her. Someone yelled for help as he secured the line and kicked open the dumbwaiter door. "It's the end of the road, anyway."

"My God," a man shouted. "The fire's between us and the lifeboats!"

"Figures," Malone muttered. "Are you all right?" he asked Bella.

"Never better." Ignoring his hand, she jumped out—and a second later was nearly bowled over by a three-hundred-pound man in a tux.

"Watch it," Malone snapped, then immediately wished he'd left well enough alone, because the man rounded on him, grabbing him by the vest and dragging him upward.

"Where are the boats?" he demanded.

Bella circled swiftly, pointing. "That way. You have to go up the stairs."

The man dropped Malone the way a child might discard an unwanted toy. Malone felt Bella's hands on him but couldn't hear her voice. His head spun. Had he hit it on something or was the smoke just incredibly thick up here?

A blurry face with shorn blond hair swam into view. Malone swore sharply. "They're everywhere." He caught Bella's hand. "We have to get to the upper deck."

"But the lifeboats—"

"Aren't accessible through the fire."

"What about that man?"

"He'll get out. I'm not so sure about us. Rudge is here."

"So is either Lady P. or Lady S. Crowe, too, Malone. We're cut off."

"Not quite. There's still the outside ladders." Malone wedged open a port window. "How are you at climbing?"

"Lousy."

"You go first, then."

She glanced doubtfully into the darkness above, then drew back. "I can't."

"You have to."

"Look, isn't there—"

"No, there isn't. Go, Bella. Now."

She hated being ordered about. Temper flared briefly in her smoky eyes. But there were tongues of flame licking at the entry curtains, and Rudge was searching through the fleeing people, trying to find them. She had no choice, and she knew it.

It took five precious minutes for them to reach the upper deck. Even there, smoke poured through the portholes. Below them, in the water, people splashed and kicked and cried for help. The hourly cruiser had picked up some of them, but it couldn't hold everyone.

"Oh, God," Malone said heavily. "We'll have to swim for it. Take off your clothes."

"Go to hell, Malone."

With the deck heating up beneath them, he glared at her and then started to do it for her. His deft fingers undid three of her uniform buttons before she slapped them away.

"All right, all right," she said through her teeth.

Irritated, but too aware of the danger now to ignore it, she stripped down to a navy blue teddy with antique-lace trim. Malone suppressed a groan. That scrap could have passed for an extremely sexy bathing suit. Sheer panty hose, no bra, legs that went on forever... his blood couldn't have boiled faster if the fire had had him surrounded.

But the fire was only one of many problems. No doubt Rudge and Tock were still on board and hunting for him.

Malone tugged off his vest and shirt. "Jump," he ordered Bella.

A cloud of smoke and fog obscured her body for a moment, but he saw her nod. Swinging her legs over the rail, she paused briefly, then took a deep breath and dove.

Twenty feet away, Rudge hauled himself onto the deck. He had his gun, but didn't raise it even after he spotted his quarry.

"I won't give up, Malone, you can count on it," he shouted above the furor. "I've got my orders, and Tock's got his. And you'd better hope to hell that I win, because Mick Tock's orders are sweet and simple. Shoot to kill."

THE WOMAN KEPT A REIN on her temper long enough to reach their Chinatown headquarters. Hobby's rat hole, she called it. She made a sound like a snarl. London was her home. She didn't like it when they had to visit San Francisco, wouldn't have come here now if Hobby's ambitious, eagle-eyed assistant hadn't, one cold, pre-Christmas afternoon, happened to spot Bella Conlan in a fifties-style nightclub near the bay.

The man was a brownnoser. Not that the woman minded people who groveled, but this one tended to spit when he talked.

"I saw her, I did, saw her plain as day," he'd gushed, first to Hobby, then two days later, after they'd flown in pell-mell from London, to her and Charmaine. "I knew it was her— I mean, it had to be. But, you know, it was crowded and I lost her and no one there knew her last name. It'll be okay, though, because I've heard of this guy called Rudge. He'll track her down. All he needs is a picture. . . ."

"All he needs is a picture," the waterlogged woman mimicked, marching up the dingy staircase. "I'm thinking that what he really needs is a good swift kick in the butt." She waited until she'd reached the top and stomped into her office before shaking herself like a dog. "I hate being wet!"

"Don't we all." Charmaine's dry retort emanated from the corner. "Still, better wet than roasted alive. Did Hobby deal with the authorities?"

"Yes." The woman pointed to where Charmaine sat, shoes off, on the only piece of furniture she liked, the green-and-blue silk sofa. "You're soaking the cushions. Get off or get a towel." She turned, then gasped in horror. "Oh, my God, look at my hair." Shocked, she stared at herself in the ornate wall mirror. "I look like a drowned cat. What's that music?" she interrupted herself to snap. "You know I hate Gilbert and Sullivan, Charmaine."

"I know you have no taste." Calmly, Charmaine spread a red-and-black blanket over the sofa cushions. "Robert used to say the same thing. He had no taste either."

If the woman hadn't been so appalled by her bedraggled appearance, she would have argued the matter—but dear God, what a fright she looked. Her hair stuck up like purplish porcupine quills. It shouldn't do that, wet or not. Her idiot stylist must have used a bad brand of color. Who'd have thought Burgundy No. 4 would have side effects when mixed with salt water? Didn't manufacturers prepare for contingencies anymore?

"Is the ship a write-off?" Charmaine asked when the woman, still horrified, didn't speak.

"I guess—yes, I'd say so. Of course, *you* wouldn't know, seeing as you were one of the first people to jump."

Charmaine shrugged and sipped the Dubonnet she'd poured for herself. "Hobby jumped. So did Tock. It seemed the smart thing to do." Eyes lowered to her ruby red drink, she added casually, "I thought I saw Rudge on board tonight."

The woman could be coy, too, even if she did currently resemble an electrified duck. "Really? I didn't notice. Not that I'd have minded, since I hired him to *find*—" she paused, emphasizing the word "—Bella."

Charmaine smiled. "I see. Shall we play clever games then or talk straight?"

"That's up to you."

Charmaine regarded her, unflinching. "I had Rudge locked away. He's a leech. He also saw my face. I wanted him out of the picture."

The woman turned. "I know. I had him released. All bounty hunters are leeches. And if he saw your face, it's your own fault. He hasn't seen mine."

"So you think. He's very cunning, to say nothing of slimy."

"His job requires sliminess. And you needn't worry. I'm paying him enough to feign blindness. He's a talented leech, and I want him in the picture." Her expression grew grim. "She's mine, Charmaine. I want her alive."

Charmaine stood. "Belladonna is mine," she countered evenly.

"I have more right to handle this than you do."

"Don't be absurd. Think who you're talking to."

A tremor she strove to conceal ran through the woman. She refused to show fear to Charmaine. Why should she? She could be just as dangerous as her, more so if necessary. She'd watched Robert operate. She knew the moves. She knew a lot of things, actually. For a moment, her fingers caressed the sleeve where she kept the slender pink weapon, her memento.

Eyes cold, she retorted, "Rudge stays."

Charmaine studied her, then said calmly, "So does Tock. However," she added, when the woman opened her mouth to object, "I will agree to leave Rudge alone."

The woman didn't trust her for a minute. But neither did she pursue the subject. Better to wait, and watch and plot.... *And fix her damned hair,* she thought, noting her reflection once again. Yes, absolutely, destruction of Belladonna was imperative. But first she must see to her hair.

Chapter Eight

Romaine, Romaine, Romaine... The name buzzed in Bella's head. By midnight Sunday, soaked to the skin and wearing nothing except her damp teddy under the plaid blanket Malone had thankfully located in the trunk of his car, she found everything was buzzing, even Malone's voice.

She huddled in the front seat as he wound his way through the eerie veil of San Francisco fog.

Veil... Now there was a word. So, she had a name—Romaine—and now a word. She'd seen an invoice signed "Romaine" and two female Birds wearing veils of heavy black tulle. Who were these people chasing her?

Whoever they were, they'd murdered Lona. And they'd known her mother—at least Hobson Crowe and Lady Parret had.

At a stoplight, she became aware of Malone watching her. "Are you awake?" he asked.

Opening her eyes a fraction, Bella surveyed him in profile. God, he really was handsome. And trustworthy, she had to admit. He'd proved it several times that night.

"No," she answered, then added, "The boat sank, didn't it?"

"It will."

"Do you think anyone died?"

"There was enough warning. I doubt it." A frown marred his forehead as she suddenly sat up straight. "What's wrong?"

"This isn't the same place as last night. Where are we?"

"The Noe Valley."

Bella looked around, intrigued. She should have guessed. The crowded old Victorians lining the street needed repair—at least the one rising up like a foggy black giant before her did. And yet it had certain old-world charm, mostly from the excessive amount of gingerbread trim on the front.

"Who lives here?" she asked as he reached across to open her door.

"Ronnie." His hair brushed against her cheek and mouth, making her shiver. "Are you cold?"

She forced back the rush of desire that shot through her. "I'm . . . impressed. Is he home?"

Malone almost smiled. "I doubt it. Ronnie prefers the night shift."

"Less chance of gunmen firing at you over tea and scones." Bella looked down at her lap. She hoped he hadn't heard the catch in her voice.

He might have, though, because he didn't respond immediately. She sensed his hesitation and knew he wanted to say something. She heard the sigh that issued from him.

"Bella . . ."

"It's all right." She waved off his concern. "I didn't mean anything. It wasn't Ronnie's fault, or yours, or anyone's except Tock's and, I guess, the Birds'." She turned perplexed eyes to his shadowed face. "I can't get it straight, Malone, no matter how hard I try. There's a knife." She raised her bare fist and held it clenched in front of her face. "It's right there in my dreams, and yet the child in my dreams can't see it. But it's there when I look into the mirror. It's hanging right in front of me."

"Hanging?"

"Well, someone's holding it, but I can't tell who it is."

He studied her, meditatively running a thumb across his lower lip. "It's a pink knife, right?"

Her surprised reaction caused the blanket to fall away. "Pink?"

"That's what you said."

"I did? When?"

He seemed vaguely discomfited for a moment. "Uh..."
His eyes flitted briefly away, then returned to hers, composed and unrevealing once again, damn him. "You had a
dream last night," he explained carefully. "You cried out in
your sleep, so I came to see why. When I got there you were
talking about 'them' seeing you and about a pink knife
covered with blood."

A jolt like an electrical shock rattled through her. Yes, of
course it had been pink; she'd forgotten that. But she could
see it now. Pale, metallic pink with some kind of animal
carving on the handle. She could only glimpse a portion of
it, however; the hand holding it covered the rest.

The hand... She closed her eyes. What about the hand?
She needed to concentrate, but she couldn't, not fully, not
with Malone sitting there, so dark and dangerous and close.
And staring.

Outside, the fog floated in weird patterns, like ghosts
slinking across the windshield, watching her, watching him,
pressing in on both of them, urging Bella to follow her instincts and...

She shivered deeply. Misreading her, Malone pushed her
door open and motioned her onto the sidewalk. "I'll start
a fire," he offered when she climbed out. "It'll cut the
chill."

No, it wouldn't, Bella thought, but she didn't argue. The
feelings rolling around inside her were too confused and
precarious for her to fully comprehend. What if she fell in
love with Malone? It could happen, but would it be fair to
either of them? Who was she, really? Had she witnessed
some dreadful crime, or worse, committed some unspeak-
able deed?

No, she wasn't evil; she wouldn't believe she was. And yet
she'd blocked out the first nine years of her life for a reason. She hadn't hit her head in the crash that had taken her
mother's life. She'd simply been found, scared and hunched
next to a snowdrift—next to a dead raven, Lona had told
her—not panicking, not speaking and not remembering any
part of her past.

The buzz in her head increased as she climbed from the car. She felt chilled, despite the blanket that Malone had secured around her. She preceded him to the creaking porch, waited while he hunted through the flower boxes and, when he located the key, followed him wordlessly inside.

The entry hall could have accommodated a woolly mammoth. Although shabby, the pale pink-and-green velvet wallpaper looked original. The newel post was carved mahogany, the chandelier a dusty tribute to the nineteenth-century artisan who'd fashioned it.

Oriental flourishes were visible in the folding screens, vases and charcoal etchings in the hall and on the upper landing. There was even a Japanese tapestry hanging in the stairwell.

In Bella's head the music of *The Mikado* began to throb. Normally, she loved it, but not right now. Now it reminded her of the *Sun Sen* and the nightmare that had unfolded there only a few short hours ago. Romaine...

Preoccupied, she didn't realize that Malone had halted until she quite literally collided with his elegant spine.

Why elegant? she wondered, rubbing her nose. Must be the British accent. "Sorry," she said when he turned to steady her, a frown on his face. She loved it when he frowned. The expression made his eyes darker, his mouth fuller and more sensual.

She managed to avoid any more mishaps while he stacked dried logs on the drawing-room hearth. That chore accomplished, he lit the kindling, then went off in search of some dry clothes. When he returned, he handed Bella a red terry robe, thick and long and obviously made for Ronnie.

Malone had already changed into a pair of baggy jeans and a soft black sweatshirt—Ronnie's clothes again, Bella imagined. Black suited Malone, however, staring at him was disturbing, so she gazed around the room instead. It had vaulted ceilings, faded rose and moss-toned furniture, fringed lamps, tintype pictures of Chinatown, and now a crackling fire and an old Cowsills song on the radio.

She'd left her purse in Malone's car earlier, so it hadn't burned in the restaurant fire. Opening it, she drew out the antique picture case Lona had given her.

While Malone banged about behind the bar, she touched the photos tentatively, studying each by firelight. In one, a little girl in pigtails played with a cat; in the other, the same little girl smiled like the cat that swallowed the canary. And Amanda, wearing a denim pantsuit and what looked liked a silver ring on her right forefinger, was in both.

But it was the building in the background that intrigued Bella most. If she squinted hard and used the miniature magnifying glass attached to her key chain, she could almost make out the writing on the hanging sign.

"Excuse me, what are you doing?" Malone inquired with exaggerated politeness.

He was bending over her, two tumblers in his hands. At the sound of his voice, Bella jumped, pressing a fist to her racing heart. "Couldn't you clear your throat or something halfway across the room?"

"I thought the clinking ice would be sufficient."

She narrowed her eyes at him. "You're really irritating, Malone, do you know that?"

He held up one of the amber-filled glasses. "So you won't be wanting this, then?"

Something in the ironic way he said that sparked a memory in Bella's mind—a pleasant one this time. She brightened. "One of your parents was Irish, right?"

When that familiar ridge of displeasure rose between his eyes, she knew she'd guessed correctly.

Drawing her long legs underneath her, she continued, oblivious for the moment to the significance of her remarks, "We had an Irish gardener once. His name was Shannahan or Shawnigan, or something like that. His wife used to work for a New York fashion designer. My mother hired her to make her clothes. Well, most of them. My mother was incredibly picky about her wardrobe, but then I suppose most women . . . are." Her voice trailed off as the import of her babbling finally dawned on her. "How do I know that?" she finished in wonder.

Crouching, Malone set the drinks on the marble hearth and regarded her through somber, unreadable eyes. "Is there more?" he asked.

She searched, then shook her head. "I don't know where that came from. It's gone now. I don't even remember what Amanda looked like—except from the pictures Lona gave me."

The ridge formed again between Malone's eyes. Bella longed to smooth it away with her fingers, but resisted the urge when she noted the abstracted look on his face. "She told me she'd seen something," he said quietly.

Now Bella frowned. "Who told you?"

"Lona."

Pain, like a hot knife, twisted in her heart. She swallowed hard to ease it.

"Right before she died she told me she'd seen something, and then she said that Amanda wasn't... something else."

Bella experienced a moment of annoyance. "Why didn't you tell me this before, Malone?" she demanded in a low voice.

He saw the danger and captured her icy fingers before she could withdraw them from her lap. "Because I didn't think it meant anything, and you had enough on your mind already."

"You should have told me."

"I just did."

"Don't be obtuse. I mean before now."

His gaze unflinching on hers, he countered levelly, "Who's Mr. Shannahan, Bella?"

She wanted to snatch her hand away, to snatch herself away—do anything to escape his powerful sexual presence. She remained seated instead and replied, "I don't know. I doubt if that's his name."

"I could run it through Ronnie's computer."

"You could also run Romaine through the computer."

"Yes, thank you, I had planned to do that." He nodded at the glass on the floor. "I thought you might like a drink first."

Releasing a breath, Bella said softly, "I'm sorry, Malone. I'm being rude, but it occurs to me that I don't really know who or what I am."

Her candor seemed to confound him—or maybe any display of vulnerability would have had that effect on him. Whatever the case, he stared at her for a long, heart-wrenching moment, then let his shoulders slump. "Oh, damn," he replied simply.

The old Victorian drawing room smelled of wood smoke, rain and roses. Malone... well, she wasn't sure what he smelled of, but whatever it was, it excited her. *He* excited her. Danger emanated from him yet, oddly, so did dependability. Such a contrary mix.

But was it a good mix? she wondered.

She picked up her glass and studied the contents. Glenlivit on ice; fire warming her cheeks, holiday lights glowing on the foggy street, a New Year about to commence. What might it bring for her? Old memories, or maybe, just maybe, a new love....

Her eyes came up suddenly to confront his. Damn, he'd said as if resigned to some feeling he'd rather avoid. Fine. She certainly wasn't going to push him. Well, not much.

"Look, Malone," she began, but he stopped her with a small shake of his head—and a swift, agile movement that brought him disturbingly closer to her on the hearth rug. Eyes steady, though still looking as if he were resigned to some nameless fate, he lifted his hand to her face, stroking the silky hair from her cheeks and forehead.

"You're a complication I don't need, Bella," he told her quietly, somberly.

She noticed he said "need" rather than "want." She held herself very still. "What *do* you need, Malone?"

"I don't know." His thumb grazed her lower lip. His expression became troubled. "I only know that need is an unhealthy thing."

She drew a shaky breath and, reaching up, touched his hair. It was surprisingly soft. "You must want something, Malone. Everyone does."

''Well, I—'' his eyes closed briefly ''—don't. Oh, God,'' he murmured. Then slowly, as if he couldn't help himself, he inclined his head toward hers.

Where his lips brushed Bella's throat, her skin burned. He traced the line of her jaw upward to her ear, then to her cheek and back to her jaw, until, finally, he captured her mouth with his.

It was heaven, delicious yet shocking, wonderfully intense. A hunger born of desire and curiosity formed in Bella's mind and body. It shot downward into her stomach, then lower still until the area between her legs felt cramped and wet.

He'd awakened her sexual appetite, she realized, sliding her fingers through his hair and pulling him closer. Until this moment she hadn't been entirely sure she possessed one. Few men in her life had done more than incite a fleeting interest, possibly a glimmer of desire, but nothing close to what she felt now. This was male-female longing in its most primitive form. This feeling robbed her of breath even as it fueled her strength.

''Bella,'' Malone said softly into her mouth, but he wasn't trying to draw away or end the kiss. He wanted her, too. Whether against his will or not, Bella didn't know, and right then, didn't especially care. All that mattered was that he did want her.

His hand slid to her breast, pushing aside the thick terry of her robe and grazing her lace-covered flesh with his palm. She groaned in her throat as her sensitive nipple made contact with the hardness of his hand. She pressed herself into him, wanting more, a great deal more.

He smelled wonderful, like the night, dark and mysterious. But she knew so little about him, and even less about the formative years of her own life. This was crazy. She should stop it, now.

She felt his mouth traveling across her ear and shivered inside. He nipped at the delicate lobe with his tongue and teeth, breathing against her until she released the cry that swelled in her throat.

The hard, lean muscles of his body beneath her exploring fingers made her heart race. His skin was satin over sinew and bone. Oh, she wished this moment could go on forever.

But as aroused as Bella was, as she knew Malone was, too—the evidence of that was digging into her thigh—sanity prevailed, as she sensed it invariably would for him. His tongue delved into her mouth, tasting her one last time before he reluctantly removed his lips from hers.

A sigh of regret issued from him. Words, however, appeared to elude him. While Bella watched, he closed his eyes and dropped his head forward.

It wasn't fair, her heart cried. He'd taken her to a point far beyond anything she'd ever known, then had pulled away. She didn't want to stop. She wanted to know and understand everything about him, about herself.

"Bella, I'm..."

"Sorry?" she finished for him.

"Yes, but not in the way you think."

She managed a smile, but only a small one. Truthfully, she was too disappointed for clever games. She wanted to go to bed and not think about what had just happened, or more correctly, what might have happened but hadn't—and probably never would, if she knew Malone, which she sensed she did in that regard.

No Ties, No Attachments, No Love—that was his motto. Why, she had no idea and right now was too emotionally weary to ponder. Better to make a graceful exit and try to pretend that none of this mattered to her.

She felt Malone's eyes on her and forced herself to meet them. Damn that self-control of his. Why couldn't she look that unaffected?

His words, however, surprised her. "You do realize that you're a problem, don't you? A big one."

"Because of Rudge and Tock?"

He met her challenge with mild vexation, as usual. "No, not because of Rudge and Tock. Don't be a pain, Bella."

She hunched her shoulders, a familiar gesture of defiance. "I'll be what I want to be, Malone, and right now I feel like being a pain. I don't understand you—or me, for that matter. I shouldn't want you, I shouldn't want any part of you, not after the horrible things that have happened lately." The lingering sting of his withdrawal deepened her confusion, but, thanks to Lona, her practical streak now rushed to the fore. "Maybe you were right to stop it. After all, we're strangers, probably as much to ourselves as we are to each other. At least I am. Strangers make lousy lovers—lousy in the long term, anyway, unless you get very, very lucky."

She didn't know how she pulled it off, but she rose to her feet in a single, easy movement and, sweeping up her un-touched Scotch, walked carefully across the carpet and into the hall.

He'd told her earlier which bedroom to take—top of the stairs, turn left, third door on the right. It was Ronnie's room and the most comfortable in the house.

Good, Bella thought wearily, trudging up the staircase. She needed sleep desperately. Forget Malone—if she could. Forget fires and fog, Birds and boats, hit men and mysteri-ous invoices signed "Romaine." Forget the horror, but re-member the silver photo case with color pictures of herself and her mother, taken before that freakish night in Alaska when the rented Subaru had plunged ninety feet off an ice-covered cliff.

Remember, too, that other thing—Lona's dying words, which Malone had neglected to pass on to her until tonight. She'd seen something, she'd said, and Amanda wasn't... something else.

Wasn't what? Lona's daughter? Obviously not, since Lona wasn't Bella's grandmother.

As silently as the fog that slunk about the lead-paned windows, Bella opened the door to Ronnie's bedroom and stepped inside.

A tremor she'd been battling for hours started deep in her stomach. As inviting as the high bed and feather mattress looked, she was afraid to fall asleep. What if she dreamed about the past again? The tremor became a shudder. What if she dreamed about the present?

She stared at the Glenlivit in her hand, and the amber liquid shook slightly as she did so. *Oh, God, please,* she prayed, *please don't let me dream. Not of him.*

But would God listen?

Bella hesitated, then, raising the glass to her lips, tossed down the double Scotch in one long, fiery swallow.

NO INFORMATION EXISTED on Romaine. There was nothing in the police files, either U.S. or European, nothing in the whole damned Internet computer system.

By four a.m., Malone was bleary eyed, cross and frustrated. A headache throbbed in his temples. He'd tried everything he could think of, and while he was no expert, he knew computers well enough to be fairly certain that Romaine as a person had no substance. So what did that tell him?

"Not a bloody thing," he muttered, starting the long, slow climb up the stairs. The Birds used the name Romaine to sign invoices, but Romaine, as far as he could tell, was a nonentity. Some clue he'd turned up.

He swore to himself in Gaelic as he climbed. His eyes flitted to the shadowed nook area that held Ronnie's bedroom door. Bella would be in there, lying in Ronnie's old-fashioned feather bed, probably sound asleep by now. She'd guessed at the Irish heritage that as a rule he preferred not to flaunt. His mother had been Irish to the core—and passionate to a fault. How on earth his father had put up with her all those years was beyond him.

Bella had a similarly passionate nature, albeit without the shrewish attitude. He should have guessed five seconds after meeting Lona Conlan that Bella couldn't possibly have been her real granddaughter.

Belladonna Conlan. But Conlan wasn't really her last name.

And Shannahan probably wasn't the name of her parents' gardener. Malone had run it through the computer without much hope and had come up empty. It hadn't surprised him. What had was Bella's earlier burst of memory.

Her mother had liked fine clothes. She'd had her own personal seamstress, an ex-designer. The family had had a gardener. Obviously, then, they'd also had money.

But what was their name? Not Romaine. Not Parret or Crowe, either, at least as far as Malone could determine. He'd found no information on either Charmaine Parret or Hobson Crowe anywhere in the police records.

Of course, there should have been something, but the Birds were powerful, and power could still buy a modicum of anonymity, enough to keep amateur hackers like Malone from unearthing their secrets.

Moving his aching shoulders, he let his gaze flick one last time to the room in which Bella slept. No, he wasn't going there, he told himself irritably. Yes, he had feelings for her, but they were controllable, even if the Irish in his nature was rearing its lusty head.

He contained the growl that swelled in his throat and turned right at the top of the staircase. All right, fine, so her skin was as soft and smooth as silk and her legs were long enough to bring a stab of desire to his loins every time he thought of them. And, yes, her breasts were the perfect size, to say nothing of perfectly responsive to his touch. So what if she tasted like fire and fine wine and sex? What did any of that matter to him? He didn't *want* to be involved with her. His resolve should put an end to things right there.

It should, but it wasn't going to. Malone could will away his desire all he liked; the damage was done. Bella had stirred his emotions, and that, he knew from experience, was a deadly thing.

With his head slamming like a bass drum, his heart heavy and his mind too muddled to think clearly, he didn't bother to switch on any lights in the only guest room that Ronnie had gotten around to renovating. The bed was a four-poster double, the mattress not feather, but comfortable and fortunately directly in front of him. Leaving the door open a crack and the shades up, he forced his weary body across the floor.

He thought he heard a creak in the hall and turned to identify the source. But he saw only Ronnie's calico cat, strolling in like a queen. Her name was Aberdeen, and this, he recalled, was her room. She was simply allowing him to share it.

She meowed twice, then jumped onto the mattress and made herself a patchwork nest. Too tired to find humor in the feline ritual, Malone tumbled onto the far side, burying his face in the pillow and his thoughts in a dream of Bella that started with a stealthy creak on the floorboards at the top of the stairs....

Chapter Nine

There was a mouse under the table with her. In her sleep Bella searched for it, although the dream child that was she didn't seem to notice.

The little girl huddled under the table was alternately fascinated by her reflection in a mirror far across the room and frightened by the sound of angry voices far to her right.

In her dream, soft footsteps approached. She ignored them in favor of the raised voices. How many were there? Two? No, three. Two men and a woman. Fear of those voices paralyzed her muscles and her lungs. What if she hiccuped and they heard?

Wide-eyed, she listened, with only the occasional uneasy glance at her face in the faraway mirror. Her hair tumbled over her shoulders, but not over her features. She didn't look half as terrified as she felt. Maybe she should be an actress—like her mother had tried to be once.

"Mother..." The formal address fell from her lips. She felt cold all over. Shivering, she wished they would stop yelling.

"Marriage vows are sacrosanct, Robert!"

Who'd said that? Amanda? Bella strained to see, but couldn't. Everything to her right looked fuzzy and dark.

She heard rain pelting the window, and then the mouse squeaked again. It must be getting closer; its squeaks echoed in Bella's sleeping brain. She drew the pillow over her head and willed herself back into the dream.

In the mirror she saw herself staring openmouthed at the shouting people. The mouse scuttled closer, distracting her. How could she see or hope to think with all that noise?

Her sleeping mind began to wander. Out of the darkness a knife emerged. No, not a knife—a brightly colored parrot attached to a pointy stick. It hopped toward her on the stick, squawking, "Romaine, Romaine!" Then, suddenly, it sprouted wings and flew away.

Another voice emerged to take its place, a man's disembodied voice. He said softly, "Belladonna. Yes, Belladonna will inherit everything...."

"Oh, no!" The horrified whisper came from behind and slightly to the left of Bella. "Dear God, no."

Now only the men argued. Something about poison and Belladonna and the dissolution of a partnership. She didn't understand what they meant.

She felt someone touching her, but was too absorbed in the argument to look. The parrot on a stick had shrunk. Before her fascinated eyes, it transformed itself into a skinny pink knife. The knife flew into a hand that wore a black glove.

The men's voices rose. "It's monstrous!" one accused. "You are monstrous. Children can have no part in our operation. They're meant to play and ride ponies. Not until they are older and well taught should they be permitted to make decisions of this caliber. When they are *older,* Robert. When they've acquired the knowledge and the wisdom to decide for themselves."

The voices became a jumble after that. Only the mouse's squeaks and a woman's whispered, "We have to get away...have to escape this nightmare," registered in Bella's brain.

She saw a glint of silver in her peripheral vision as the woman attempted to pull her covertly out from under the table. In the mirror her dark eyes seemed overbright, almost too large for her rapt face. Why was she so engrossed? Why couldn't she see the whole picture?

"What are you doing?" An outraged male voice cut through the clatter in Bella's head. She heard his cry of astonishment, followed by a sickening thump.

The pink knife floated into view. The blade was stained bright red, the hand holding it clenched as if in anger.

"Robert!" the woman behind Bella gasped. A lock of blond hair fell onto Bella's shoulder, covering her own dark pigtail. Amanda? The woman's voice, with its Southern accent, shook. "Come on, darling, we have to get out of here. You must move."

Bella wanted to run to the outstretched arms, to hide her face and blot out everything that had happened. But what *had* happened? Who was Robert? Who were the other man and woman?

Lona's voice penetrated the dream. "It's just like Romaine," she said sadly. "That's what Amanda told me."

Amanda. Romaine. Malone...

His name joined the clamor in Bella's sleeping mind. Her neck and body arched, as if toward him. She saw the parrot attached to the stick again. It flew between her and Malone as they jumped from the dumbwaiter on the burning *Sun Sen.* "Beware of the Birds!" it squawked, then flew off, its black, pointed tail dripping blood all the way.

Bella couldn't seem to move, not even when Malone shoved her forward. The squeaking mouse had boarded the ship with them. A mouse and three Birds.

She saw Charmaine Parret—at least she supposed that's who it was—concealed beneath a veil, a black hat and round sunglasses. Bella's gaze was drawn to her vivid mouth. Soon that was all she could see—Charmaine's beautiful, smiling mouth.

Submitting, Bella let Malone pull her away. He propelled her from the smoking ship to a more-intimate fire. He gave her a drink with a pink swizzle stick in it. He touched her breast and sent a tremor of renewed desire through her. Then he kissed her.

Bella moved needfully on the bed. The mouse squeaked close beside her in the dark. Rain slithered down the window. She thought for a moment that Lona's ghost was out there in the night, but that was just wishful thinking, like the dream of Malone making love to her.

The mouse gave a protracted squeak, then stopped. Bella felt it bump against her. *Big mouse,* she thought distantly. She envisioned the kangaroo that always terrified Sylvester the Cat, and smiled. She wondered if Malone liked kangaroos.

Drowsily amused, Bella would have turned onto her side, except some obstacle prevented her from doing so.

Unthinking, she kicked at it. The squeak emerged as a grunt now. A man's grunt. The horrifying realization brought Bella's eyes wide open and her body to an upright position—or would have if the man hadn't used his own body to pin her to the mattress.

Too startled to scream, Bella stared up into a pair of gleaming eyes—and knew in that grotesque moment of time how a trapped animal felt right before its death....

A SHRILL SCREAM shredded Malone's dreams of Bella and feather beds, of New Year's Eve and sailing on the foggy bay. It was the second time in as many nights that he'd been jolted in this way from a sound sleep, except that tonight the scream had a different timbre and was followed by the sound of a scuffle.

He shot from the bed, dimly aware that he was still fully clothed, and ran down the hall to Bella's bedroom door. When he realized it was locked, he stared at it, unbelieving, banged twice with his fists, then stood back and, teeth bared, began kicking at it with his bare foot.

"Malone—!"

She screamed his name this time, then something he couldn't decipher. He pictured Tock's fat hand closing over her mouth, or worse, pressing a pillow to her face.

He grunted with each hard kick.

"Malone, help!" she screamed again.

He ground his teeth, raising his foot one last time to the door. The wood barrier gave with a sickening crunch. Using his shoulder as a lever, he thrust it open and ran inside.

He saw the hulking shape before he spotted Bella. Someone was on top of her, attempting to do—God knew what. No doubt Tock would be cursed with an inventive nature.

As Malone darted across the floor, he saw Bella's knee come up. It caught the man squarely in the groin.

"Shee—ahh!" Her attacker shrieked.

Malone's eyes focused. Skidding to a halt, he yanked the man around, his face a thundercloud. "Ronnie, you idiot! What are you doing here?"

The best Ronnie could do was topple sideways, his face in the pillow. "She-devil," he gasped. "She kicked me in the bloody crotch! Let go of my collar, Malone. You're choking me."

Malone reached over him to help Bella scramble out of the bed. "You're drunk," he remarked in disgust.

"Damned right." Ronnie sprawled over the sheets while Bella, pressed against Malone's arm, looked on in relieved silence. "Went to a holiday party, to ring in the New Year early." He lurched onto one elbow. "Am I in the wrong house or something?" His bloodshot eyes moved to Bella and blinked. "What were you doing sleeping in my bed?"

Fighting the urge to giggle, she laid her forehead against Malone's shoulder. "You sound like Papa Bear. I thought you were Mick Tock."

Ronnie's nose wrinkled as if he smelled something decomposing. "That scum? What would he be doing in here? One thing this house has got is a good alarm system."

Malone, still annoyed by the scare he'd received at his cousin's hands, said wryly, "We had a run-in with Tock earlier tonight." But he'd forgotten about the alarm system. Tock would never have been able to circumvent it.

"He tried to kill us," Bella added. Unable to stop herself, she giggled again. "Sorry, Malone," she said apologetically at his exasperated stare. "It's just that I thought I was going to die, and now I find out it was only your tipsy cousin crawling into his bed."

"My tipsy idiot cousin," Malone said, not mollified.

Ronnie snorted. "Well, it *is* my room, Malone, and my house. And I'll thank you, lass, to watch those knees of yours next time you and this vagabond cousin of mine decide to invade my home. Go to Annie's, why don't you, Malone? You're welcome to leave Bella here, mind, but you're bad news. Where you go, so goes trouble."

"Where I go?" Indignant, Malone stabbed a finger in Ronnie's face. "Now see here, you great Highland prat."

"That's an ass," Ronnie translated to Bella.

"I know," Bella said, then she knit her brow. "How do I know?"

"Because it's obvious." Malone continued to glare at his cousin. "And you're one to talk about trouble. Who bailed who out of jail for causing a ruckus in a London pub?"

"I was defending myself," Ronnie protested. "Or Annie was."

Bella tapped Malone's arm. "Who's Annie?"

"Diana's sister."

"Who's—"

"Ronnie's cousin," Malone said crossly. "And you were hardly defending yourself, Ronnie. You were playing Gulliver on a burning chair."

"Someone tipped a candle onto a chair seat," Ronnie explained, grinning lopsidedly. "I was a wee bit ratted and thought to put the fire out in the fastest possible way—like Gulliver in Lilliput."

Evidently, Bella knew the story because she laughed, which was amazing after everything she'd been through. Malone, however, found humor in this situation sorely lacking. Maybe he should have tried coaxing her into his bed, after all.

While Ronnie elaborated on his burning-chair story and the less-than-gentlemanly manner of extinguishing the flames, Malone let his gaze travel to the window. It would be dawn in three hours. For the most part, the fog had given way to rain. A slight mist remained to shroud the trees and neighboring houses, yet not so much that he could make out definite shapes below. He saw Ronnie's car and his own, then beyond them for an instant, a movement. It could have been a branch blowing in the wind—or something else entirely.

"What is it, Malone?" Bella appeared at his elbow. "Do you see something?"

He gave his head a small shake, eyes intent on the ground. "I'm not sure. The fog's still pretty thick. I thought I saw a movement."

"Ach." Ronnie flopped dismissively onto his back. "That'd be Mrs. Bellinsky's St. Bernard. Bloody great behemoth. Her husband's off to work at four every morning, so she's up at three fixing his breakfast, and once she's up, Toby wants straight out, to do his business, if you take my meaning."

"He likes to imitate Gulliver, too," Malone said with heavy sarcasm. He sighed and turned to regard Bella as benignly as he could. "You can use my bed for the rest of the night. I'll sleep in the living room."

Bella made no response, except to say good-night to Ronnie, until they reached the top of the stairs. Then she laid a hand on his arm. "You don't have to sleep downstairs, Malone."

Oh, God, no, don't do this, Malone thought. He swayed a little on his feet and a great deal more in his mind. She looked like a sylph, standing there in her silk teddy with Ronnie's red robe opening to reveal her slender body. Temptation he could resist, but this—this was nothing short of torture.

He got through it, but only by using the last vestiges of his control to force the words from deep in his brain—and only from his brain, because if he allowed his heart to get involved, he'd be in bed with her in a minute.

"Yes, I do, Bella," he answered evenly. "I have to sleep downstairs and you have to sleep up here, and we both know the reason why."

If his answer stung, she didn't let it show. Head raised, she looked him straight in the eye. "The reason," she said serenely, "is that you are a self-deluded, pigheaded fool. But just to prove that I can be pigheaded, too, I'll tell you now that I'm going to see Lona tomorrow, before she's cremated."

"You can't do that," he countered, outraged. "They'll be waiting for you to show up."

"Then I'll have to sneak in, won't I? There's no point arguing," she said when he opened his mouth to protest further. "I'm going. If you won't tell me where she is, I'm sure Ronnie will."

"Like hell he will."

"He will. But even if he won't, I'll find her myself."

She was angry, at him and everything, but mostly, he suspected, at him.

Dammit, though, he was angry, too, and with reason. She'd waltzed into his life, made him care about her against his will, and now she expected him to cast aside all those years of restraint and self-control and fall in love with her.

Trust a bloody woman, he thought, grimacing as the guest-room door closed with a muffled bang. No man would be so irrational.

He heard another click, and Ronnie's hazy face appeared to his left. "Hey there, Malone, you need a drink?"

"Shut up and go back to bed," Malone snapped.

Ronnie merely smiled a drunken, knowing smile. "So it's like that, is it?"

"No, it bloody hell is not."

Grinning broadly, his cousin teetered over to him. "Scotch or whiskey?" he asked.

Malone sent him a black look. Drinking solved absolutely nothing, never had, never would. He needed to keep his wits about him, for his sake and Bella's safety. He needed sleep and blessed oblivion.

Jaw set, he regarded his unwieldy cousin. He kept his answer short and tight. "Scotch."

"HAPPY NEW YEAR TO YOU, ma'am."

The milkman greeted Bella cheerfully late the next morning. She was alone in the kitchen, drinking coffee and endeavoring to sort through the mire of last night's dreams and the events that had followed.

In spite of everything, she responded to the man's pleasant attitude. "Why the whistle?" she asked.

He deposited two quarts of milk, a pint of cream and a container of cottage cheese on the counter. "Hardly any work to do is why. Most everyone's out of town for the holidays."

"Lucky them," Bella said into her cup.

She heard a noise behind her and realized that Malone had wandered into the kitchen. He offered something halfway between a snarl and a grunt by way of a greeting and headed straight for the coffee machine.

"Morning to you, sir," the milkman chirped. "I was just telling your friend here how easy my job is this week. Normally I deliver to the whole block. Today there's only your place and three others five houses farther down this street. I'll be home by one o'clock, easy. How's that for a belated Christmas present?"

Malone made a sound of indifferent acknowledgment, leaving it to Bella to nod and say, "It's very nice." She darted a quick look at Malone's back, hesitated, then lowered her voice and added discreetly, "Uh, would you happen to know where the Harper Funeral Parlor is? Ronnie—the man who owns this place—doesn't have a phone book, and I couldn't get clear directions out of him this morning."

The man scratched his head. "Let me see. I think it might be that funny green brick building just off Castro."

"That's the Murray Harper Rest Home," Malone said in a dry tone. "I know where the funeral parlor is, Bella."

"Thank you anyway," Bella said politely to the man. She smiled, wished him Happy New Year and, the moment he was gone, rounded on Malone, whose back was still toward her. "I don't want you to go with me," she said, then gasped out loud when he turned to face her. "My God, you look like death."

"Yes, we shook hands early this morning. What time is it?"

He was three feet from the stove clock and apparently unable to focus on it. "Eleven fifty-five." Bella fought a grin. "Monday morning," she added just to provoke him. He deserved it for turning her down flat last night. "I'm leaving at twelve with or without you." She propped her elbows on the table. "What were you drinking at three in the morning that has you looking so hung over nine short hours later?"

He shuddered, squinted out the window, then probed the area over his left eye with tentative fingers. "Ask Ronnie. All I know is it was potent as hell."

"Like drinking a cup of the devil's ale?" Bella longed to stroke the rumpled hair back from his forehead, but pride kept her in her seat.

"I take it you've been hung over before."

"No, but Irish Max has, and my father...." She disclosed the last uncertainly. Where had that come from? She knew her mother had been an actress once; she knew that a "prat" was an ass, and now she knew that her father had been hung over. Yet as quickly as the knowledge came to her, the source of it vanished. The information itself remained; the wellspring was too fleeting for her to retain. The previous night's dream returned to the forefront of her mind. "My father," she said slowly. "He was there. And another man. And a woman."

Malone's fingers stopped their rubbing motion. "What about your father?"

"I had a dream last night. There were two men and a woman arguing in it. I couldn't see them. I'm not sure if I recognized their voices or not. But I remember now that my father was one of the men. I think."

Malone came to stand in front of her, setting his hands on her upper arms and causing a tiny flutter in her chest. "Think or know, Bella?"

"Think," she maintained. Easing free of his grasp, she circled the butcher-block table. "It was just a flash, Malone, nothing tangible. I can't picture his face. But I think his name was Robert."

"Robert what?" Malone leaned over the table too quickly. He gave a groan of pain and immediately backed off.

"I don't know." She hastened to his side, catching his arm. "Are you all right?"

"No, but I'll drive you to the funeral parlor anyway."

She retreated to the safety of the sink. "I can drive."

"So can lots of people, but not my car, not without a long list of dos and don'ts.

"That's sexist, Malone."

He raked exasperated fingers through his hair. "For God's sake, Bella, I said 'people' not 'women.' Now get your things if you want to go. I'm not in the mood to argue."

If she'd been within punching distance of his nose, Bella might have given in to temptation, but for Lona's sake, she let logic prevail and picked up the black raincoat she'd borrowed from the front-hall closet.

"Ready when you are, Mr. Malone. I assume you're not planning to go barefoot."

The look he shot her was not a promising one. "Wait in the car. I'll be out in two minutes."

More like ten, Bella thought, but she refused to respond to his snappish tone. "Better watch out for Mrs. Bellinsky's dog," she cautioned in parting. "Ronnie says he likes to jump on people."

"Yes, well, if he jumps on me we'll both go down."

Men were such babies, Bella mused in his wake.

She would have found his grumpy attitude humorous if her dreams hadn't begun crowding in on her again as she walked down the driveway. Parrots with pointy, stick tails; a violent three-way argument; her mother trying to coax her out from under the table; the rapt look on her face in the mirror as the parrot on a stick turned into a pink knife— none of it made any sense. And yet, somewhere in a cobweb-filled corner of her mind, Bella suspected it did.

Malone never locked his car, doubtless because of that long list of dos and don'ts he'd mentioned. What chance would a thief have of making it go? Bella had to tug three times before she could get the passenger door to open.

Her task accomplished, she slid in and contemplated the lowering sky. To call this daylight was stretching a point. The clouds overhead were bruised and angry, although they paled by comparison to the ones hanging over the bay. She'd never seen such a sinister, overcast day. If it had been midnight in Scotland in the dead of winter, the sky couldn't have been any blacker.

A man's voice reverberated gently in her head. She detected an English accent. "Come, Belladonna, come and see this. A winter night in the north is like the inside of a chimney, as black and sooty as a footprint made by the devil himself...."

She concentrated hard. Did she recognize the man in that memory? Had he been in her dream last night? Had she heard him somewhere before? Last night on the *Sun Sen* perhaps? Good Lord, had the second man in her dream been Hobson Crowe?

Possibly, and yet there was something about his voice now that was different from the one in her memory. She couldn't picture his face, either, which bothered her. But Robert—yes, she was sure now that Robert had been her father's name. Robert what, though?

Eyes squeezed shut, she leaned back in her seat. The driver's door opened and closed. Eyes still shut, Bella said, "Not bad, Malone. That took less than two minutes."

"Glad you approve, angel."

She jerked upright so fast that she almost banged her head against the windshield. There in the driver's seat, grinning at her around the stub of his unlit cigar, sat Larson Rudge.

"Sorry to disappoint you," he apologized cheerfully, "but as they say, all's fair, especially in my line of work." With one hand he connected the wires that Bella hadn't noticed dangling under the dashboard. The other hand, casually resting on the steering wheel, held a Magnum that was aimed not so casually at her head.

When the engine roared to life, Rudge's smile widened. Dipping into his coat pocket, he removed a loosely wadded handkerchief. "Happy New Year, Bella Conlan." Chuckling, he brought the handkerchief toward her. "I'm about to get my money for the second time around. And you, pretty lady, are about to meet your match."

Chapter Ten

"He's got her," the woman crowed triumphantly. "Did you hear that, Hobby? Rudge is bringing her in. So much for that idiot, Tic-Tac."

Legs crossed, Hobson Crowe regarded her over the rim of his coffee cup. "You seem happy," he drawled.

She whirled away from the mirror. She was still thanking God that her hair hadn't turned green from the ocean water. "I'm delirious. Soon Belladonna will be history."

"Then you really do intend to kill her."

"Of course. Why does everyone keep asking me that? I want Belladonna gone. Period."

Sometimes she hated Hobby's unflappable manner. Even Charmaine, for all her composure and self-restraint, succumbed to the odd fit of temper, if only for a few moments. Hobby never lost his head; he never even lost his cool. It was disgusting.

Was it also dangerous? she wondered, then dismissed the notion. Hobby plot a mutiny? Might as well ask Robert to rise from his grave—wherever that might be—return and take back the imperial reins.

She chuckled at the thought. Poor Robert. Stupid Robert, too, but she could still summon a glimmer of pity for him. Men must be the weakest-minded creatures ever to inhabit the earth.

"Where did Rudge find her?" Hobby was asking now. "Surely not at Mr. Malone's apartment."

The woman gave an inelegant snort. "He'd be a fool to go back there, wouldn't he? And something tells me Mr. Malone's no fool." She shrugged and went back to rearranging her spiky hair. Maybe she should grow it long, let the dye wear off.... "He mentioned a cousin. Ronald MacDonald, or something like that."

"Ronnie MacMalkin."

Surprised, she regarded him via the mirror. "You know the man?"

"I know of him. I did some checking early this morning."

"Bravo, Hobby. I'm impressed. Maybe I should have sent you after Bella Conlan instead of Rudge." The corners of her mouth turned down. "Where's Charmaine, by the way?"

"Still in bed. I believe her arthritis is acting up after last night's dip in the bay."

"Good—I mean, what a shame. What about those two shipments from South America?"

"All taken care of." Hobby finished his coffee, then, uncrossing his legs, rose from the sofa. "Still, it's best to stay on top of them." His expression blank, he inquired, "When does the boat for the Orient sail?"

"New Year's Eve." The woman plucked peevishly at her bangs. She couldn't see long hair flattering her more, but maybe she should do a quick mirror check anyway. "Is it full yet?" she asked, referring to the boat.

"Getting there."

She halted halfway to the wall safe. "What does that mean? How full is 'getting there'?"

"Two thirds at last count."

She pulled an oil painting of a brightly colored peacock away from the wall and spun the lock. "Fill it, Hobby," she ordered darkly. "I want a full delivery made. And tell Tic-Tac or someone to get me some belladonna, will you?"

Hobby's brows went up. "I beg your pardon?"

"Deadly nightshade. Poison." She gave the small brass handle a twist, peered inside and drew out a green shoe box. "I have an idea."

"I hate to think."

"Hah!" The woman sniffed. "Bella Conlan should be flattered that I'm the one who's going to get her. Charmaine... well, she won't do it right. Bella would be dead before she even knew the reason why."

Hobby said nothing to that, merely offered her a vague half smile, inclined his head and walked out of the office.

"You can be such a spook sometimes, Hobby," she said after him. But her thoughts didn't linger on that point. Tossing aside the top of the shoe box, she drew out a slightly disheveled wig and, returning to the mirror, settled it over her own hair.

Not bad, she thought, eyeing her reflection critically. But she'd have to alter her makeup—oh, and get rid of a few things, too. Amanda had told her once that life was a sea of endless possibilities. Of course, a free spirit like Amanda would say that.

Still, the idea had merit. All she herself had to do was take the possible and turn it into a reality. She removed the slender pink weapon from her sleeve and smiled at it. One way or another she would blot out the name Belladonna. Forever.

THE ROAD UNDER THEM felt rough, as if it were comprised solely of potholes and ruts. Bella's head spun in lazy, drug-induced circles. Sometimes those circles would spiral into blackness, but then the car would jolt and she'd snap back. Not to consciousness, but to a certain level of awareness.

Rudge had chloroformed her again, must have done so. Her mind lurched every time the car hit a bump, hopping from Malone to the Birds, from parrots to pink knives, from Ronnie to Robert.

Ronnie was Malone's cousin; Robert had been her father. Her father was dead now—she knew that instinctively. She didn't know what he looked like. In fact, she had no memory of him at all, not even a vague impression of his face.

"Hell of a burn last night," Rudge was saying conversationally. "Nah, don't close your eyes and try to fake me out, sweetheart. I didn't give you a big enough dose to put you under completely. I just wanted you docile.''

"Go to hell, Rudge," she managed to retort in a slurred voice.

"Docile but gutsy." He gave a rough laugh. "You dove off that railing like a pro. Me, I went in feetfirst. Tock just belly flopped." He laughed again. "Yeah, it sure was a great burn."

Bella smelled the smoke again in her mind. She saw the parrot from her dreams flying into that smoke, squawking, "Beware the Birds."

"Who are the Birds?" she asked Rudge.

It took him a moment to understand her fuzzy question.

"The what? Oh, the Birds. Parret, Crowe and Madame X?" He chuckled as if at some private joke. "Man, she took a dive, too—Madame X, I mean. She's got a good figure—better than yours, I'd say, but then I like my women curvy. If you ate better, you'd look more like her."

Where was Malone? Bella wondered blearily. Had he seen the bounty hunter take her? "How do you know what I eat?" she demanded, afraid to let her eyes close all the way. Where were they? Heading for Chinatown, by the looks of the blurry buildings. Chinatown and one very nasty storm, if the black sky was any indication.

Rudge shrugged. "I saw you earlier this morning. You pick at your food, pretty lady. You eat like a bird, while, as far as I can determine, the Birds eat like pigs." He lit his cigar, puffed, then continued, "I wonder how old Hobby Crowe is today. The headwaiter practically had to throw him into the water. He kept trying to put out little patches of fire with an extinguisher."

"He should have tried Gulliver's method," Bella said, too sleepy to be frightened. Had Malone heard his car start up? she wondered. Had he seen it drive off?

"Gulliver." Rudge blew smoke through his teeth. "Is that the giant who got shipwrecked on an island of midgets?"

"Lilliput." Bella propped her eyes open. "Why are you doing this, Rudge?"

"Money, of course."

"Don't you have any morals?"

"Not many. Lilli—what was that again?"

Her head cleared slightly. "Lilliput. Jonathan Swift wrote the book."

He puffed on his cigar. "Swift. I've heard that name before. American?"

"British." Irish, actually, but who except Malone would care about the difference? She closed her aching eyes and prayed for Malone to be close behind them.

"This Swift guy—did he write anything else?"

"A Modest Proposal."

He chuckled. "Sounds dirty."

Rudge was assessing her through half-closed eyes, Bella noticed. Wisely, she let her head bob. "Maybe it was," she agreed. "Maybe he was a perv—" Her eyes snapped open midword. Swift! Jonathan Swift. He was the author, but there was another Swift—Robert Swift, who'd been her father.

Fortunately, Rudge was watching the road now. Even so, he was canny enough to remark, "I think maybe you're waking up, pretty lady." He slid her a sidelong look. "Are you waking up?"

Bella heard him but didn't answer. Her father had been Robert Swift. She had a name, a real name. Not Bella Conlan, not Romaine, but Swift. Belladonna Swift.

She thought for a second. She didn't like it. Bella Conlan had a much nicer ring to it. Or Bella Malone....

As her thoughts cleared, fear began to haunt her. What if Malone didn't know that Rudge had taken her? Could she escape from him on her own?

Aware that he was watching her again, she abandoned contemplation in favor of reason. "How can you do this, Rudge? You're not like Tock. Malone said you weren't."

"I don't give a tinker's damn what Malone said, lady. I'm a bounty hunter. You're bounty. It's my job."

"But you must have a conscience," she persisted.

"No morals, no conscience. Now shut up before you piss me off."

"They're going to kill me, you know."

Swearing, he slammed the steering wheel with the heel of his hand. "Knock it off, will you?"

"I don't want to die, Rudge."

"Damn!" Squealing to a halt on an eerily still side street, he brought out the handkerchief again, holding it up threateningly. "Knock it off or you'll be asleep. Just sit here, keep your mouth shut and prepare."

"For what?" she challenged, eyeing the cloth.

"For a shock, lady." He returned the handkerchief to his pocket. "One hell of a nasty shock."

"You still here?" Ronnie wandered into the kitchen, where Malone was hunting through his jacket pockets for his keys. "Nice leather," he said in passing. "I thought I heard your car just now."

"Must have been Mrs. Bellinsky's dog," Malone retorted with ill-concealed irritability. He was digging through his inner pockets when something clicked in his brain. "'Your place and three others five houses down this street,'" he repeated. His head came up. "Oh, my God!"

"Hey, what's your hurry?" Coffee slopped onto Ronnie's hand as Malone wheeled around and ran for the back door. "The dog won't hurt her."

"There's no dog," Malone muttered. He grabbed Ronnie's keys from a hook by the door. "I'm borrowing your Bronco."

"Yeah, sure but be careful of the—"

Malone didn't catch the last word. He was halfway down the overgrown driveway before the door slammed shut.

How could he have been so stupid? Hangover or not, he should have picked up on the milkman's remark. Ronnie had heard his car start. Had he himself heard it, too, without realizing it? He'd definitely seen something out there early this morning, and where there were no Bellinskys there would be no dog.

Cursing his mental reflexes, he yanked open the door to his cousin's aging Bronco. Sure, his Jaguar had its quirks, but the truth was Bella could have driven it, no problem. And so could Rudge or Tock.

Grinding the Bronco's gears, he floored the engine. Where would the bastard take her? Not back to that first house. To the Birds' San Francisco offices then? Fine, but where the hell *were* their offices?

Thankfully, Ronnie had a cellular phone. Snatching it up, Malone punched in his cousin's home number.

"Malone?" Ronnie sounded mystified. "But you just left, man."

"I need some information. What do you know about the Birds' headquarters?"

"Rumors mostly. Why?"

"Because I don't know where the hell to go, and one of their henchmen has Bella."

"Well, you might try Chinatown."

"Where in Chinatown?"

"If I knew that I'd be a rich man. Off Grant, maybe, on Commercial Street. Somewhere inconspicuous."

"Thanks a lot," Malone retorted. "When did you hear my car start?"

"Thirty seconds or so before I told you."

"So they can't be far ahead. Thanks, Ronnie."

"Yeah, sure. Uh, Malone, about those—"

Again Malone cut him off, tossing the cell phone back on the dash and taking a sharp right at the next corner. All he had to go on was an educated guess, but if he could beat them to the gate, he might just catch a glimpse of them. Yes, but what if he'd guessed wrong?

The unacceptable thought sent a shudder along his spine. Jaw set, he took another hard right. He hadn't guessed wrong. For Bella's sake, for her life, he couldn't have.

"WHAT THE . . . ! Hold on, lady," Rudge snarled. "Your champion's on our tail, and he's flying."

"He is?" Twisting around, Bella glimpsed Ronnie's Bronco. "Thank God," she breathed, then promptly banged into the passenger door as Rudge yanked the steering wheel to the left.

"Bastard's like a leech," he growled. His eyes were glued to the rearview mirror. "How can he be gaining in a Ford?"

Bella, facing forward, paled. "Rudge," she cried. "This is a one-way street!"

"What?" His curse was short and crude. He dodged a Thunderbird, then a Honda Civic, swore fiercely and hit the brakes.

They were going to die, Bella decided. Rudge was going to plow into the vegetable truck in their path, and they were going to be squashed.

Another thought stuck her and she turned, clawing at the headrest. Malone! Wouldn't he follow them into this nightmare of oncoming traffic?

She was straining to see when Rudge fishtailed the car and sent it careening rear fender first into the truck. Bella's neck gave a sickening crack as her head snapped back, then abruptly forward.

The impact left her dazed and seeing spots—tiny black spots to match the tingling in her skull. Names flashed in her mind in quick succession—Malone's first, then the others. Lona, Amanda, Robert Swift, Charmaine Parret, Hobson Crowe. Swift, Parret, Crowe—the Birds. But her father, Robert, was dead. She was sure of that now. Unfettered, her mind slipped backwards....

"How dare you!" a woman's angry voice exclaimed. "Romaine stops here, Robert—Belladonna, too, at least for you. It's over. Do you hear me, Robert? It's over! Do you hear me, Robert...? Do you hear me...?"

"Can you hear me, Bella?" Another voice took over, a man's voice, familiar and oddly comforting. She swam upward through the black murkiness of her past toward that voice. Her eyelids fluttered.

"Bella!" It was Malone who held her, Malone who shook her gently until her eyes slowly opened. His face came hazily into view. He really did have the most mesmerizing eyes. And then there was his mouth...

She reached up to touch his lips wonderingly with her fingers. They were alive, both of them. But what about Rudge?

She tried to look, but her head refused to move. Pain dipped right into her spinal column.

"You need a doctor," Malone said. Was that concern in his voice? Was it more than concern?

"Shouldn't move her, Mister," an old Chinese woman advised. She knocked her forehead. "Might be she hit her head, got concussion."

Bella managed a weak protest. "I just...snapped my neck. My head didn't hit. Chloroform, too. I'll be all right. Where's...Rudge?"

"Out cold," Malone told her. "Forget him."

"Is he...?"

"Alive, yes, just unconscious. Now, put your arms around my neck and hang on."

Bella didn't ask where they were going. Truthfully, she didn't care, as long as he took her there. But there was something she needed to say, a name hovering on the tip of her tongue that had to be spoken.

She forced away the blackness that wanted to engulf her. "Swift," she whispered as Malone lifted her out of the wreckage. "It's Swift, Malone."

He pulled back just far enough to stare at her. "Swift? What's that?"

Her head dropped onto his shoulder, shadows filling her mind. "It's his name. My father's name. Robert Swift..."

"ROBERT SWIFT, born July 12, 1943. Birthplace, South Shields, England." Malone made a sound of disgust. "Lord, he's a bloody neighbor."

"To you," Ronnie said, hanging over his cousin's shoulder.

Malone made a indistinct response. He ran a considering forefinger across his upper lip while Ronnie reached around him to move the cursor on the computer screen.

Bella had been thoroughly examined by a Chinese doctor Malone knew. Lo Chow had pronounced her "okay, but with a bitch of a headache." He'd ordered her to stay in bed for the remainder of the day.

In bed at Ronnie's house was what Lo Chow meant and where Malone had reluctantly taken her. But in his opinion, if Rudge knew about the place, so would Tock. They should have gone to Annie's or Diana's. On the other hand, Ronnie had argued, neither Annie nor Diana had a security system.

Grudgingly, very grudgingly, Malone had submitted to logic. Now they were huddled over Ronnie's computer, while Bella slept upstairs.

Ronnie glanced at Malone's bandaged hand, injured in the accident. "I did *try* to warn you about the brakes," he said, calmly tapping the keyboard. "What did you do, smash my Bronco into your Jag as it was smashing into that vegetable truck?"

"Something like that," Malone agreed, distracted. "I realized I couldn't slow down on the curves, so Rudge had to go the same speed in order to stay ahead."

Ronnie didn't look at him as he noted softly, "She could've been killed, you know."

"Yes, I know," Malone returned snappishly. "The thought hasn't been out of my mind since I saw them crash."

"Don't get touchy. I understand how you feel."

"No, you bloody do not."

"Wanna bet?"

"Move the cursor, Ronnie, and tell me something I can use."

Ronnie knew better than to sound amused, so he adopted a serious tone. "Well, for starters, you're in love with her."

If looks could kill, he'd have been a dead man. He hid a smile behind his red beard.

"Would it help if I told you that I think she's in love with you, too?"

"Information, Ronnie," Malone said, stony faced. "From the computer."

Ronnie recognized this defense mechanism. "Bingo," he said. His ambiguity was deliberate—and successful, he noted, intercepting Malone's dark glare. He nodded at the computer. "It seems Robert Swift was in the import-export business. Herbs and spices."

Malone frowned. "What?"

"That's what it says. Herbs and exotic spices. A profitable business, apparently. He got into veggies next, then tea, rice and cocoa beans. Owned a few factories in England and South America had offices in London, Sao Paulo, Hong Kong, Shanghai, Tokyo, New York and San Francisco."

"Why so many?" Malone looked closer. "Did you say 'had'?"

Ronnie pointed to the upper right corner of the screen. "Pre D," he read. "Presumed dead."

"When do they presume he died?"

Ronnie tapped more keys. "Uh—twenty years ago."

"The same time that Bella lost her memory."

"If you say so. You, uh, want me to check on her?"

Malone didn't bat an eyelash. In a level tone, he simply said, "No." Which could have meant a number of things, but probably didn't.

"Wanna do it yourself, huh?"

"Shut up."

He'd better, Ronnie decided. Malone aroused to anger could not always be handled. "So what do you figure happened?" he asked more seriously. "Bella saw something she shouldn't have, right? Something involving a pink knife. But her mother—Amanda, did you say?—got her out before whoever was chasing them could stop them. They were going to this woman Lona's place in Alaska when their car flew over an embankment. Bella was thrown clear, but her mother went down with the car. Neither car nor mother were ever found."

Malone's brows came together. "Who told you that?"

"About the mother's body? Lona. We had a chat that day, before you and Bella showed up at the hotel. She seemed upset. I thought I was being nice."

"So Amanda's body was never recovered." Malone stared at him, or possibly through him, and Ronnie made a dismissive gesture.

"The car went into a gulch, Malone, an ice crevasse. Those things can go on forever."

Malone returned his eyes to the computer screen, setting his thumbnail meditatively against his lower lip. "I wonder how Lona got that picture case?"

"Maybe it fell out of the car with Bella."

"Yes, I suppose Amanda could have pushed her out." He paused, then seemed to sink deeper into thought. "'I saw...'" he murmured. "'Amanda's not...'"

Ronnie straightened, yawning. He detected a movement in the darkened library doorway and smiled. "Well now, you're looking better."

Malone's brow furrowed. "What are you blathering about?"

Ronnie indicated the threshold, where Bella stood, or rather leaned, arms folded, wearing his red robe and a skimpy, dusty rose chemise, watching them.

"You ran into us, Malone?" she asked in a tone that was halfway between exasperation and disbelief.

Malone's frown deepened. "Just how long have you been standing there?"

"Long enough to hear that you think my father, my late father, was a crook." She pushed off from the frame. Her expression, Ronnie noted, gave little away. The faint tremor in her voice was another matter. "That was really stupid, Malone. You could have been killed."

"Yes, well, I didn't know about the brakes." Malone's gaze flicked to Ronnie's ingenuous face.

Arms stretched over his head, Ronnie sauntered toward the door. "Listen to that wind, will you? I'd start a fire if I were you, Cousin. Bay storms blow like the devil with his tail in an electric socket. Black as pitch out there already and it's only three o'clock. Perfect night for a fire and a cup of mulled wine. A little pre-New Year's cheer."

He felt Malone shooting daggers at his spine with his eyes, but it was Bella who brought him to a halt halfway out the door.

"What's that?" she asked, bending over Malone's shoulder. "I think your computer's caught a virus, Ronnie."

He jogged back. "What's it doing?"

"Talking to us." Malone moved the cursor. "It's not a virus, it's a message."

"On my computer?" Ronnie blinked at the screen as, one by one, words appeared in capital letters. Bella read them out loud.

"Do not be deceived. Ro maine lives on. Bella Donna is mad. Search your mind. Remember..."

Remember...

The last *R* flashed as Charmaine's eyes calmly scanned it. "It would seem we have a problem," she said to the woman whose fingers pecked away at the keyboard.

"No kidding." She gave the keys a swat. "Damn him, I can't erase this thing. Why did he do it? *How* did he do it? I didn't think he understood computers."

"Some people will surprise you." Charmaine turned on *The Sorcerer,* her favorite Gilbert and Sullivan CD, lit a pot of jasmine incense, waited until it was smoldering, then glanced at the rain that spattered the outer windows. "Where's Rudge?"

"You mean you want his help? He'll be flattered. Unfortunately, he's in the hospital with a concussion."

"Pity."

The woman kept tapping keys. "It wouldn't matter anyway, Charmaine. He's bringing Bella Conlan to me. Deal with the rogue yourself." Her tone grew sly. "Unless you want me to do it."

Charmaine laughed, and the sound was not a complimentary one. "We'll see," she said. "Any luck?"

"No." The woman glanced sourly at the screen. "He deserves a dose of belladonna for this, Charmaine. How dare he send a message to the enemy? This is mutiny."

"With your permission," Charmaine said, her manner only slightly mocking, "I'll deal with this particular problem by myself and in my own time. He won't be difficult to catch. His type is unenviably predictable."

Ignoring Charmaine's sarcasm, the woman replied, "Do what you want with him. Just leave Bella Conlan for me."

"Bella Swift," Charmaine corrected. "You seem to forget she's Robert's daughter."

"Yes, and how fortunate that I have you here to remind me." Straightening, then distracted by the bamboo wall mirror, the woman touched her spiky hair with her palm. "What do you think, Charmaine? Should I grow it or keep it short?"

"A pressing question." Charmaine flipped her own dark hair over one shoulder. "Why not toss a coin? Or better yet, ask the mirror? You like that."

"I don't talk to mirrors!"

Charmaine struck a theatrical pose and began to mimic the old rhyme.

"Mirror, mirror, in my hand.
Who's the fairest in the land?
Never, never, *ma pauvre soeur.*
Not Charmaine—no, never her.
And not—"

"Shut up!" the woman shouted. Her chin came up in defiance. "All right, so maybe I'm a little vain. You're not entirely unfamiliar with the trait yourself."

"The difference being that I acknowledge my faults."

"Do you also acknowledge your mistakes?"

Charmaine's smile contained no trace of malice. "Yes." She switched off the computer and covered the incense pot. "I do. And what I screw up, you can rest assured I will also put right."

The woman's lips thinned. "Not Belladonna, Charmaine."

Charmaine looked over, noted her partner's body language, shrugged and replied more amiably, "We'll see. The fact remains he sent her a clue that could conceivably jog a critical memory. We have to get to her now, before she remembers specifics, namely who and what we are. On that point, at least, we can agree. Belladonna must die.''

Chapter Eleven

"No," Bella argued staunchly.

"Yes," Malone retorted.

"No! Malone, I'm tired of playing musical houses, and I don't want to hide out at Annie's place, or Diana's or any of your other female friends."

"Oh, God." His shoulders sagged. With his thumb and forefinger, he massaged the bridge of his nose. "For the tenth time, Bella, Annie and Diana are Ronnie's cousins."

"On his father's side. You and Ronnie are related through your mother's. They're not your cousins, Malone."

Bella knew she sounded bitchy, but she refused to apologize. She was tired and frightened and sick to death of being chased all over San Francisco by a bunch of faceless Birds. She wanted to sit with Malone in front of the fire Ronnie had mentioned and sip mulled wine. She wanted glitter and ballroom dancing at a forties-style nightclub. She wanted to attend a stage play, something by Shakespeare or Gilbert and Sullivan or an opera by Tchaikovsky. She did not want to remember that her father was dead; that she'd probably witnessed his murder; that her name was Swift and that some unknown ally had sent her a cryptic computer message two hours ago.

"We're going, Bella," Malone insisted, placing his leather jacket around her shoulders and taking her firmly by the hand.

She dug in her heels. She would have tried wrapping her arms around him and kissing him, but in his present mood she doubted that would have worked. Too bad, too, because in a black, three-button jersey, faded black jeans and boots, with his hair rumpled and his eyes still vaguely bloodshot from his earlier hangover, he looked extremely appealing. Or so her senses told her every time she set her eyes on him.

"Look," she said more reasonably. "Let's talk this over, huh? It's pouring rain outside. No one's showed up yet, Ronnie's got a fantastic security system and that stack of firewood lying next to the hearth is just begging to be burned."

"No."

Exasperated, Bella jerked her hand free. "Honest to God, Malone, you're the most stubborn, irritating person I've ever met. Rudge is in the hospital."

Malone stabbed a finger in her face. "Tock isn't. And it's not me who's stubborn, it's you. What *I* am is practical. Any security system, state-of-the-art or not, can be circumvented, given tools and time. For all you know, Tock could come smashing through the drawing-room window any minute now and..." He stopped, switching his gaze sharply to the north wall. "What was that?"

Bella rubbed her wrist. "Thunder. And no matter how many dire predictions you make, I'm still sick of running. I can't run forever."

Crossing to the heavy velvet draperies, Malone eased them aside and glanced out. "Yes, well, forever won't be long with an attitude like that. Romaine lives, Bella. That's what the message said."

"It also said Belladonna was mad." Annoyed, she yanked the leather jacket on over the moss-green blouse and jeans that Ronnie had loaned her. His sister's clothes, he'd explained, although his surreptitious wink at Malone had conveyed a somewhat different message. Not that Bella cared as long as the so-called sister in question wasn't a close friend of Malone's.

Shoving down her spurt of unwarranted jealousy, Bella zipped up the tobacco brown jacket with a vengeance. "Well?" she demanded when Malone remained at the window.

"Well what?" His eyes continued to scour the rain-soaked street.

"I thought you wanted to leave." She crossed to him, ignoring the ripple in her stomach that was part fear, part desire. "What are you looking at? Malone, you did this last night. What's out there?"

The oath he muttered answered that question. Grabbing her wrist, he spun her around and started for the cellar.

"Malone!"

"Shut up and run."

Had she offered a protest, it would have been drowned out by the sudden screech of security claxons around them.

Ronnie! she thought, then checked her panic. He'd left for work an hour ago.

"Down here, quick!" Malone shoved her through a door into a black pit. Even with him behind her and his fingers wrapped around her arm, she had to grope her way along the wall. A damp stone wall, she reflected with a shiver. When her hand got tangled in a spiderweb, she had to bite her tongue to stifle her scream.

The claxons stopped as abruptly as they'd started. "Quiet," Malone warned in her ear. "They're coming."

They? In her haste, Bella stumbled. She would have fallen outright had Malone not caught and steadied her.

Above them the door burst open. A powerful beam of light swept the cellar floor.

"Gotcha this time," Tock snarled. "Down here," he shouted to someone behind him.

"Damn!" Malone swore, tossing crates one on top of another. "We'll have to go out through the root cellar."

Bella cast an apprehensive look up, then a quick one behind her. "Shouldn't there be a ladder or something?"

"Probably." Malone hoisted himself up. Grunting, he applied his strength and body weight to the trapdoor. It took him three tries to knock it free. By the time he did, Tock was stumping with amazing dexterity down the stairs.

Malone didn't waste a second. He hauled himself through the opening and reached back for Bella. However, in her rush to scramble onto the crates, her knee knocked the top one over. On tiptoe she could barely brush Malone's fingers.

"Jump!" he ordered.

But the only thing that jumped was her heart into her throat as a thick hand suddenly closed on her ankle.

"Not this time, lady," Mick Tock snarled nasally. "You're coming with us. As for you..." He pointed the gun upward at Malone's shadowed face, grinned broadly—and to Bella's horror, squeezed the trigger.

"NO, YOU CAN'T!"

It was the only thing Bella remembered screaming. She didn't recall kicking Tock's arm with her booted foot, but she must have, because the gun went flying into the darkness, its discharged bullet burrowing deep into a wooden cross beam.

Wind and rain rushed in as Tock, furious and swearing, shrieked at his accomplices, "Shoot the bastard. And get her!"

"Run, Malone!" Bella shouted. Then she felt an agonizing blow across the base of her skull. It was Tock's flashlight, and although it didn't knock her out, it did send a shower of pain through her head and down her neck.

"What's he doing?" The hit man stared, incredulous, then shocked Bella by emitting a high-pitched giggle. "He ran." The giggle became a guffaw. "The great Limey hero took off like a jackrabbit. What do you say to that, lady?"

But Bella was too dazed to answer. Her voice seemed to have become lodged in the middle of her throat.

Tock's blurry grin was tinged with triumph. Belatedly, Bella realized that there were two men holding her arms.

"Forget Malone," Tock said, chuckling. "Just bring her. We snipped the alarm wires too late. The police'll be on their way."

His helpers might have been mute, for all they said. At Tock's instructions, they hauled her off the crate and up the cellar stairs.

Tweedledum and Tweedledee, Bella thought dizzily. They resembled Mary Poppins's chimney sweeps. Their faces were smudged and stubbly, and they wore black turtleneck sweaters with grubby wool caps.

It wasn't until the four of them were seated, rain-spattered and uncomfortably close, in the clunky gray Toyota that served as Tock's kidnap vehicle, that the hit man turned to stroke a fat finger down Bella's cheek.

"You're a lucky lady," he sneered. "I got new orders. New boss, new orders. You're coming with us to Chinatown."

Which was where Rudge had been taking her only this morning.

Bella closed her eyes against her aches and fears. She'd been bombarded with so many things lately—memories resurfacing that made no sense whatsoever; a father, surely a criminal, very likely killed by someone wearing a glove and wielding a superthin pink knife. And then there was her reaction to the murder she must have witnessed. In her dreams, she felt terror; in the mirror, she looked engrossed. What kind of a child had she been?

The sedan sped like an angry shark through the winding streets, past rain-soaked houses, shops and restaurants, through the artsy Haight-Ashbury District and on toward the water. Bella had a flash of the Barbary Coast as it must have been in the 1800s and wished it was still viable today. In a den of thieves, cutthroats and con artists, she might have been able to use her wits and escape. With two guns aimed at her throat and her head spinning, she didn't hold out much hope.

By the time Tock passed through Dragon's Gate into Chinatown, darkness was descending over the city. The rain had let up, which meant the number of pedestrians had risen proportionately. Uptilted roofs, neon signs and ornate shop fronts gave the streets an air of excitement and prosperity. Dusty fruit and vegetable stands were crowded, and already several Chinese acrobats in full makeup and costume were doing back flips for money.

"Parade tonight," Tock remarked conversationally. "The Dragon Walk, in honor of the Christian New Year." He leered over his shoulder. "Not that you'll see much of it unless you look real hard through the slats. Assuming the boss wants you awake, that is."

His chuckle intimated a fate that Bella was loath to consider.

Tock's grungy helpers pulled her from the car into a typical Chinatown alley filled with baskets, garbage cans, cats and second-story balconies strewn with clothes.

"In here," Tock ordered, darting a quick look around.

The alley entrance was not the main one into the building—the building in question being a small warehouse, as far as Bella could determine. The Chinese symbols above the door had no English translation and therefore held no meaning for her.

The men bracketed her as Tock led them through a maze of dingy, odd-smelling corridors. Bits of straw littered the floor, and there were barrels and chests in most of the doorways.

"There," Tock finally said, pointing. Bella had been forcing herself to breathe deeply since leaving Ronnie's house. It helped to combat the dizziness and also to keep the panic from bubbling up inside her.

"Who—who told you to bring me here?"

"Not Lady Parret, that's for sure." Tock snickered. He indicated a cot covered with a rough brown blanket. "Get some sleep, why don't you? The big Bird'll be in soon enough."

Which big Bird? The men thrust her inside and slammed the door. To catch her balance, Bella leaned her palm on the wall. Above the traffic she heard muffled noises. Groans, perhaps, or possibly cries for help that ended in whimpers. She looked heavenward in supplication. What was this horrible place?

Pacing didn't calm her stretched nerves. Neither did pounding with her fists on the door. Her head was going to explode. Maybe sitting down would help. Lona had taught her yoga. It might work.

She sat cross-legged with her spine pressed to the slatted wall and endeavored to search deep within herself. What she saw was Malone's face, overlaid with a pink knife.

In the nearby street, she heard the rising chant of Cantonese singers. The Dragon Walk—jeweled, mystical, larger than life. Like the Birds. She decided to try a new train of thought.

If she screamed, would Malone hear her? Had he followed her here? Did he care about her romantically? Did he, could he...love her?

Seconds turned to minutes. The roof leaked in spots. Residual raindrops plopped monotonously, forming a puddle in the shadowy corner. The air was dusky and damp, cool but not cold. Bella huddled in her leather jacket and continued to search her feelings.

More time crawled by. The muffled cries continued. Her head drooped; her eyes closed. The wall felt rough against her back. And yet...

She wasn't really pressed against a warehouse wall, was she? She was on her hands and knees, peering out from under a table, a long mahogany table, and the floor-to-ceiling mirror on the wall across from her told her that she was fascinated rather than repelled. But that was a sham. She was shaking inside, shaking and wishing that Amanda would come and take her away, make the nightmare end.

Then, suddenly, magically, Amanda appeared. Her golden blond hair brushed Bella's cheek from behind. Bella recognized the silver ring on her forefinger and knew she would be safe.

At her mother's bidding, she crawled out from under the table.

"We have to leave this place, darling," Amanda whispered in the corridor. "We've seen too much. We'll give ourselves away if we stay."

Bella remembered nodding mutely. She also remembered that there was a question she wanted to ask, but she couldn't recall what it entailed. In any case, she knew it would have stuck in her throat. Funny how the mind worked. The image of the pink knife suspended before her eyes in the mirror still seemed remote to her. Had her mind been resisting the horror of the situation even as it unfolded?

On the cot, she squeezed her eyes tightly shut. "Where are you, Malone? Wherever you are, don't let them catch you. Don't let them kill you...."

Because she knew they would—at least, one of them would. The one who'd murdered her father was evil inside and out. Vicious and evil and—if Amanda's fears had been justified, which no doubt they had—fully prepared to kill again.

IT TOOK MALONE sixty tedious seconds to unlatch the sedan's trunk from the inside. He climbed out, his eyes scanning the cluttered alley while he worked the kinks from his muscles. He'd expected Chinatown; he hadn't counted on a warehouse that no doubt resembled an ancient rabbit warren inside.

So this was where the Birds stored their merchandise. Malone wondered cynically what illicit bags, bundles and boxes might be lurking on the other side of these old walls. Drugs, firearms, stolen jewels—he wouldn't put much past them. Still, Tock had brought Bella here alive. That was something to be grateful for.

"You need help, Mister?"

A canny little Chinese boy, wearing a torn '49ers jacket and olive green rapper pants, peered up at him with bright eyes.

Malone regarded him skeptically. "Maybe. How much?"

The boy grinned. "Twenty bucks. Fifty if you want me to bust up the parade."

Malone pulled a twenty-dollar bill from his wallet. "Mick Tock," he said, holding the folded money just out of reach.

The boy's eyes shone, but he tried to be nonchalant, shrugging his thin shoulders and jerking his head to the side. "He's a bad dude, Mister."

"Yes, I sensed that. Did he have a woman with him?"

"Lots of women go in there."

"Really? Why?"

"Thirty bucks," the boy said. He waited until he saw the cash, then explained, "They go in. I've never seen them come out. We live up there, me and my grandfather." He pointed to a second-floor apartment at the head of the alley. "Grandfather says it's a bad business, like the old days."

"Which old days? Here or in China?"

"Both, maybe. But that's where they take the women now."

"Yes, well, the woman I'm looking for has long dark hair."

"Pretty?"

"Very."

"Wearing a brown leather jacket and jeans?"

Malone kept his expression neutral. "Yes."

"Yeah, she's there. The fat dude and two others took her in a minute ago. You sure you don't want me to mess up the parade?"

"Not right now." Preoccupied already, Malone began to plot. "Here." He handed the boy the money. "Thanks."

The boy pocketed his take. "No problem. You can go in the back door, you know. It'll be open. If they locked it before seven o'clock they'd look supi—surspi—they'd look bad. Inside'll be tougher. Maybe I should come along, huh?"

Malone cast him a dry, sideways look. "Thanks, I can't afford it."

"Bargain rate. Twenty bucks."

"Go back to your grandfather." Malone tested the door. Though warped, it swung open easily enough. "Are you sure they took her in here?"

"Man, I got eyes." The boy stuck out his chest. "I saw a lady lose her hat and wig here one day in the wind."

Malone glanced back. "Hat and wig? Was it one of the Birds? Do you know the Birds?"

"Sure. My grandfather told me about them. The one I saw had a black wig about down to her shoulders and a hat with a net thing on it. They landed in a puddle. Man, was she mad."

"What was underneath?"

The boy raised his shoulders. "More hair."

"Yes, what kind of hair?"

"Sorta blond, I guess, or light brown. She stuck a scarf on her head real fast."

"How old was she?"

"Older than me."

"My car's older than you," Malone muttered under his breath. "Go home," he instructed the boy again, then he eased the door open and slipped soundlessly inside.

It took his eyes several seconds to adjust. Far ahead, in another part of the building, he heard a sound like whimpering. Human, not canine, he reflected bleakly.

A tap on his arm made him jump. Snapping his head around, he spied the boy, excited but solemn faced, stabbing a thin finger to the left.

"Me and my buddies snuck in here once," he revealed in a loud whisper. "The other way's all boxes and stuff. There's where the rooms are."

Malone darted a look forward. "This isn't an adventure," he answered reproachfully, his eyes on the corridor. "There are people here with guns."

"I know."

"Get out," Malone said simply. "Go to your apartment and watch the alley for me, okay?"

The boy wrinkled his nose. "That's boring. Hey, what's that noise? Sounds like my pooch with his paw caught."

"It's no pooch. Look, just go, will you? I have to find someone. I haven't got time to worry about you, too."

"I'm not a kid, you know."

"Wanna bet?" a man's voice drawled.

The boy's fingers gripped on Malone's sleeve. "Who said that?"

Malone's eyes closed in recognition. With his body, he blocked the youngster from view. "You have a thick skull, Rudge," he noted, motioning behind his back for the boy to run.

"It's hereditary." Rudge detached himself from the shadows, a streamlined rifle in one hand and a fat cigar in the other. He had more bandages than hair on his head at this point, but he looked alert and as wily as ever. "Scram, kid. The Birds eat tidbits like you for lunch."

Although Malone didn't turn—only a fool would take his eyes off Rudge—he heard the boy scuttle away.

"Well, that's one problem dealt with. As for you, Mr. People-finder—" Rudge's icy eyes glittered "—what should I do about you, I wonder?"

"You could try switching sides, but I'm not counting on it."

"Good thing." Puffing on his cigar, Rudge strolled closer. "You know, you're a real pain, Malone, and a costly one to boot. Totaled your own Jag for a bit of skirt." He chuckled. "A pretty bit, granted, but there are other women just as pretty as her in this world." He removed his cigar. "*Just* as pretty, Malone."

"Oh, really?"

"Yes, really." Rudge's eyes hardened. "And don't give me that bored look. The Birds are well out of your league. They're well out of mine, for that matter. Believe me, they're not what you think."

"Oh? You know what I think, do you?"

"I've a fair idea."

Malone's own eyes glinted dangerously as he focused on the bounty hunter's face. "Where's Bella, Rudge? Is she safe?"

"For the moment. I suspect Tock's working under new orders. Hello more money, goodbye loyalty. He won't kill her unless his new boss tells him to."

Malone's suspicions mounted. "If Tock brought her in, what are you doing here?"

"You haven't guessed?" Rudge shook his head. "That isn't the cunning Malone I know."

Although the crack smarted, Malone showed him nothing. "You snuck in, didn't you?"

Rudge shrugged. "I can't let Tock grab all the money, can I?" His fair brows rose. "What do you say? Wanna call a temporary truce—join forces, so to speak?"

Malone considered the idea. Not that he trusted Rudge an inch, but the bounty hunter had everything to gain if Bella escaped from here, and absolutely nothing to gain if she didn't.

Rudge sweetened the offer with a nonchalant, "She'd have to escape all the way, you know. I couldn't nab her at the door and expect any recompense. My Bird's quirky, but she's not stupid. Bella would have to make a clean break for me to benefit." He rested his chin on the tip of the rifle barrel. "It's up to you, Malone, but personally, I'd take the deal. It's hell and gone better than the alternative."

Malone hated this. He also knew his Achilles' heel when someone hit it. "What's the alternative?" he asked, narrowing his eyes.

"Staying here until the next cargo ship sails."

Malone kept his tone and expression level. "What?"

"Cargo, Malone. Female humans, to be precise. Bound for the Orient."

Malone's features grew darker. "Are we talking about Madame Tea's Cathouse in Shanghai?"

"You've heard of it."

"Only in legend."

"Oh, it's no legend, my friend. The old Barbary Coast slavers are alive and well and running ships out of San Francisco on a regular basis. There's one leaving New Year's Eve. And I have a hunch that at least one of the Birds intends for your luscious Bella to be on it."

Chapter Twelve

Bella gave a violent start. Her eyes flew open to darkness and the smell of wet wood. How on earth had she fallen asleep in this hellhole?

Her skin prickled in warning, as if a thousand ants were crawling on it. Something in the shadows that enfolded her felt different. What time was it? How long had she been asleep? Minutes or hours?

Her ears separated the clamor of the Dragon Walk from the beat of her own heart. The parade was still going, so she couldn't have slept for very long. Why didn't that make her feel better?

She raised her knees, wrapping her arms defensively around them. She'd always relished the danger posed by Alfred Hitchcock's *The Birds*, but these human Birds were another story. They hired hit men, stayed mostly anonymous and had a grisly penchant for guns.

An almost imperceptible rustle of fabric from the deepest shadow brought Bella's head up.

"Who's there?" she demanded.

"A friend of sorts."

Hobson Crowe! She hadn't expected—or wanted—an answer, and so had to steady her voice before she could ask, "What do you want?"

"To do what I can. It won't be much, I fear, but at least you'll be alive and able to put your wits to use."

If she searched very hard, she could distinguish his outline from the wall against which he sat.

Afraid to move in case this was a trap, she said, "I've seen you before. I know you, don't I? I remember your accent, your voice. You were with Robert, my father."

"You remember Robert?" He sounded sharp, wary... relieved?

"No, I only know that Robert Swift was my father." Of his murder, she said nothing.

"I see." He shifted position carefully, as if digesting the information. "Do you remember your mother, as well?"

Bella shrugged. "I know her name was Amanda and that she took me away, but I was told those things."

He tapped a finger to his lower lip. "Yes, I'm sure you were told many things. You don't remember me at all?"

"No."

"What of Romaine and Belladonna?"

"I don't know who Romaine is, and Belladonna's just my name. I still can't remember the first nine years of my life."

Bella felt his eyes assessing her. "But you don't recall me specifically, is that right?"

"I'm sorry—" she began.

"Don't be," he interrupted. "I'm not a good guy, Bella. Far from it. I simply don't want to see you die. You don't wish dead a child to whom you once gave a pony."

A pony? "So I do know you." She hesitated. "Were we close?"

"I'm not a good man or a close one, Bella. I was fond of you and you of me. Suffice to say I'm not the type to give ponies lightly, and not even a shiny red bicycle could disguise that fact."

Bella had no idea what he meant, nor did she dwell on it. If he'd given her a pony, she must have known him well indeed.

A minute portion of her tension subsided. "Hobson Crowe," she repeated softly. It sounded wrong somehow. "Hobson. Hob—Hobby?"

He stood in a single, jerky motion. "Don't," he warned.

"But..." She paused, regarding his indistinct face. "It was you, wasn't it? You sent me that message on Ronnie's computer? I don't understand. You wanted me to remember when you did that."

His composure restored, he propped his fingers in a steeple. "That was before, and in any case, I was wrong. I suspect—in fact I'm certain—they discovered the message. Fortunately, I was able to intercept Tock before he left to fetch you here."

"Yes, but if they know you sent me a message, won't they be after you?"

His mouth curved in a ghost of a smile. "Oh yes. But in their own time and fashion. You're uppermost in their minds at this point."

"Would it do me any good to ask you who they are?"

"No."

Bella battled the icy trembling that started in her chest. "What are you going to do with me now that I'm here?"

"Send you on a little trip."

He sounded apologetic, but hard, too, under that veneer of gentility. The tremor Bella fought to offset tore through her. "Where to?"

"Best you don't know, just as it's best you don't remember the truth."

"That's not fair," she retorted, then immediately wanted to bite off her tongue. To her relief, he offered her a sad smile.

"Believe me, Bella, life is not fair. You'll survive. Moreover, you'll be safe. One place they won't think of looking for you is aboard our own Shanghai-bound *China Rose*."

"You're shipping me to China?" Shocked, Bella hunted frantically for a deterrent to his mad scheme. "What about Tock? He knows where you're holding me. If he tells the others, they might figure out your plan."

"I can handle Mick Tock." His head bowed slightly. "I mustn't stay any longer," he said without inflection. "I've done my best for you, little as that may be. You'll say I haven't, of course—that I should help you to get out of San Francisco, falsify your death or something equally workable. But as I explained earlier, Bella, I'm not a selfless man. That message was a mistake. For your sake and for mine, I would prefer that you don't remember the past, at least not all of it.''

"'Romaine lives...Belladonna is mad.' Can't you at least tell me what that means?''

He gave his head a tiny shake and said nothing.

Lashes lowered, Bella endeavored to sift through the clutter in her mind. She caught another faint rustle above the noise of the parade and brought her gaze back up.

Hobson Crowe was gone; he'd vanished. It seemed impossible, yet the shadowy corner was empty. He'd left her here alone with a host of unanswered questions and absolutely no reassurance as to her fate.

The word *slavers* burned in her mind. She pictured Chinese brothels, toothless men and terror like nothing she'd experienced before in her life.

But there was more, so much more than fear and confusion crowding her thoughts. She'd known Hobson Crowe as a child; it stood to reason that she must have known the other Birds as well. Yet the name Charmaine rang no bells, and no one would tell her who the other woman was.

Hobson Crowe had given her a pony. How could he now send her off to a Chinese brothel? Did he really consider that preferable to death?

Tears scalded her eyelids. The lump of fright in her throat climbed higher, threatening to erupt in a terrified sob. She wanted Malone to come, yet at the same time she didn't. He could be killed. She'd never be able to live with the knowledge that he'd died for her.

The parade had circled. Once again the cacophony swelled. Dragons' fire, smoke, incense—she smelled the last two mingled with the acrid odor of exploding fireworks.

The noise became a deafening roar. Standing, Bella paced, palms pressed to her ears. But there was no shutting it out—the screech and bang of bursting rockets, the rat-a-tat of firecrackers, the shouts and cries and laughter as the colorful procession wound past.

Without warning, a pool of light, barely perceptible, formed on the wall opposite the door. Bella whirled, but not quickly enough to evade the person who slipped across the threshold. Before she could utter a sound, a man's hand was clamped across her mouth. She felt the heat from his body and his hair brushing her cheek. It wasn't until he gave her a gentle shake that the scent of him penetrated her panic.

"Malone!" Her mouth moved against his hand. Relieved, she stopped struggling. Looking up, however, she found herself staring straight into Rudge's square Germanic face.

She stiffened. He must have been lying in ambush in the corridor, but Malone merely hissed at her, "Pax, Bella. He's on our side." His wry comment, "For now at any rate," did nothing to alleviate her tension.

Irritably, Bella smacked Malone's hand away and, turning, glared at him accusingly. "Are you out of your mind, trusting this snake? He's on no one's side but his own."

"True enough," Rudge agreed. He checked the passageway in both directions. "Okay, it's clear."

"I'll explain later," Malone said. "Right now we have to get out of here before Tock or one of his goons spots us."

Bella had faith in Malone; she had none whatsoever in Rudge, and so studiously avoided him as she ventured across the threshold.

"Did you see Hobson Crowe?" she whispered to Malone.

"Crowe, here? No... oh hell."

Without looking, Bella interpreted his meaning: Mick Tock.

"Other way." Malone eased her behind his back. "I don't think he saw us." A shot ricocheted off the wall, and he ducked, pulling Bella down with him. "Maybe he did at that."

"Go on." Rudge motioned them forward. "I can slow him down without him knowing I'm here."

Malone glanced at him doubtfully. "I wouldn't count on it. Straight ahead," he said to Bella.

As Bella ran past, Rudge extracted what appeared to be a fine wire from his inner jacket pocket. He fastened one end to a protruding bolt on the baseboard and, winding the other end around his hand, vanished into the shadows of a narrow entranceway.

Even running for her life, Bella was aware enough to notice movement in several of the niches. Shanghaied females bound for China on New Year's Eve? Not if she could help it. She'd go to the police. She'd... A hard yank on her jacket brought her up short.

"Not that way," Malone told her roughly. "We have to circle back to the alley."

A surprised "Oomph" followed by a spate of Greek swearing seemed to bear out Rudge's claim that he could slow Tock down. Unfortunately, Tock must have the reflexes of a cat because his footsteps behind them scarcely faltered.

"Figures," Malone muttered.

"It's a maze," Bella panted as they ran on. "We're going in circles."

In answer, Malone grabbed her again, this time by the wrist, pulling her into yet another dingy corridor. The revelry of the Dragon Walk grew more pronounced. Exhaust fumes blended with the silk, dust and water scents of the warehouse. As Tock closed in, Malone shouldered open an outer door, and together they burst into the alley.

Malone darted a look past her. "Quick, Tock's car."

"*Psst.* Hey, you! Mister, lady, over here!"

A youthful voice hailed them from behind a stack of broken crates. Malone swore under his breath as a boy's skinny arm gestured frantically to them. "Hurry!" the urchin called in a loud whisper. "There's a door here. We can get away."

"Don't kids learn obedience anymore?" Malone grumbled, but he nudged Bella forward as he spoke.

The boy couldn't have been more than eight or nine years old, yet the clever expression in his eyes strongly belied that age.

"Go in there," he bid them, pushing open a small door.

"No, you go in there," Malone countered. "I'm going to lead Tock on a wild-goose chase."

Bella clutched his arm. "That's too dangerous, Malone. We can't outrun him."

"Not we, me. You go with the Artful Dodger here. Stay out of sight till I get back."

"Look, if you think—"

The boy tugged on her jacket. "It's okay, lady. We'll go to where my grandfather lives. Your mister knows the place. It's safe. Grandfather says the bad dudes are scared of him because he knows the old ways."

"Yes, fine, the old ways," Malone said impatiently. "Just get going. And don't leave without me," he added pointedly to Bella.

She would have challenged his attitude if Tock and the same pair of henchmen who'd brought her in hadn't suddenly lurched into the alley. Instead, she placed her hands on either side of Malone's face and kissed him hard on the mouth.

"Be careful!" she ordered.

She barely had time to glimpse his startled reaction before he disappeared into the glittering Chinatown night.

As expected, Tock spotted him instantly. "There they go," he shouted, beckoning with his gun to the men. "This way."

"Get down, lady," the boy whispered, but Bella was already down and concealed behind a splintered barrel.

Her eyes lingered on the spot where Malone and now Tock had vanished. "Tock'll kill him if he catches him," she murmured.

The little boy's head surfaced next to hers. "Maybe not. He didn't kill you."

Bella summoned a faint smile. "Only because he was ordered not to."

"Why not?"

Taking the little boy's hand, she started for the low door. "Probably," she said softly and with one final, worried glance over her shoulder, "because the *China Rose* carries only female cargo."

"So, YOU ARE KNOWN to the Birds. That is very interesting."

The old man seated in a red, high-backed chair before Bella was, to say the least, a prepossessing figure. The boy's name was Matthew and the old man, Chen-Li, was in actual fact his great-grandfather.

White hair, scraggly and long, skimmed the shoulders of his black silk jacket. Although his body was stooped with age, his eyes bespoke a wisdom that few people could expect to achieve in their lifetime. His bearing, as much as his words, commanded respect. He had a beard, a Fu Manchu mustache, and he wore a flat round cap on his head. His manner was calm, his skin yellow as parchment, his fingers spidery and gnarled. When he lifted his delicate china teacup, his hand hardly shook at all. An amazing feat in Bella's eyes for a man who must be close to, if not past, his centenary birthday.

She answered his question cautiously, aware that he was scrutinizing her. "I'm told I know them. I gather they know me."

Matthew, who was ten, poured more tea, then went back to his milk and Oreos. "They have offices here in Chinatown, don't they, Grandfather?" he chirped.

"I believe so," the old man replied. Every movement was made with great deliberation. Bella had never seen such control before. Even Malone would be impressed. "It is certain that they are wicked and immoral. However, you do not seem to be this way. It is most intriguing to me that Hobson Crowe would incur the female Birds' wrath and thus risk his own life in order to send you away. Easier and more in keeping with his character simply to kill you."

"Yes, well, I'm grateful he chose the alternative."

The old man's smile was faint. "Death is, I agree, most final. And yet—" all trace of the smile vanished "—had you not escaped, you would perhaps not have been as grateful to him as you think for sparing your life. There are many types of death. Some we suffer even as we breathe."

Bella studied his lined face. "You know all about this Shanghai operation of theirs, don't you? Why haven't you gone to the police? Or have you?'' she added, as he folded his hands in his lap.

"Once," he said, "many years ago. Ah..." His eyes rose. "Here's your young man."

"Malone?" Bella frowned. "But how—?"

A knock on the apartment door interrupted her question and had Bella glancing mistrustfully at Chen-Li as Matthew trotted off to let the caller in.

It was Malone, a fact that didn't seem to surprise Matthew, but that caused Bella to wonder quite seriously about this old man. If he possessed such a profound knowledge of the Birds and disliked them as strongly as he appeared to, why didn't he do something to bring them down?

The question was forgotten when Malone entered, out of breath from the chase and out of sorts because of it.

"I knew he wouldn't catch you!" Matthew declared, leading him through a red-and-gold-beaded curtain into the living area. "Tock couldn't chase down a three-legged tortoise."

"He could on a motorcycle." Malone regarded the old man, and at his silent bidding, sat on the embroidered sofa next to Bella.

He smelled of fireworks, sea spray and incense, and Bella couldn't resist brushing the sweat-damp hair from his face. "How did you lose him?" she asked.

As mistrustfully as she had earlier, Malone glanced at the old man, whose gaze embraced them both. "I had to go through the parade."

"Cool!" Matthew breathed, then, at a tolerant look from Chen-Li, added hastily, "I mean, that's too bad." He paused, but couldn't resist asking in an awed tone, "Was it neat?"

His expression dry, Malone answered, "Yes, well, that would depend on your definition of neat. Tock ran his stolen motorcycle right through the middle of the dragon."

"Wow, you mean he T-boned it? Was he hurt?"

"Not much. Fortunately for me, he fell off the bike and into the crowd."

"Were they pis—I mean, mad?"

Bella smiled at Matthew's substitution. Malone merely shrugged. "I'd say so. They went for him like a pack of hyenas."

"Or Birds," Bella murmured. The remark drew three pairs of eyes to her. Sighing, and solely for Malone's benefit, she described once more her puzzling encounter with Hobson Crowe.

At a nod from Chen-Li, Matthew rose from the collection of red-and-green-velvet pillows where he'd been sprawled and, shoulders slumped, started dejectedly for his bedroom. Halfway across the carpet, he jerked his head up. "Hey, you can't go back home, can you?" he exclaimed.

Malone and Bella exchanged glances. "We haven't actually been home for several nights," Bella told him.

Matthew looked excitedly at his grandfather, who inclined his head in the faintest of assents. "You will stay here with us," the old man said, in such a way that, had they refused, Bella sensed he would have been insulted. "The attic is empty save for a number of wooden chests. There is a cot, a feather pallet for the floor and folding screens for privacy, hand painted by my granddaughter-in-law before her death. Go to bed now, Matthew," he instructed the boy. "If it is our guests' wish to stay, you may visit them in the morning."

"Use the dolphin screen," Matthew whispered to Bella. "It was my mother's favorite."

"Melina, Matthew's mother, was not Chinese," Chen-Li revealed after the boy had scampered off. "When she married my grandson, she strove to learn our ways. She had great talent and great beauty." He kept his gnarled hands calmly clasped in his lap. "The Birds took her eight and half years ago, when Matthew was a baby."

A chill crawled over Bella's skin as the old man closed his eyes.

"I knew of their operation, yet, like many down here, I turned a blind eye to it. The Birds did not bother us and we did not bother them. It is less like that today, but still they are mostly free to perform their evil deeds.

"The day Melina disappeared, my grandson, Yung, became enraged. He searched through all of Chinatown, with the exception of the Birds' warehouse here, their fireworks factory in Ton Alley and of course, the House of Mann.... Mannequins," he clarified, at Bella's puzzled look.

"I take it he never found her." Malone reluctantly accepted the cup of green herbal tea that Chen-Li passed to him.

"Yung was one man, alone and upset. His mind was not clear. He had only his purpose to drive him, and the Birds are notoriously thorough."

"Couldn't he have gone to the police?" Bella asked.

"The Birds learned many years ago how to evade the authorities. Perhaps a few of them are paid to look the other way. I only know that Melina was taken, Yung was distraught and the result was that Melina died attempting to escape. Melina and three other women. Their bodies were discovered floating in the bay. They were strangled, then placed in the water."

Malone frowned first at his teacup, then at Chen-Li. "How do you know the Birds were responsible?"

For an answer, the old man tapped his temple. "I have knowledge of many things. You ask me did I contact the police, and I will tell you now that I did, yes. Once. But few people believe in mysticism and magic anymore. They said I was an old fool, that Melina simply left Yung for another man. I know the Birds kidnapped her, yet the authorities insist that she was murdered by person or persons unknown, likely for the modest sum of money she carried the night she went missing."

Bella wanted to ask about Yung's fate, but couldn't bring herself to do it. Instead, she edged closer to Malone on the sofa. Whether consciously or not, he wrapped his warm fingers around her cooler ones.

A sad smile touched Chen-Li's lips. "Yung grew reckless after Melina's death. He loved Matthew very much, but Melina had for many years been his main reason for living. He drove his car into the back of a truck one night on the Golden Gate Bridge. It was foggy and he was not obeying the speed signs. The accident happened at 8:13 p.m. on a Friday, but the police did not have to telephone for me to know that, because at precisely 8:13 a raven came to perch on my windowsill."

"Is that an omen?" Bella asked.

"It is a sign of death, Miss Conlan." Folding his hands inside the bell of his sleeves, he surveyed her through half-closed eyes. "I saw another raven today. It didn't land, but glided slowly past my window. Death will be indirect this time, nevertheless, it has been portended. You must take care, Bella Conlan, and you as well, Mr. Malone. For tonight, I feel you may be safe, but for tomorrow night, I cannot say. It will be the eve of the New Year for you. I only hope that you will both live to see it, and that the raven will not land in your path."

Bella recalled the raven discovered at the scene of the accident that had taken her mother's life, but decided that was silly. Ravens couldn't possibly portend death. She resisted the urge to help Chen-Li as he stood.

Malone rose as well. "Thank you for your hospitality, Chen-Li," he said politely. "You've put yourself and Matthew at great risk for us."

The old man summoned a modest smile. "To thwart the Birds, I would risk a great deal more." He inclined his head. "Sleep well, both of you. You will find the stairway to the attic at the rear of the kitchen. Please help yourselves to anything you need. Fortune willing, we will speak again tomorrow."

Small, dignified footsteps carried him almost silently across the floor and through the beaded curtain. Bella waited until she heard his bedroom door click shut before rising herself.

A bed and a pallet, Chen-Li had said. Heaven knew, with all the turmoil in her head, she should leave it at that. But logic, like her memory, was a fickle thing. And Malone had risked his life in a big way for her tonight.

Moving with deliberate seductiveness, she switched off the lamps. In the glow that filtered up from the alley, Malone watched her. He reminded her very much of the raven Chen-Li had mentioned, except that he posed no physical danger to her, only danger to her heart.

"Do you want to go up?" she asked, and in the dusky shadows, she thought she saw a glimmer of unease in his eyes.

"I suppose...." He drew his answer out slowly, at the same time eyeing her with circumspection.

For most men that response wouldn't have meant much. Coming from Malone, it meant a lot. Smiling, Bella held out her hand.

He hesitated, "Bella..." he began, then sighed and met her halfway.

No death tonight, Bella thought, moving closer to him. Chen-Li had hinted that they would be safe. But he'd also said something else, and the memory of it struck her with a suddenness that brought her to a halt in the middle of the kitchen floor.

"Miss Conlan," she repeated, and turned to look up at Malone.

"He called me Miss Conlan."

"I don't think he'd be familiar with the concept of Ms., Bella."

"That isn't what I mean. I told Matthew my name was Bella. That's how he introduced me to Chen-Li."

"So?"

He sounded mildly impatient now, and Bella, gripping the front of his shirt, shook him to emphasize her point. "So," she countered softly, "I never told either of them my last name. How did Chen-Li know I was Bella Conlan?"

"CHARMAINE. Charmai—oh, my God!" The woman jumped, pressing a hand to her chest. "Don't do that!"

"Do what?"

"Sneak up on me like that. Where have you been, anyway? I've been searching for you for hours. Please don't tell me you've been talking with Dr. Peters again."

"I have." Shedding her coat, Charmaine hung it on the brass rack and, in an uncharacteristic move, slowly peeled off her black wig. "I don't expect you to understand my feelings at this point in your life, but you will. One day you, of all people, surely will. What do you want?"

"Hobby."

Charmaine gave a short laugh. "Well, don't look at me. I haven't got him."

"I know. That's the problem." The woman controlled her exasperation at Charmaine's disinterest. "He got to your precious Tic-Tac, did you know that?"

"No, but I'm not surprised. What did he do?"

"Hobby paid Tic-Tac to bring Bella to the warehouse. He was going to ship her off to China."

Charmaine fluffed her naturally blond hair with her fingers. There was gray creeping in, the woman noted smugly. No one, not even Dr. Peters, could stop the clock forever.

"You were supposed to deal with him, Charmaine," she said, giving her own hair a pat. "Instead, Hobby's on the loose. God only knows where Rudge is because he checked himself out of the hospital late this afternoon, Malone ran Tic-Tac into a giant dragon, which in turn had Tic-Tac running to the phone to beg me for mercy, and then, to top it all off, Bella got away."

"I see."

"That's it? I see? That's all you have to say?" The woman flung out an angry arm. "No 'Tic-Tac's an ass' or 'Where did Bella go?' or, worst of all, 'How much do you think Hobby told her?' "

Charmaine lit a cigarette. "Nothing," she said calmly.

"You sound like an oracle. How do you know he didn't tell her anything?"

"I know him."

Hands on her hips, the woman glared. "Well, I know him, too, Charmaine. He's a cold fish, with one and only one exception. We have to get him before he gets us. If you insist on using him, put that idiot Tic-Tac on his trail. He obviously can't handle Malone, but Hobby's not quite so agile.''

"If Mick Tock disobeyed my orders, as you claim, then you can put him out to sea in a bucket as far as I'm concerned. As for Hobby, I'll deal with him in my own way.''

The woman's eyes narrowed. Something in Charmaine's tone sounded an alarm in her brain. "You knew, didn't you? You knew he'd try to help her.''

Charmaine shrugged. "It crossed my mind. I hadn't bargained on Tock switching allegiance, for the simple reason that I didn't think Hobby would lower himself to bribe someone of Tock's ilk. Hobby's always been such a fussbudget. Unfortunately, as you say, with one exception. Do you have any idea where Bella might be hiding?''

"None, but wherever she is, she knows now about our deal with Tea in China—and don't you dare laugh. That wasn't a pun. We have to get her, Charmaine. Every minute she's out there, she poses a greater threat to our operation.''

"I agree. Can we ship our 'cargo' ahead of schedule?''

"Only by a few hours. I'm having it moved to another location in the meantime.'' She tipped her head to the side. "Why don't you lose the wig? Your hair would look nice with some highlights.''

Charmaine's brows rose. "You know very well why. Now, if you'll excuse me, I'm going to take a bath.'' She plucked the heavy gold band from the third finger of her left hand and dropped it into a jade bowl. "I'll handle Hobby,'' she promised in parting. "You just keep the business on an even keel.''

"Haven't I been doing that for years?'' the woman challenged softly as the bathroom door clicked shut. "Romaine hasn't been in control for a decade now. And Belladonna never will be.''

On that solemn vow, she spun away. As she did, she caught a glimpse of herself in the mirror. The image jarred her, as it often did, then she smiled in satisfaction.

Forget growing her hair. That would be a mistake all around. She would dye it a brighter shade of red, something more flamboyant and rich. Like blood, she decided, testing the spiky ends. Yes, blood was power, and she was the power, make no mistake about that. She controlled the kingdom, she was the power and soon she would have the glory. But only when Bella was dead. When Belladonna was gone, forever.

Chapter Thirteen

How had Chen-Li known Bella's last name? Did it matter right then?

Not much, Malone decided, although maybe it should, because he was scared, bloody scared of this beautiful woman whose life he felt driven to protect even as he opened his own to attack. He didn't mean physical attack, either. That he could handle, but this sweeping assault she'd leveled on his emotions was something he couldn't begin to fight.

How did you combat love? But he shouldn't call it that, should he? Call it lust or sexual attraction, but for God's sake don't use the word *love*.

He stared at her in the gauzy beam of moonlight that poured through the tiny attic window. The room was cramped but clean and smelled of sandalwood. As if he'd known there would be guests staying here that night, Chen-Li had laid the feather pallet on the floor. The pallet was large enough for two; the cot, folded and stored against the wall next to a collection of camphor chests, would accommodate only one. It was also the pallet, Malone noted wryly, that had been piled high with sheets, blankets and pillows.

Bella regarded him, expectant but covering up the fact. "Well?" she demanded, and Malone, acknowledging the challenge in her tone, to say nothing of the one his own body was offering, shut his eyes.

She moved closer. Malone felt the warmth of her body where it brushed tantalizingly against his. He felt himself harden at her touch and knew with the barest twinge of regret that he was utterly lost.

Opening his eyes, he let his gaze slide downward to the gentle swell of her breasts, exquisitely delineated by the pearly winter moon. He wanted to gather her into his arms, to crush her against his body so that he could feel every part of her—her hips, her legs, her stomach, her breasts, her mouth on his, hot and greedy and longing. But if he did that, he'd be giving up every last vestige of his control, and self-control was a fierce point of pride with him.

As if sensing his struggle, Bella let her fingers travel over his cheek to his temple, then into his hair. "Give it up, Malone," she said softly. "I'm not poison, you know, no matter what my name might imply."

Not poison, no. But deadly just the same. He swayed on his feet, swayed unconsciously toward her. Dropping his forehead down onto hers, he murmured, "I won't make promises I can't keep, Bella."

Her tongue traced a sensuous line over his brow. "I don't expect promises, Malone. I'm not that greedy."

Malone's gaze roamed her face. She reminded him of a Gypsy, one of those magical Irish witches he'd heard about as a child. One touch, one kiss, and a man was enchanted for life.

A groan rolled from his throat. *Sorcery,* he thought. She'd played a tape called *The Sorcerer* once. She'd been wearing Ronnie's robe at the time and beneath it a silk teddy, and he'd felt drugged simply looking at her. She was all long limbs, smooth lines and slender curves. Even her hair was witchy, long and dark and silky. And those eyes of hers...

He sighed in resignation. How could he hope to fight her when he couldn't fight himself?

Desire for her swelled up inside until it threatened to consume him. He must be mad. But if he was, then wasn't madness preferable to sanity?

His lower body throbbed. Bella's fingers strayed to his lips. She stared at him boldly out of large, dark eyes. "I love you, Malone," she said simply. "I love you, and I want to make love to you. I want you to make love to me. I want..." She hesitated, and he saw, for a split second of time, the fear that haunted her. "I want tonight."

Oh, God, don't, he thought. *Don't let this happen. Give me the strength to fight it.*

But Malone knew that he could no more stem his feelings for this woman than he could reach up and touch the moon.

His eyes steady on hers, he trapped her wandering fingers with his own and, bringing her hand to his mouth, kissed her palm.

In the back of his mind, he heard fragments of childhood fights, his mother screaming lustily at his father. But it was a distant sound, insignificant after all these years.

Bella didn't scream, just moaned softly as his lips, moving from her palm, traced the delicate veins of her inner wrist. Her skin, like warm silk, was tinted golden in the opulent wash of moonlight.

An old sixties song about flower children in San Francisco drifted across the alley from another apartment. At thirty-eight, Malone had a vague recollection of the hippie days for which San Francisco was known. Peace, love and rebellion. Funny how all of that fit a Gypsy witch.

He eased aside the soft cotton of Bella's shirt, exposing her creamy shoulder to his sight. Hunger rose in him, unchecked. With his mouth, he grazed the line of her collarbone. He heard her release a shaky breath and felt her head tip backward.

"Malone..." She dug her fingernails into his back. It was both a question and a plea.

"I'll be careful, Bella," he promised, and knew by the tightening of her grip that she understood.

Fear shot through him, then immediately began to disperse. She pressed herself into him, her breasts lush and soft and unbearably exciting.

Malone had no choice but to abandon reason. He captured her mouth and, sliding his tongue between her lips, proceeded to kiss her long and hard and deep.

If he'd expected her to object, he was surprised. When she placed her palms on either side of his face and kissed him back, he might even have been shocked.

He explored her mouth hungrily, needfully, dampening her lips, running his tongue over her teeth until it found hers. Every muscle in his body felt taut. The friction between them was electric. He'd explode in a minute if he didn't get inside her.

Yet even as that thought occurred to him, Bella pulled away, just far enough to smile faintly at him. "One night," she promised, and although he sensed it would be a great deal more than that, he nodded.

"One night."

Slipping a hand beneath her legs and one around her waist, he scooped her into his arms. And with hippie music playing softly in the background, he carried her through the moon-washed attic to Chen-Li's feather pallet.

BELLA'S EXCITEMENT WAS mounting in direct proportion to her anxiety. At twenty-nine, she'd never been with a man before. Not that she'd had occasion to regret that decision, but how might Malone react to the knowledge?

As he laid her on the pallet, she reached up to touch his mouth. "Malone, I haven't . . . I mean, I've never—"

He kissed the tips of her fingers. "I sensed that," he said, and there was no trace of amusement in his dark eyes.

Relief coursed through her, followed closely by a renewed surge of desire.

He pressed her onto the pallet, but didn't trap her. When his mouth covered hers in a deep, probing kiss, the last vestiges of fear seeped from her mind.

She wrapped her arms about his neck, tugging him closer. His skin smelled of soap and the dampness of the night. Her fingers slid through the silk of his hair, tangling in the curls that tumbled over his neck. With her free hand, she unbuttoned his shirt, all the while kissing his mouth and face.

Malone's lips traveled from her brow to her eyelids, across her cheeks to her mouth and from there along the line of her jaw to the highly sensitive spot at the base of her throat.

He unbuttoned her shirt slowly and then set his mouth on one lace-covered breast. Her nipple hardened instantly. Bella arched her back in reaction, twining her fingers into his hair and pulling him nearer.

Her mind and body were on fire. She felt him removing her clothes piece by piece, first her shirt, then her jeans, then her bikini briefs and bra. She saw his dark gaze linger on her lower limbs and shivered inside.

With careful fingers, Bella unzipped his fly. She was trembling and hot; the area between her legs had grown cramped and wet. God, but she loved this man.

No one before him had ever made her feel these things. She was exposed and vulnerable and not sure she liked it. But then his eyes met hers and, as if he'd zapped it away by magic, her uneasiness fled. Her trembling, rooted in uncertainty seconds earlier, became a shudder born of desire. She wanted him inside her. She wished she could crawl inside him, through his pores and straight to his heart.

His breath on her face was warm and unsteady, but he took his time, caressing her with infinite tenderness, suckling first on one nipple, then on the other. Emotions like none she'd ever experienced swelled in Bella's throat. Feeling needful more than bold, she closed her fingers on the vital, throbbing part of him.

Her lashes fluttered down as something jumped wildly in her chest. Malone was pinning her to the pallet with his weight. She could have escaped, but it never crossed her mind that she might want to. No, this above all things felt right.

The horror and the nightmares receded until they were nothing but a blur. Radio music and the distant sounds of Chinatown enhanced the darkness. Bella felt a mood, an indescribable sense of mystery and mysticism, of past and present mingling in the colorful City by the Bay, of gumshoes and gambling dens, Chinese healers and shanghaied sailors....

Shanghai. Now there was a word that conjured up all manner of shady horrors. And yet in the heat of her current passion, Bella had trouble retaining that image of horror, especially with Malone's mouth doing the most amazing things to her equilibrium.

He stroked her, caressing her with his hands, his mouth and his tongue, exploring her body inch by exquisite inch. Prompted by his touch, she moved on top of him, hesitantly at first, then, when she witnessed the response of his body, with increasing fervor. But it wasn't until she put her mouth on him that she realized how much he truly wanted her. He hissed, drawing in a quick breath, arching his hips and reaching for her in the same instant.

A delighted smile curved her lips. Maybe he did love her a little at that.

Moonbeams dappling the polished attic floor created an atmosphere of magic. A moan escaped her throat as Malone drew her upward and positioned her gently but firmly on top of him. His hands steadied her hips, raising her slightly so that she could fit herself against him. She felt a tiny stab of pain and then ... Euphoria, maybe, though no word could accurately describe the host of sensations that shot through her.

"Slowly, Bella," Malone said. "The night's plenty long."

But Bella didn't want to go slow. She wanted him, now, and she knew—she could feel—that he wanted her just as badly.

Unwilling to break the spell of her desire, she moved first to the rhythm of his body, then with increasing energy to the demands of her own.

His skin was slick with perspiration. She allowed her fingers to run over the satin-smooth expanse of his shoulders, through the dark patch of hair on his chest, then down to where it narrowed into a tantalizing V below his stomach.

Her back and hips arched as she and Malone moved together. Her head fell backward; her eyes closed. She heard the ragged sound of his breathing coupled with her own. It was heaven, and the silvery darkness and the scent of sandalwood merely completed the picture.

A shudder swept through her. She had to lean forward with her palms on his shoulders in order to recover. But it was a slow thing, a beautiful moment that made her feel at once safe and loved—and excited all over again.

When at last she opened her eyes, it was to find Malone staring up at her. He said nothing, just stared. Then, in one deft movement, he brought her down and tucked her in beside him, dragging a blanket over both of them.

Bella wanted to say something, but what it was she couldn't fathom. Maybe later, she reflected sleepily. Snuggling happily against the solid warmth of Malone's body, she fell into a deep, blissfully dreamless sleep.

TIME MOVED in inexorable patterns, the woman thought, gazing around the quiet pier. So, she supposed, did life. New Year's Eve eve, and here she was in San Francisco on a semiclear night, gazing on one hand at the Golden Gate Bridge and on the other at Alcatraz.

She saw him and had no doubt that he also saw her. Of course he would come to a place like this; she'd had only to search inside herself, to dredge up that long-buried part of her nature that allowed her to do such things, to know where he'd be.

She drew nearer, her heels clicking on the wet pavement. Stopping, she pushed her hands into the pockets of her raincoat. A raven swooped silently, landing close to him. "Why did you do it, Hobby?"

He didn't flinch, didn't move a muscle, just sat there on the waterlogged pylon and gazed calmly over the darkened bay. "If I told you, you wouldn't understand," he replied.

She bristled, but hid the fact. "You always say that, but how do you know what I feel, what I'm capable of understanding?"

His gaze flicked to her bloodred hair, then returned to the water. "You haven't changed in all these years. I find it hard to believe you ever will."

The woman absorbed his words like blows. She should leave this to Charmaine, she knew, but spite had been a longtime part of her nature. She retaliated stridently, "I have feelings, too, Hobby. So does Charmaine. We trusted you, and you turned on us. How do you think Robert would feel if he knew what you'd done? You were his brother—well, half brother—and now you're jeopardizing everything that he built and I built upon."

A sad smile crossed Hobby's mouth. "You really are a mad little thing, aren't you?"

"I am not mad," she declared hotly.

He gave his head a small shake. "You don't even realize what you just said."

She hesitated. "Which part?"

He shook his head again, but didn't explain. Instead he said, "Robert didn't build the business alone, not by a long shot. And while we're on the subject of friends and relatives turning on each other, what gives either you or Charmaine the right to preach? Think about it. Yes, you trusted me, but Robert trusted you and Charmaine just as much, and where is he now? Dead."

"Missing," the woman corrected automatically.

For the first time in her life, she saw anger flash in Hobby's eyes. "Don't be an idiot. That's the official lie. We all know what really happened that night. Amanda—"

"Is also quite dead," another female voice interjected. "Dead and gone twenty years ago. Is that a raven?"

Hobby sighed. "Hello, Charmaine. I can guess how she found me, but not you. Intuition's never been your strong suit."

The woman was tempted to laugh. Talk about an idiot. Charmaine had hovered on the outer fringes of the business for several years now, becoming involved only when the need arose. She herself preferred to be in London. That made San Francisco Hobby's territory. Hong Kong and the rest of the Orient was also under his jurisdiction. He'd gained so much from Robert's death, and yet here he was playing with a loaded gun. Might as well pull the trigger and be done with it.

As was her wont these days, Charmaine ignored the gibe, or appeared to. Moving closer, she studied the raven. "What an intriguing bird. If it makes you feel good to be right,

Hobby, the answer is I followed her, because, as you say, intuition never has been my strong suit. With that in mind, I now find myself wondering how many other times you've deceived us over the years.''

The woman's heart gave an unexpected thump. She prided herself on her suspicious mind; however, the possibility of an earlier act of treachery by Hobby hadn't occurred to her. Dammit, Charmaine would have to come along and one-up her. Well, she'd just have to even the score, wouldn't she? Use her authority to put this particular situation to rights.

As usual, Hobby gave no indication as to the veracity of Charmaine's remark. But the suggestion had merit, nauseating though it might be to admit that.

Poking Charmaine, the woman whispered discreetly, "I'll take care of him. Let me do it. Alone."

Did a poignant little smile flicker across Hobby's lips? Well, he must know, mustn't he, that payment had to be extracted for his treason? And she'd try to be quick if she could. No pain, nothing along the lines of what she had planned for Bella.

Charmaine's gaze strayed to the raven, which was ruffling its feathers. "Yes, all right," she agreed at length.

The woman wished she could read the expression in her eyes, but there were times when Charmaine Parret took on the characteristics of a chameleon. God knew she had a complex nature. She'd be one way one minute, completely different the next. You couldn't predict people like her; you could only hope to stay one step ahead of them in all things.

The woman adopted a pleasant smile that didn't fool Hobby for a minute. She started to fiddle with her hair, but caught herself and fingered the razor-sharp edges of her concealed pink weapon instead. With her head, she made a motion away from Fisherman's Wharf. "Why don't you and I take a little walk?" she suggested.

Chapter Fourteen

Six a.m. God, was he really doing this? Malone pulled the hair out from under his jacket collar as he walked the misty city streets toward the Haight-Ashbury District. Hippietown turned human hodgepodge. And one of those "podges" just happened to be his father.

Douglas Malone lived and worked on Haight Street. He'd gone into partnership ten years ago with Ronnie's father in a pub-style restaurant that suited the trendy area to perfection.

So the retired schoolteacher was now a restaurateur. Off-the-wall in both professions, Douglas was quirky to the point of eccentricity. Not that Malone didn't love him, but they had little in common these days, only the address of the woman they both kept in touch with in Dublin and, of course, their last name.

He entered the restaurant through the kitchen door. The latch barely made a click, yet his father's shaggy white head immediately popped up from behind a counter. "Malone? Is that you, lad? What on earth are you doing here at this hour of the morning? Are you dying?"

"Not as far as I know." Highly skeptical, Malone glanced at the stove. "Is that coffee fresh?"

"Brewed it myself ten minutes ago."

Douglas stood, patting the slight paunch visible beneath his baggy black jacket. He sported the same bowler hat he'd worn in England, along with his suspenders, checkered pants and bow tie. His hair was longer now than before—in fact, it brushed his shoulders, side and back—and he had a three-day growth of stubble on his chin. But those changes were minor. A character he'd been and a character he would stay, despite the longtime nagging of Malone's mother, who was thankfully now Douglas's ex-wife.

Father peered closely at son. "Is that a twinkle in your eye, lad?" he demanded, unbelieving.

"No, it isn't," Malone snapped. "It's concern."

"Ah... For whom?"

"You don't know her."

"So there's a 'her' at last, is there?" Chuckling, his father tossed him a warm crumpet. "My, my, things are looking up."

Malone suppressed a heavy sigh. "That depends on your point of view. Someone's trying to kill her."

His father's hands stilled. "Why? Is she a gangster?"

"I doubt it, but she might be connected to one." Malone leaned against the chopping table. "Have you ever heard of the Birds?"

"Hell, yes. To call them a bad bloody lot would be high praise. You tangled up in one of their webs, lad?"

Masking a smile, Malone returned, "You're mixing your metaphors, Da. And, yes, I am. Indirectly."

"Through this woman about whom you're concerned?"

"Yes, well, I don't know that I'd call it concern, exactly."

"No?" Douglas sent him a shrewd look. "Would love be closer to the mark? Oh," he chortled at Malone's affronted reaction, "this one I simply must meet." He shook a vegetable knife accusingly in his son's face. "You never bring your female friends around to see me—and don't say you do because you don't. And don't say it's because you've never dated any of them more than two or three times, either. That's bunk."

"I wasn't—"

"If there's a female alive who can put a sparkle in those cynical eyes of yours, I not only want to meet her, I also want to shake her hand. 'No marriage for me,' you used to swear. 'No way. I've no time for vipers.' Oh, your ma's doing fine, by the way. Sent her love in her last letter.''

"I can imagine," Malone muttered uncharitably.

"Now, now, that's just her way. She has a fiery temper."

"And an icy heart. Don't make excuses for her, Da. I remember the fights. I learned from them."

"Not the right lesson, obviously."

Malone allowed his head to drop forward. His father, lovable though he could be, was also one of the most exasperating people he knew. His father and Bella. If he had half a brain, he'd see her safe, then turn and walk away from any further complications. Except that it was too late to turn, let alone walk, and the complications were already carved into his heart. God, what kind of a mess had he gotten himself into?

With an effort, he brought his mind back and his head up. "Robert Swift, Da?" he said somberly. "Have you ever heard of him? Or Romaine? Or Chen-Li?"

"Chen-Li rings a bell. No to the other two."

"Who is he?"

"Chen-Li?" Douglas screwed up his round face. "Some in Chinatown call him a prophet, but I think mystic is closer to the mark. As you know—" he speared a chunk of carrot with his knife "—I do a lot of restaurant business in that area. Chen's out and about some days. Old as the hills, I'm told, but still razor sharp up here." He tapped his forehead. "How'd you come to meet him?"

"It's a long story."

"Does it involve this woman of yours?"

"Yes—no. Look, she's not my woman. Her name's Bella—well, Belladonna, actually. She's a victim of childhood amnesia. She doesn't remember anything about the first nine years of her life, and frankly, I'm having one hell of a time turning up information. She's connected somehow to Charmaine Parret, Hobson Crowe and the mysterious third Bird.''

Douglas thrust his bottom lip forward in contemplation. "She couldn't have been too involved in the business when she was nine years old. Did she see something?"

"I think so. She has nightmares about pink knives and parrots—"

"That last thing could be representative of Charmaine Parret."

"Yes, I thought of that, but the connection isn't clear. Are you sure you've never heard of Robert Swift? He must have been a Bird once."

"Swift, Parret, Crowe." His father scratched his head. "They're types of birds, all right—spelled differently, of course, but the sound's the same. Have you tried variations?"

The coffee tasted like mud. His father never had gotten the hang of making this particular beverage. "Variations of what?" Malone shuddered, set the cup aside and reached for the teapot.

"Bird names, lad. I find it a trifle coincidental that all their names should just happen to belong to birds."

Malone studied his crumpet. "It crossed my mind," he admitted, "but there are a lot of variations. Besides which, for all we know, their names could be made up. Except for Robert Swift's. His is in the Scotland Yard and Interpol files. Not much on him, though."

"There wouldn't be. The Birds are secretive in the extreme. But it's a good bet that Hobson and Charmaine are their real first names. Why don't you put the variance to your computer? Use those first names, then question the surname, based on what you have. That being Crowe and Parret."

Malone frowned. Why hadn't he thought of that? Because Bella had his head so screwed up that he could hardly think in a straight line, let alone with the wobbles necessary for invention. "It's an idea," he conceded.

"Oh, well, I'm full of those." Douglas grinned. "Just don't know what to do with them is all."

Malone drained his teacup. "Put them in fortune cookies and open a stall in Chinatown," he suggested, poker-faced. "You'd make a bomb." God, he was slipping back into the old North-of-England dialect, he realized with a shiver of distaste. First the dialect, next the life-style.

Most of his parents' friends had had marriages like his mother and father's, with a lot of shouting and nagging and general grating on nerves. He wasn't open to that kind of a life, not for anything or with anyone. He wanted to love and be loved. He wanted, he reflected bleakly, Bella. Amnesia, Birds and all.

"Damn her...." The declaration came out with a soft sigh that caused his father to raise his brows. Malone didn't explain, and Douglas didn't press him. But the wily old codger smiled. His lips twitched before he bowed his white head.

"If it's information you're wanting, you'd be as well to take your direction from Chen-Li. He knows what goes on in Chinatown, even if the police don't want to recognize the manner in which he obtains his knowledge."

"Which is?" Malone asked, highly doubtful.

"Not by shank's mare, lad." Again Douglas tapped his forehead.

The action earned him an even deeper sigh from Malone. A mystic, for God's sake. How could someone like that help him? He needed facts, not Chinese fantasies.

"Thanks anyway, Da," he said, pushing off from the table. "But a man who babbles about ravens being omens—" *and guesses young women's last names,* he reminded himself silently "—isn't the answer I'm looking for."

Douglas shrugged. "If you say so."

"I do." At the door, Malone hesitated. Glancing back, he said reluctantly, "I might bring her around sometime—if she wants to come, that is."

"Just don't let her become Bird feed." A smile quirked his father's lips. "Or yourself, either for that matter. Take care, lad."

Malone regarded him solemnly for a moment, this colorful, good-natured man who was his father. Then he nodded and, letting his mouth twitch into a vaguely rueful smile, left the kitchen.

Lord, how he wished he could make that one small utterance that hadn't crossed his lips for more than twenty years. But with his father, as with Bella earlier, the words invariably stuck in his throat. Three simple, powerful words: *I love you. . . .*

HE WAS GONE!

Bella stared accusingly at the empty feather pallet, as if it were somehow responsible for Malone's absence. She hadn't heard him leave, hadn't felt him untangle himself from her body and slip away.

Three times, she thought, provoked and hurt. They'd made love three times on that stupid pallet, and after all that, he'd walked.

On the other hand, she'd agreed to one night. No doubt she'd said it in a way that had implied she meant it. But he must have known she hadn't. Didn't men understand anything about women?

She yanked on her jeans and the clean rose colored blouse that Matthew had shyly brought to her thirty minutes ago. "The tub in the corner works," he'd added, peeking curiously around her arm, in search of Malone. "Shower, too. Breakfast's in forty minutes."

So here she was, showered, changed and endeavoring to air-dry her hair with her fingers while alternately applying a coat of mascara to her lashes and glaring at the empty pallet. She loved him, dammit. Why did he have such a problem with that?

She worked at her damp hair for another five minutes before finally calming down. Lona would be appalled at her attitude. But Lona wasn't of her blood, was she? Would Amanda have been appalled as well? Maybe. After all, Bella wondered, who was she to ask for Malone's love? She who appeared to be directly linked to the Birds, criminals all, or so everyone who'd heard of them claimed.

Did that make her bad by association? Did she have evil tendencies? Would they surface at some later point in her life?

Biting her lip, Bella hunted through the pocket of her jeans for the picture case Lona had given her. "Who am I?" she asked the blond-haired woman photographed with her on both panels.

Her mother merely smiled, a bright, wholesome smile that fit well with the blue denim she wore and the pastoral setting.

As she had done often, Bella peered past the subjects to the building in the background. It looked like a stable, and a very prosperous stable at that. It was surrounded by a fence and what appeared to be grazing horses. But the lettering on the sign that swung from the painted eaves was too small for her to distinguish, even with the aid of a magnifying glass.

Setting the case on the pallet, she decided to try an experiment. She couldn't read the writing, but maybe if she let her mind drift toward it, she'd remember. The stable might be connected with the pony Hobson Crowe had given her.

Hobby, she must think of him as Hobby. Hobby, Robert, Amanda and herself as a child. *Think only of them. Go back in time, but not back to that horrible day. Go back to the day when these pictures were taken.*

She thought hard, but all that did was give her a headache, so she forced herself to relax. Time passed. Slowly, a foggy, distorted image began to form. Words came into her head, like echoes.

"...Going to the Borders...the Borders... Going to Scotland, to the Borders..."

Someone had said this to her—a woman, though not necessarily her mother. But Amanda *was* there, somewhere very close to her. Bella felt the loving presence even if she couldn't see her.

Truthfully, she couldn't see much of anything. Splashes of green appeared through the gaps in the fog that cloaked her mind.

"Come on, quick, quick." Hands clapped in a hurry-up fashion. "Hobby'll take the pictures. But we have to do it before—well, you know."

A tiny thrill of excitement rippled through Bella's bloodstream. She recognized Amanda's Southern accent. She could even see her as she'd looked that day, grass stained and laughing, her own golden blond hair loose as she tugged on Bella's pigtails.

But the fog remained dense. It blotted out details that Bella sensed were important.

"Oh, look!" Amanda exclaimed. "A kitten. Hobby's stable cat must have had babies. Would you like to hold one?"

A young voice intruded on the scene. It had the aspect of a snake's hiss. "I hate bicycles, especially red ones...."

Who had said that? Bella felt she should know. Had it been her?

"*Click, click.* Picture's done." She felt Amanda tickling her chin as she herself cautiously tickled the kitten's. "Ah!" Her mother feigned a sudden gasp. "Its claws are stuck in my ring. Get them out, Bella."

Bella heard herself giggle, then the first woman's voice, muffled by the wind, reached her again. "Stop pouting, I'll buy you one of your own next week."

Buy who one? One what?

"Don't lose that ring, Bella," Amanda warned. "My mother gave it to me. It's the only piece of jewelry I own. It's real Navaho silver."

"Belladonna..." A man called to her. She recognized his voice, and yet she didn't. Did she recognize the first woman's voice, too? The accent sounded Southern.

"I hate you!" Through the swirling clouds, Bella glimpsed her own face, red with rage. Dark hair fell in tangled waves in her eyes. "You always spoil everything! I hate you, I hate you!"

Bella struggled to separate the images. Who on earth had made her so angry that her cheeks had gone blotchy?

The stable drifted closer. "Gotta go now, Belladonna," Amanda whispered. "Be good, okay? You know how your father hates discord."

"Then he shouldn't have married into it," a man behind Bella remarked.

Hobby! She spun around, to find him standing in front of the open stable doors. He wore a tweed suit, had a pipe in his hand and a cap on his head.

Bella fought to bring the sign that dangled from the eaves into focus, but she was too close, and the fog was still very thick.

A chorus of murmurs started up around her. Where had Amanda gone? What did she mean, Robert hated discord?

"Belladonna." Robert, her father, walked toward her. He didn't look mean or evil. He had dark hair and even darker eyes that seemed to sparkle the closer he came. "Are you having a good birthday?"

"Yes, Papa... Ouch!" Something landed hard on the child Bella's head. Was it the stable sign? She looked up, but couldn't see it through the haze.

The scene wobbled. When it steadied, it felt different, darker and less happy somehow.

"You'll spoil her, Hobby," a woman admonished. Bella should know that voice. Was it Amanda? Something about it made her think of her mother.

She felt her hand being snatched by a woman with painted, copper-colored nails. "Come along," she was ordered sharply. "I've appointments with my dressmaker and my cosmetician. Hobby and your father have business to discuss."

Bella looked up and spied styled blond hair. She felt herself resisting the pull on her hand. *Amanda,* her mind cried fearfully.

"Stop it." The woman gave her a rough shake. "I don't have time for whining. 'I hate red bicycles, I want a pony, can I have a kitten?' Honestly, you're more trouble than ten little girls. Bella, pick up your hair ribbon and stop dragging your feet. You're going up to the house to bed. It's already after eight." There was a pause, then she said impatiently, "Stop that. I hate bugs, too, but flailing at them won't make them go away. Be thankful you didn't grow up in Mississippi. The mosquitoes would have eaten you alive."

The state name diverted Bella's attention from the rest of the disjointed memory. That was it. This woman had a Southern accent. Southern United States. So did Amanda. Hobby and Robert sounded British, but not her mother or this mysterious other woman.

Confusion swamped her. She heard knocking and endeavored to ignore it. She remembered not wanting to go to bed. She wanted to play with her pony.

She also remembered twisting her head around and seeing Robert and Hobby beside the stable door. Her eyes flicked upward to the loft.

Sitting on the pallet in Chen-Li's attic, Bella caught a quick breath. In her memory, the stable sign hung directly below the loft window. She had to concentrate, bring it into focus.

Slowly, the words became visible, despite the twilight and her creeping mental fog. The sign read:

Hobson J. MacCawdor Stables
Est. 1763
Hawick, Scotland

"VARIATIONS, RONNIE," Malone said into the telephone. "Any names that can be derived from Parret and Crowe. I need you to run the possibilities on your computer. I can't get to mine, and I don't want to leave Bella alone much longer, in any case."

His cousin snorted. "How come I get all the rotten jobs while you get to guard a pretty lass? Where are you now? Sounds like thunder behind you."

"On Haight Street in a phone booth."

"Ah, went to see your da, eh?"

"Yes, well, he needs checking on every now and then."

"Sure he does. What is he now, sixty-five? Must be on his last legs. But don't tell my da that, will you? By your count, at seventy-three, he should have one foot in the grave. Instead, he's captain of his bowling and darts teams."

Malone made a sound like an irritable snarl. "If I wanted sarcasm, I'd have called my mother in Dublin, Ronnie. Where's Rudge?"

"A car length in front of me, heading for North Beach."

"That's getting close. Is he following a lead?"

"I doubt it. He's tailing Tock."

"Well, what's Tock doing?"

"Haven't a clue. We just picked him up. A few more vehicles and we'll be a traffic snake. By the way, this grungy green Escort you told me to rent drives like a drunken turtle. If Rudge makes for the highway, I'll lose him."

"If Rudge makes for the highway, it won't matter if you lose him," Malone retorted. "Stay with him for another half hour. Give me time to get back to Chen-Li's and talk to Bella."

"Talk?" Ronnie asked in a knowing tone.

"Yes, talk," Malone said evenly. "Let me know if you come up with anything."

"Humph," Ronnie responded succinctly.

Rubbing his temples with his forefinger and thumb, Malone rang off. His thoughts automatically returned to Bella, but not in a helpful way. Damn, he should never have made love to her. If he could have resisted that, the rest would have been a piece of cake.

"Happy New Year!" A group of teenagers passing in a white Rabbit shouted the premature greeting.

New Year. New Year's Eve. The *China Rose*... The ship sailed tonight with its female cargo, bound for Shanghai. Bella could easily have been among them. How could Hobson Crowe have considered that fate preferable to death?

"Bastard, Crowe," Malone swore under his breath. "You won't get away with this."

With that thought in mind, he made his way back to Chinatown and Chen-Li's apartment. He entered using the key that the old man, already up and dressed at five a.m., had given him.

Bella was nowhere in sight. Neither was Matthew. Only Chen-Li was present, sitting in his high-backed Oriental chair, hands folded serenely in his lap.

"She is safe," he said in answer to Malone's unspoken question. "No one has come here searching for her."

"Matthew?"

"I've sent him to fetch Miss Conlan from the attic. There is information that you will both be interested to know."

"Here she is, Grandfather," Matthew chirped, dragging Bella in by the hand. "Hi, Mister—uh, Malone."

Malone managed a brief smile and glanced at Bella. He only had to look at her face to melt. She merely gave him a bewildered shrug and came to stand beside him, and he took the hand Matthew had just released.

"What is this information, Chen-Li?" he asked. "Is there something in the morning paper?"

"I don't take the paper."

"No, I didn't think you would," he murmured. Louder, he pressed, "What then? Have you seen one of the Birds?"

Chen-Li met their combined gaze. "Yes, I have. Indirectly."

The admission both surprised Malone and caused his suspicions to rise. "What do you mean, indirectly?"

"I didn't see him in person."

Bella's fingers tightened around Malone's. "Please just tell us, Chen-Li."

Head high, the old man closed his eyes. "I see the Bird you call Hobson Crowe. He is floating facedown in the water near a seldom-used pier."

"Is he . . . ?" Bella began, and Chen-Li nodded.

"Yes, he is dead. But he didn't drown. There is a bullet hole in the center of his forehead."

Chapter Fifteen

By nine a.m., Rudge had effectively ditched Malone's cousin, who'd been on his tail since dawn, and followed Mick Tock to an underground hovel that had once been a storage cellar in a dingy downtown alley. Rain had been falling intermittently since eight o'clock. It fell now in a torrent that had pedestrians scurrying and Larson Rudge grinning as he strolled toward Tock's makeshift hideout.

Very makeshift and very poor, in Rudge's opinion. A rank amateur could sniff this place out. If they chose to, the Birds could have another hit man here long before the clock struck midnight.

He estimated that he was about fifteen minutes behind Tock. The Birds' hit man would be into his whiskey bottle by now. But not heavily, if he knew what was good for him. He'd switched allegiance midstream. A stupid move, in Rudge's opinion. You shouldn't switch sides unless circumstances forced your hand. In Tock's case greed had blinded him to the wiser way.

Rain slithered down Rudge's neck as he descended the cracked concrete steps to the cellar. The alley smelled of wet garbage, of spoiled food and stale beer. Even the raven perched on the rusty metal garbage can didn't seem interested in the soggy scraps.

Rudge pushed open the door, which, surprisingly, wasn't locked, and stepped inside. The room was dark and damp, leaking in several places. The furniture consisted of two overturned orange crates, a foam pad tossed on a plywood bed, a Durabeam lamp and an old radio playing forties swing music, a tune by Tommy Dorsey.

Normally, Rudge would have snapped his fingers to the beat, but his probing eyes glimpsed a large lump in the corner. A lump roughly the size of Tock's bulky body.

He stared at it for a moment, then decided to check. Tock's death—if indeed he was dead—meant nothing to him. Knowledge of the manner in which it had come about might prove valuable should he too become a liability in the Birds' eyes. Who knew how long they would tolerate his own greed?

Reaching down, Rudge plucked at Tock's wet jacket. The hit man rolled over slowly, much like Norman Bates's mother in the closing scenes of *Psycho*.

As a bounty hunter, Rudge had seen corpses before. In many ways this one was no different. And yet it was. Tock had been shot five times, from his knees to the final lethal bullet in his back. But it was the sight of his hand, his right hand, that made Rudge recoil.

All of Tock's fingers had been cut off. Cleanly, Rudge had to admit, but severed nonetheless.

He squatted, biting thoughtfully on his cigar. Who would cut off Tock's fingers? And why?

A sound behind him brought his head up. He didn't turn, didn't need to. A female shadow formed on the damp concrete wall.

Whether she'd just come in or had been there all along and simply moved when he entered, he couldn't say. He sensed, however, that it wouldn't be prudent to ask.

She came to stand behind him, her hands hidden in the pockets of her raincoat. The wall shadow revealed a hat and veil, but he knew which Bird it was by her voice. They did not sound alike, these two Bird woman.

"Is he dead?" she asked.

Rudge sat back on his heels. He scrutinized every movement of the shadow before him. Maybe she hadn't killed Tock, but if she was a Bird, she was capable of murder and more. "He switched sides," Rudge noted shrewdly. "I assume that didn't sit well."

"It doesn't look like it."

He indicated the severed fingers. "Was there a reason for this?"

She showed no surprise, merely shrugged and said sourly, "There always is. She's not what she seems, Rudge."

He stood finally, cast one last dispassionate look at Tock and turned to face her. "Are any of us?"

"Probably not, but most of us who would kill would also leave it at that. For all my nasty tendencies, I don't enjoy mutilation."

Though his gaze never deviated from her, he felt bold enough to inquire, "So what's the next move?"

She stared at him. "Find Bella. Bring her to me and only to me."

Rudge considered for a long moment, then motioned with his head toward the dead man. "I was planning on squeezing some information out of Tock. It won't be as easy to locate her with him gone."

"Then you'll just have to be inventive, won't you?" Her voice hardened. "I want Bella found, before midnight."

"What about—" he made a vague gesture toward Chinatown "—your counterpart?"

"Avoid her. Do it, Rudge, or take my word for it, you'll be as dead as your onetime assistant. I'm not stupid, you know. I'd be willing to bet you had some part in Bella's escape from our warehouse." She flapped a hand at Tock. "Look where greed got him. Is that how you want to end up?"

Rudge studied her veiled face. "You're sure she did this? It wasn't Crowe?"

"No, it wasn't Crowe."

"How do you—?"

"I know because he's dead. Savvy?"

Rudge's brows shot up. "Like Tock?"

The woman before him remained unflappable. "If you mean was he butchered, that's none of your business. He's simply dead. That makes two gone in a single day. We Birds aren't known for our benevolence. Trust me, she'll be more than happy to bring the total to three. So unless pain is something you enjoy, I'd keep my distance from her. Not that she'll be looking for you particularly, but under the circumstances, your paths could easily cross."

He regarded her for a long, measuring moment. Was she telling him the truth, or had she in fact killed and mutilated Tock? After all, Tock had only been fifteen minutes ahead of him, and now here she was, at the scene of the crime.

He let ten more seconds tick by before slowly nodding. "I'll watch my step," he agreed. *And my back,* he thought. He allowed the Bird woman to precede him through the door—in fact, he insisted on it. This time, no games. He would locate and capture Bella Conlan before the clock struck twelve.

"CAN'T IMAGINE WHY, but someone's painted two red circles on his cheeks. And there are a bunch of lines radiating outward from the center of those circles." The policeman scratched his head in perplexity. "Done in lipstick, too. That might give us a lead, but I doubt it'll amount to much. Probably a woman's doing."

Absolutely a woman's doing, Bella thought, resting her forehead against Malone's shoulder. Chen-Li hadn't established the gender of Hobson Crowe's murderer, because, as he'd explained, his visions didn't extend to such things. He'd been accurate about the location, though, and also about the bullet hole in the late Bird's forehead. But a woman was responsible, all right. A deadly Bird woman.

Stroking Bella's hair, Malone murmured disgustedly, "He was shot from behind."

Bella battled back a jumble of disconnected memories. "How do you know?" Although she didn't want to, she looked at the corpse again. Something about the circles on the dead man's cheeks unsettled her.

"I've seen exit wounds before." Malone felt her shiver and drew her closer. "Look, let's get out of here. We've already told the police everything we can."

Everything they could, but not everything they knew, Bella reflected. They hadn't mentioned her connection to Hobson Crowe, or the fact that, if her memory was accurate, his name was really Hobson J. MacCawdor—"Caw" being the key to the change, Bella presumed. The police knew he was a Bird, which was a sufficient coup for them. If that satisfied them, she supposed the rest could wait.

As if sensing their predicament after his vision, Chen-Li had volunteered to contact the police. He'd explained calmly and patiently the nature of his vision. Although skeptical, the police had responded. But they'd wanted Chen-Li present at the pier, and that meant Bella and Malone had had to accompany him.

"A most distasteful business," Chen-Li said now, joining them. "I think it's time we returned to my apartment."

We? Bella wondered about that. She was putting all of them in jeopardy. Hobson Crowe had, in his own twisted fashion, tried to help her. Now he was dead. It would be too easy for Malone, Chen-Li, Matthew and even Ronnie to wind up in the same state. The question was, how could she slip away without them seeing her?

They drove back to Chinatown in another rental car procured by Malone. The old man shuffled into the building via a narrow outer staircase. Bella would have followed if Malone's fingers hadn't closed firmly about her arm.

"Uh-uh. Not so fast. We have to talk."

She pushed down her fear and former frustration over his vanishing act. "About what?" she returned calmly. "Us?" She eased her arm free. "You can relax on that score, Malone. I'm not going to make any demands of you. I don't expect you to change your entire outlook because of one night."

"One beautiful night."

Oh, yes, it had been beautiful, all right. If Bella's thoughts hadn't been in such a tailspin, she would have searched for a deeper meaning in his words. But as things stood now, she was no longer certain she wanted to find one. The Birds were killers, and like it or not, she was tied to them. Maybe that made her a bad person, maybe it didn't. She only knew for certain that it made her a definite danger to Malone—trouble, as Lona would have said, with a capital *T*.

To her relief, Malone let the subject slide. When she started up the staircase, he followed without another word. If only he would stop staring at her with those beautiful Irish eyes of his.

Chen-Li was waiting when they entered the apartment. He sat in his high-backed chair and motioned for them to join him. "Perhaps if we review all that you know of this situation, together we'll be able to sort matters out."

Oh, matters would be sorted out, Bella thought, but not by the three of them. Rather by her alone, the moment the opportunity arose.

Nodding at Chen-Li's suggestion, she searched discreetly through her pockets for the packet of prescription sleeping pills she'd been given the day of her accident with Rudge.

"Please, start your tale at the beginning," Chen-Li invited.

With Malone's help, Bella poured out her story, down to the smallest detail. She removed from her jeans the silver case that Lona had given her, and would have showed it to Chen-Li had Malone not reminded her of a detail she'd neglected to mention: Lona's last words.

"'I saw . . .'" he repeated. "'Amanda's not . . .'"

"Not what?" Chen-Li asked. He poured the tea that Matthew had brewed and left steeping for them.

Bella eyed the pot, but made no move toward it. "Not a Bird?" she suggested with a feeble attempt at humor. She wasn't sure why she bothered. Maybe she was hoping to divert their attention from the teapot. In any case, the attempt failed.

Malone's dark eyes flicked to her face, but as usual, she couldn't interpret their expression. Lounging back on the sofa, he made an impatient gesture. "We know that Amanda wasn't Lona's daughter, so what does that leave?"

"Well, let's see." Bella ticked off items on her fingers. "We know that Hobson Crowe is, or rather was, really

Hobson J. MacCawdor. We know that someone, presumably Mick Tock, shot and killed Lona instead of me.''

"We don't know that for sure, Bella," Malone replied with aggravating logic. "He could have been aiming at Lona, intending to kill her before she could tell you something that might conceivably jog your memory."

"Maybe. But he came after me, too, and Rudge *did* say that Tock's orders were shoot to kill."

Malone pressed a thumb to his lip. "Yes, he did. But those weren't *Rudge's* orders. He was told to bring you in alive, or so he implied the night of the restaurant fire."

Bella sighed. "Whatever. One of the Birds apparently wants me dead on the spot, Hobby was going to ship me to Shanghai and the third Bird would prefer that I was brought in alive. Somehow I don't find the differences comforting."

Chen-Li's gaze shifted to the window, but when Bella looked, she saw nothing of interest on the other side. "It was a shadow," he assured her. "Do not trouble yourself." Malone's eyes narrowed suspiciously on the old man, but he made no comment. A moment later, Chen-Li said, "Tell me more about your dreams, Miss Conlan. What is this pink knife you spoke of earlier?"

"It's a long, skinny knife with some sort of funny carving on the handle. First it was a parrot on a stick in my dream, but then it turned into the pink knife."

"And you saw this knife clearly?"

"Not at first, but I do now. It's funny though, Chen-Li, but when I look at it in my dreams, the knife isn't really clear to me. I can only see it in the mirror across the room from where I'm hiding. It's visible in the mirror, but not in front of me, where it should be."

"I see," Chen-Li said.

"Then would you mind explaining it to us?" Malone asked, exaggeratedly polite.

For a moment Bella forgot her worries and hid a smile at his tone. Why couldn't he love her? Why couldn't they have met under less-horrific circumstances? Why was he staring at her again?

Chen-Li sipped his tea. "I cannot explain what I did not witness," he said at length, "but I'm intrigued nonetheless. You say you cannot see the face of the person who murdered your father. Do you see the face of the woman who led you away from the stable?"

Bella thought back. "No..." She drew out the word. "But she was wearing a black silk coat, and she had blond hair. And a Mississippi accent. They both had that."

Malone frowned. "Both?"

"The murderer and Amanda. At least they sounded similar. Hobby and Robert—my father—sounded British."

"What about you?" Chen-Li inquired. "How did you sound?"

"I..." She paused, uncertain. "I'm not sure. Like I do now, I suppose."

"Were you angry?"

"In the dream? No. Well, except for once or twice. The first time when I said I hated red bicycles, and again when I shouted that I hated someone."

"But you don't know who that someone was?" Malone questioned.

She opened her mouth to answer, but exclaimed, "Bicycle!" instead. Her fingers found Malone's forearm. "A red bicycle, Malone!"

"Yes, what about it?"

"Bicycle tires. That's what those circles on Hobson Crowe's face reminded me of. Red bicycle tires. The lines radiating outward from the center could be spokes."

"Bella..." Malone began wearily.

"No, listen." She shook his arm to emphasize her point. "It's a message of some sort, a symbol. It must be."

"Bicycle tires are a symbol?"

"Yes. I told you, Malone, Hobson Crowe mentioned a red bicycle to me. It could be..." Bella caught the skeptical look in his eyes and her enthusiasm subsided. "Oh, all right," she said with a resigned breath. "Have it your way. But what else could those circles represent?"

"An unwell mind?" Chen-Li suggested.

The look on Malone's face would have brought a smile to Bella's lips if she hadn't consciously stopped it.

"Yes, presumably," he said, his tone dry. "But for the moment I'd rather concentrate on this blond mystery woman in Bella's latest dream. You said that she said she had an appointment."

"Two," Bella confirmed. "One with her dressmaker and another with her cosmetician."

Malone knit his brow. Bella wished he wouldn't do that. It made him look even sexier than he already did, and she was having a difficult enough time just sitting next to him.

"Your mother had an ex-designer dressmaker—didn't you tell me that once?"

"I think so. But I don't think the woman in my dreams was my mother. I mean, she sounded a little bit like Amanda, but she didn't act the same way at all."

"Really," Malone said enigmatically.

The telephone rang, and a moment later the beaded curtain clacked. Bella noticed that Chen-Li's eyes were once more fixed on the window, yet again she saw nothing. When she turned back, the old man was staring at her from under half-closed eyelids.

"Hey, Malone," Matthew called through the curtain. "Phone for you. Says he's your soon-to-be ex-cousin."

"Sooner than he thinks, making cracks like that," Malone muttered, rising.

The moment he left, Chen-Li removed his hands from the bell of his sleeves and, leaning forward, gripped Bella's cool fingers. "I have seen the shadow of the raven, Miss Conlan," he told her without preamble. "Twice since I have been sitting here I've noted it outside my window. Not the bird itself, but its shadow."

Not normally superstitious, Bella nevertheless felt a chill feather along her spine. "What are you implying, Chen-Li? That I'm standing in the shadow of death?"

His troubled eyes offered no solace. "Perhaps. I cannot say for certain what any shadow portends. Let us drink more tea and discuss your dreams on a deeper level."

Drink more tea . . .

"I'll pour," Bella promptly offered.

Chen-Li's eyes closed, as they tended to do when he wanted to think. Seizing the opportunity, Bella emptied the powder from several of the prescription sleeping capsules into her palm. On the pretense of stirring the tea, she uncovered the pot and dropped the powder in. She was pouring when Malone returned with an excited Matthew trotting on his heels.

"They're gonna meet in an hour," Matthew revealed, his black eyes shining. "Malone says I can go, too. May I, Grandfather? Please?"

Bella's fingers tightened on the china handle. She'd forgotten about Matthew. Could his young system handle this drug? But if she didn't put him to sleep with the others, she'd have to explain her actions to him.

She set the teapot down carefully. She could always wait until Malone and Matthew left, but then who knew where they were meeting Ronnie, or how long the rendezvous would last? They might return and spot her, or worse, she might run into them.

"You may go," Chen-Li was saying to his grandson. "But first you must do your reading exercises."

Bella's heart gave a relieved thump. Thank heaven for homework.

Matthew made a face. "Aw, Grandfather. It's New Year's Eve."

"For you it is simply a new day of learning. Go upstairs and begin. Mr. Malone will call you when he's ready."

Matthew looked at Malone. "You won't forget, will you?"

Bella picked up one of the teacups. "He won't forget, Matthew. Do as your grandfather says."

Reassured, Matthew ran off to his bedroom. Bella fought the lingering pricks of her conscience long enough to give Chen-Li his cup. For herself, she picked up a cookie and sat back.

Both men drank, first Chen-Li, then Malone. Since neither of them said anything, Bella assumed the powder was tasteless. Still, Malone, being British, was picky about his tea, and Chen-Li with his visions might have "foreseen" her plan at any time. Her fears were assuaged when they emptied their cups and even took refills.

Returning his hands to his sleeves, Chen-Li regarded her through calm dark eyes. "May I see the picture case given to you by your grandmother?"

Bella handed it to Malone, who opened it before passing it on to the old man. "Mississippi," he said, stifling a yawn. "She looks more like Utah to me. Very wholesome. Not the type..." His head bobbed, but he recovered and blinked. "Not the type to have a dress...at her beck and..." His head dipped forward; his grip on the silver case relaxed.

Chen-Li blinked deeply as Bella rescued the sliding case. "He has been worried about you."

Bella hadn't realized how strong guilt pangs could be. "Yes, I know." She stroked the hair from Malone's eyes, then laid his head back against the sofa cushions. "He's helped me a lot. I didn't trust him at first, but I do now."

"And you love him?" At her reaction, an impish smile tugged on the old man's lips. "You needn't look so surprised, Miss Conlan. I understand love quite well. I loved my grandson and his wife very much. And of course Matthew is part of my soul." He sat back in his chair. "We do many things in the name of love. Will you hold up the picture case for me to see?"

Bella couldn't bring herself to talk. How could she have done this horrible thing? This was a Bird tactic. Maybe she was as ruthless as they were, after all. She ran her fingers through Malone's hair one last time, then held up the picture case.

"The woman—you called her Amanda?—she wears a silver ring on her right forefinger."

Bella nodded. "Uh, Chen-Li? I think there's something I should... Oh, my God, are you all right?"

The sudden widening of Chen-Li's eyes had her catapulting from her seat. He was an old man. She'd put the contents of five pills into his small teapot. What if the drug proved too strong for his system? He might be allergic, for all she knew. Malone, thank heaven, was sleeping peacefully, but he was young compared to Chen-Li. Young and heathy and—oh, Lord, what had she been thinking?

Panic gripped her when Chen-Li gasped out what seemed to be his last painful breath. Then his startled expression melted into one of understanding. He whispered gently, "Ah, Miss Conlan," before a smile settled on his lips. Eyes closing, he laid his head against the chair back.

Bella immediately checked his breathing. It seemed fine to her—deep and steady, like Malone's.

Should she wait? she wondered. No. For all her anxiety, the pills weren't that strong, not diluted in tea. She'd been letting her nerves rule her brain. They were asleep—which was precisely what she'd wanted. All she had to do now was escape before Matthew came trotting downstairs in search of cookies and milk.

She donned her leather jacket, considered for a moment, then crossed to the desk and scrawled a hasty note. She signed it instinctively "Love, Bella," placed it in Malone's hand and, bending, kissed him on the mouth and forehead.

"Please understand," she whispered. Then, taking a deep breath to bolster her courage, she marched to the door. It was time for the remaining Birds to flock together. Before midnight struck and the *China Rose* sailed for Shanghai.

"MALONE! Wake up, man. Come on, now, wake up. Malone, can you hear me? It's Ronnie, your cousin, Ronnie."

Malone heard the familiar voice, but couldn't place it until the man shaking him repeated his name. What was Ronnie doing shaking him awake in the middle of the night? "Go away," he mumbled crossly, but Ronnie only shook him harder.

"Malone, you have to wake up. It's Bella. Matthew says she's gone."

Bella?

Malone forced his eyes open, but felt too groggy to concentrate. "Oh, damn," he groaned. "Don't tell me the little idiot . . ." With Ronnie's aid, he hauled himself upright. "She must have slipped us a mickey. How could she be so stupid?"

Ronnie sniffed the teacups, then the pot. Dipping in his pinky, he tasted the residue. "It's a bit chemical, all right—probably those sleeping pills that doctor of yours gave her."

Malone rubbed his eyes with his fingertips to clear them. "Chen-Li?" he asked.

"I'm here," said the old man. He sounded weak but awake. "I didn't expect... Should have, though. A most resourceful young woman."

"A most foolish young woman, you mean," Malone countered, scowling. "How long have we been out, Ronnie?"

"Two hours, give or take. Matthew came down to remind you of our meeting and found the pair of you sound asleep. When he couldn't wake you and couldn't find Bella to help him, he came to our arranged meeting place alone."

"I thought the big blond dude might have taken Miss Bella and knocked you and Grandfather out cold," Matthew interjected from Chen-Li's side. "I never figured she'd go off on her own."

Neither had Malone. But, dammit, he should have. She'd been too studiously polite earlier. Why on earth had he drunk the stupid tea—if you could even call the noxious green concoction tea? It had tasted like steeped dandelions to him. No wonder he hadn't detected the drug.

He stood despite Ronnie's protests. "Give yourself a minute, man," his cousin advised, his Scottish brogue heavier than usual with concern. "You're still under the influence."

Malone swayed, but steadied himself on the mantel. His head throbbed like it had when he'd been five and had the measles. Groaning again, he closed his eyes. How bloody many pills had she slipped them?

"What is it, Grandfather?" Matthew asked. "What are you pointing at? That silver thing? The paper?"

"Both," Chen-Li said weakly.

What paper? Malone frowned. He followed Matthew's finger and spotted it on the sofa—a folded sheet of paper. "Let me see," he said to Ronnie.

"Hand me the picture case," Chen-Li told his grandson.

Ronnie unfolded the paper before relinquishing it. "'Malone,'" he read over his cousin's shoulder. "'You've placed yourself in enough danger for me already. The Birds are my problem. I'm going to find them and try to remember. Please don't be angry. Love, Bella.'"

Again, Malone's eyes closed. "I don't believe this," he muttered. When he looked again, he saw Chen-Li staring avidly at the picture case. "What is it?" he asked, his tone just short of snappish.

"A puzzle." One by one the old man's gnarled finger traced the human subjects. It stopped on the left side of the case, on Amanda's face. "Did you tell me that you originally found Miss Conlan through a photograph given to you by Larson Rudge?"

Malone nodded warily. "Yes. Why?"

"Do you still have it?"

"It's in my wallet."

"May I see it, please?"

Ronnie tapped his cousin's arm, then his own watch. "If your legs are firming up, shouldn't we be off after Bella?"

"What's this all about, Chen-Li?" Malone said, impatient to follow Ronnie's suggestion. "What do you see in these pictures?"

"Perhaps a great deal, but it would require a keen eye to spot the differences."

"What are you talking about?"

For an answer, Chen-Li indicated Amanda. "You must at least notice the obvious discrepancies," he said, tracing the line of her body. "She is wearing a loose denim pantsuit, and her only piece of jewelry appears to be a silver ring that she wears on her right forefinger."

"Yes. So?"

"This woman had a dressmaker, did she not?"

"Lots of people wear jeans, Grandfather," Matthew said piping up. "They're cool."

Malone kept his gaze fixed on Chen-Li's implacable face. He had a vague idea of what the old man was hinting at, but he needed to be sure. "What exactly are you saying? That there was something wrong with Amanda?"

Chen-Li raised his eyes to Malone's. "Much is wrong here, I fear," he said softly. "All is not as it appears in these photographs. They are, all of them, misleading." His finger stroked the face of the young girl in pigtails, who was holding a kitten. A gentle smile curved his lips. "All," he amended, "but one."

Chapter Sixteen

Bella discovered nothing in the warehouse across from Chen-Li's. Plenty of boxes for shipping, but no women or other cargo.

She crept from shadow to shadow, her heart in her throat, until she realized that she'd searched the entire building. There were cots, blankets and bindings, and even piles of questionable refuse, but the only people she saw were workers, bored and thankfully unaware that an intruder lurked on the premises.

Obviously, the Birds had moved the women. Where to? Bella wondered, concealing herself behind a stack of barrels. What other places had Chen-Li told her they owned here in Chinatown? A factory, for one. Yes, a fireworks factory in Ton Alley. And something called the House of Mann. Surely neither of those places would be difficult to find.

She had to wait, cramped and scarcely breathing, for fifteen minutes before she could escape from the warehouse. When the way was clear, she slipped out a side door. How long those pills would continue to work on Malone and Chen-Li was anyone's guess, and she'd been inside for the better part of two hours now.

A clock chimed the half hour as Bella emerged onto bustling Grant Avenue. The sky seemed dark, but that was deceptive, since it was only two-thirty in the afternoon. Black clouds rolling in from the bay gave the sky a brooding aspect that boded poorly for the commencement of the New Year. On the other hand, if the storm kicked in in full force, the *China Rose* would be unable to sail on schedule. Unless, of course, it sailed early.

She'd tried earlier to tell the police about the warehouse, but the first officer she'd spoken to had stared at her as if she'd lost her mind, and the second, a woman called Sergeant Moller, had merely nodded and jotted her statement down in a worn notebook. Malone had probably summed it up best when he'd said that by the time the authorities could show sufficient cause for a search warrant to be issued, the Birds would long since have flown the coop with their female prey. So much for justice, Bella reflected in distaste. Who said the Barbary Coast no longer existed?

With the aid of the Yellow Pages, it took her no time at all to locate the fireworks factory. The place was called Lee's, undoubtedly the Chinese equivalent of "Smith."

Ton Alley was a crowded, crooked lane. The factory stood at the far end, a dark, dingy place with two equally dingy buildings on each side. The windows were high, narrow and dirty, the doors small and, unfortunately, secure. With one exception . . .

Bella knelt behind a rusty fire-escape ladder and watched as a pair of Chinese men carried an assortment of crates through that lone door. No one appeared to be checking them in and out, but Bella knew better than to take that observation on faith. She considered the truck. With luck, she might fit into one of the crates, assuming the contents weighed as much as she did.

She waited until the men went in again, darted a quick look down the alley, then ran to the truck. Hauling herself onto the platform, she headed for the nearest crate, pried off the top and peered inside.

"Damn," she said in frustration. "They're empty." Her fingers balled into fists. She'd have to sneak into the factory.

The men returned just as she finished replacing the lid. Grunting, they dragged out another pair of crates. They

spoke Chinese the whole time, laughing and displaying rows
of gold teeth. Evidently, the Birds paid very well indeed.

Breath held, Bella huddled in a niche at the rear of the
delivery truck. The men gave no indication that they saw
her. They removed their crates and started for the factory.
She counted to ten, whispered a heartfelt prayer and hopped
out.

The door remained open. Bella crept along the wall until
she could see inside. The blackness in the passageway
matched that of the clouds overhead. Only a forty-watt light
bulb burned to break the murkiness.

She ventured in cautiously, flinching at the gritty sound
made by her boots on the concrete floor. On the other hand,
why was she creeping? She wanted to find the Birds, didn't
she?

Find them, yes, but not confront them directly, not in a
place where they had every advantage over her.

She hadn't really thought this plan through, she realized.
Yet what else could she do? If she waited, the *China Rose*
might sail. And Malone wouldn't have sat still for very long
in Chen-Li's apartment. He already had Ronnie checking on
the name MacCawdor. If that name led him to the other
Birds, he'd plunge in headfirst, and the consequences of that
rash act Bella simply could not accept. Better that she
should be rash. The Birds wanted her—not Malone.

The deeper she ventured into the building, the stronger
the smell of fireworks grew. Strings of firecrackers hung in
rows along the passageways. There were rooms stuffed with
metal boxes, some open, some closed, but all, she suspected, brimming with flares, "bombs" and glitter rockets.

It wasn't long before other smells intruded—those of
perfume and perspiration, of human hair and skin. Beneath them Bella detected the aromas of food and wine.
Why wine? She frowned and continued toward the source.

Before long, she caught a familiar sound—those same,
muffled whimpers she'd heard in the warehouse. But these
cries she could follow.

Five minutes later, she reached a fork. The cries came
from the right, so she went that direction, careful to avoid

the workers who occasionally came and went along the corridors. Three times she had to duck into the shadows, but only once did a man pause and glance in her direction. When nothing stirred—Bella couldn't imagine how he missed hearing her thundering heart—he shrugged and carried on about his business.

The passageway ended in a series of hallways lined with what appeared to be cages. Bella stared at them, aghast. The thought of animals in cages disturbed her enough, but women? God, the Birds must be totally devoid of conscience to indulge in such a grotesque practice.

One of the women spotted her, wrapped the fingers of her bound hands about the bamboo bars and rattled them. *"Hemph!"* she pleaded through her gag.

Bella motioned her to silence, waited for a moment, then slipped closer.

The lock of the cage was easily picked with a bobby pin. Thanking Irish Max and Lona for all they'd taught her, she drew the door open and, after untying the cloth gag, began to work at the leather ties on the captive's feet and hands.

"Oh, thank you, thank you," the woman moaned. "I thought I was going to die. I never—I was working my usual corner on the Strip and suddenly out pops this guy and bags me."

"The Strip?" Bella repeated. "You're from Los Angeles?"

"Yeah. Hey, keep going, okay? They'll be coming with wine soon. They give us a shot glass every couple of hours during the day to keep us fuzzy. But after a while it stops working. My—my name's Florrie. That's my friend Disa across there. We got bopped at the same time."

Bella undid the bands around her ankles. "Can you stand?"

"Oh, sure. They make us walk and stuff every day. Told us we need to be in some sort of shape when we get to China. 'China,' I said when I first heard that, and this guy who walks us around says, 'Yeah, Shanghai. But only some of you will stay there. Plenty of other countries pay to import hookers.' That's what he said, I swear. They import hookers. Can you believe it?''

"I believe it." Bella hastened to her feet. "Can you untie your friend?"

"Yeah, but there's lots more. Who are you, by the way?"

Almost one of you, Bella thought. "Another friend," she said. "How many corridors are there?"

"I don't know, but they'll be coming for us soon. We heard Jepson—he's the assistant here—telling someone to feed us good today because we're shipping out right after the apple drops in New York."

"That would be nine o'clock on the West Coast. We'd better hurry."

At Bella's urging, the women continued their muffled whimpering. To stem the sounds would be to invite suspicion, and they could scarcely overpower armed guards. Thankfully, and perhaps due to the recent, unexpected move from the warehouse, guards were few and far between in the fireworks factory. Still, those few carried guns and looked mean.

When Florrie noticed one of them approaching, she signaled frantically to Bella. Together, the women snuck up behind him. One swing of a two-by-four and he lay facedown on the cracked concrete floor, alive but blessedly unconscious.

Wary of more guards, but grimly determined, Bella left Florrie to bind him and returned to the task at hand—undoing the Birds' barbaric deed. Only when that was accomplished would she go in search of Hobson Crowe's associates, whoever they might be.

Whoever she might be in relation to them.

"WE HAVE TO DO SOMETHING, Charmaine." Fingertips tapping in agitation, the woman paced the floor of her office like a caged tiger. "Where is she? What's her game? Why haven't the police searched our warehouse yet?"

Charmaine lit a cigarette, took a deep drag and, more hastily than usual, blew the smoke out in a gray cloud. "Maybe they didn't believe her."

"Yeah, right, and pigs fly. They'd love to pin a shanghai operation on us. And you know she told them."

"Maybe Hobby's death shocked her into silence."

The woman turned her head. She didn't trust Charmaine's tone, but she couldn't quite interpret it, either. Was that mirth or annoyance she heard, sarcasm or indifference? Surely, it couldn't be fear.

"Have you seen Rudge?" she asked suddenly.

"No. Have you?"

"No. Uh, what about Tic-Tac—I mean, Tock?"

"No again, I'm afraid."

The woman watched as Charmaine's long fingers slid in apparent abstraction over her pen holder, her paperweight, her letter opener and her stapler. She held her breath for a moment, releasing it in silent relief when Charmaine moved away.

Charmaine had her black wig on today, as well as her usual amount of clever, age-concealing makeup. She looked as she often did—calm, cool and collected. And yet something didn't seem right.

Don't trust her, a voice in the woman's head whispered. *You can't trust someone like her, you know that. You can only be more clever.*

But had she been more clever? Was Charmaine several steps behind her or several steps ahead?

As was her wont, Charmaine paused beside the stereo and flicked the FM dial until she came up with a classical station. No Gilbert and Sullivan, thank God, but Strauss could be just as tedious under trying circumstances.

The woman knew better than to reveal her rising agitation. She fingered the slender pink weapon in her sleeve, then shook herself. A diversion, that's what she needed—something to take her mind off the gargantuan problems facing her. Problems she blamed mostly on Bella Conlan, and to a lesser degree on the woman before her—the Southern beauty whose blood was a mishmash of nationalities, whose face these days was an indecipherable mask and whose thoughts few if any had ever been privy to.

Thank heaven for mirrors, the woman thought, catching sight of herself in the Chinese lacquered one on the wall next to her desk. It wasn't the prettiest, by any means, but it was the largest, which in turn made it the best.

A rhyme came into her head. The woman liked rhymes, always had. She had a knack for making them up. Not that she'd ever been praised for her talent, but then she'd never been praised for anything that she could remember. It was always Belladonna this, Belladonna that. She'd never been singled out—and she should have been. Robert, at least, could have noticed, but no, he'd been all wrapped up in Romaine, and later in Belladonna.

Well, she wasn't wrapped up in Belladonna, not one bit. She was who she was and what she was. She ran the business—and she was prettier than Charmaine. Yes, much, much prettier . . .

Like a magnet, the reflecting glass drew her forward. The verse bubbled up in her mind, bubbled until it spilled from her lips. She touched the spikes of her bloodred hair.

"Mirror, mirror, on the wall,
Who's the fairest one of all . . . ?"

A shadow of sadness passed over her features, but she couldn't let it show, didn't dare display any weakness around Charmaine. She let the verse dance back into her head.

"Where are Rudge and Hobby, Tock,
And Robert? Can she beat the clock?
Did she kill Amanda or
Did Amanda know the score,
And leave with Bella, run away?
How then could Belladonna play,
The role laid out by Romaine who,
Like Belladonna's really . . . ?"

Her eyes focused with a swiftness that froze her lips mid-word. "What?" she said softly, not moving. Why was

Charmaine staring at her? What lay behind those unrevealing hazel eyes?

"Nothing." Inhaling on her cigarette, Charmaine turned away. But there'd been something. The woman had seen a glimmer of some unrecognizable emotion on Charmaine's face. Oh, to be able to read that wicked, scheming mind, to follow the twisted lines of logic that drove her.

But, no, that would never happen. Now as in the past, her wits were her only defense against Charmaine's wiles.

Shoving the rhyme from her mind, the woman left the mirror to rest her hip against the edge of her desk. Her fingers drummed on the top. Strauss became—God help her to survive this—the Maiden song from *The Mikado,* Charmaine's favorite operetta from as far back as she could recall.

"You haven't answered my question," she said, striving to conceal the edginess in her tone.

Charmaine stubbed out her cigarette in the polished jade ashtray. "Which question would that be?"

The woman repressed a growl. "Bella. I think we should search for her ourselves."

"Where?"

That stopped her. "I don't know, but we can't wait for Rudge or Tic—I mean, uh..."

"You mean Tock, the traitor, don't you?" Charmaine separated the blinds and peered into the alley, where Chinese vendors, even late on New Year's Eve, hawked their wares.

"I mean," the woman said, getting angry, "that we have to do something ourselves. If you don't want to, that's fine, but I do. I'm not going to sit idly by while someone else does the hunting. That time is long past. Rudge has my cellphone number. If he manages to locate her, he can call me. In the meantime, I'm going to do a little private detecting."

"In the rain?"

"If I have to, yes. Are you coming?"

"Not right now. I'll see what transpires first, then maybe I'll condescend to a hunt on foot."

The woman didn't trust her. No, not for a minute would she trust that expression on Charmaine's face. Like the timbre of her voice, it was too serene, too dispassionate. What nasty little counterplot did Charmaine have up her elegant black sleeve?

For the first time in years, the woman's mind flashed back to the day Robert had been killed. There he'd lain on the floor in a puddle of his own blood, staring sightlessly at the ceiling as the fine pink blade was pulled from his body. He'd understood so much about business, yet he hadn't understood the most basic part of his wife's nature at all. Jealousy had ruled her from birth. It had ruled Robert into death. Jealousy—and the woman they'd called Amanda.

RUDGE KNEW HE POSSESSED an uncanny knack for blending into his surroundings, no matter what they might be. He used that ability now to melt into the shadows of a Chinatown alley. Ignoring the rain that fell in great blowing sheets and the thunder that crashed like an earthquake, he watched the door through which Malone's cousin Ronnie had passed some fifteen minutes earlier.

She wasn't with them; he'd eavesdropped and learned that much, though precious little else, thanks to the storm. It didn't matter. Malone would go after her. He'd find her, too. Love did that to a man—gave him second sight where the object of that feeling was concerned.

From there it would be easy. Rudge would incapacitate Malone and take Bella. If he took her where he was supposed to take her, though, watch out, devil, because fur and feathers would fly—as all hell broke loose in the City by the Bay.

CHEN-LI SAT ALONE in his apartment after Malone and his cousin left. Matthew had been dispatched to a friend's home—under protest to be sure, but he'd gone. So now, at last, Chen-Li could contemplate in peace the pieces of this most-intriguing puzzle.

Romaine. He didn't know what that name meant or to whom it belonged, but of Belladonna, he had an idea.

Should he have told Malone all that he suspected? No. He was old, and his visions had their flaws. The shadow of the raven had passed by his window twice. Only once when he'd looked at her had Chen-Li's mind flashed a picture of Bella dead.

He'd been unable to hold the image or to summon it again. If he could have done that, perhaps he could have laid to rest some portion of his fear.

He studied the photos in Bella's picture case again. The blond woman in both of them was called Amanda. But not Amanda Conlan, as Bella had been brought up to believe. Bella's father had been Robert Swift, so that had likely been Amanda's surname as well.

Bella's surname was also Swift. Her mother had died in a car accident in Alaska. The body had never been recovered. Her father had been murdered, stabbed with a pink knife. Where his body was or whether his death had been reported were mysteries to Chen-Li.

Oh, there was so much more to all of this than Bella realized, more even than Chen-Li understood.

She was related to the Birds of San Francisco. But who were the Birds now? Robert Swift was gone. So was Hobson Crowe, né Hobson J. MacCawdor. That left only the females—Charmaine Parret and an unknown commodity.

The puzzle shifted subtly in Chen-Li's head, and quite unexpectedly, he saw it. Rather, he saw a snippet of it, perhaps a very important snippet. He closed his eyes. Charmaine... Yes, of course, Charmaine and Robert.

Breathing deeply, he allowed his mind to expand. He saw again the shadows of two ravens and Bella lying dead. Bella, whose sole recollection as a child had been a name—her name, she had told the woman who'd taken her in. Belladonna...

Chen-Li rested his head against the chair back. Perhaps he had found one of the keys to the riddle, but the shadows of the ravens had still crossed her path. It could go either way. Just like Romaine. And therein, he suspected, lay the truth of Belladonna.

"I HATE CRYPTIC CHINESE," Malone grumbled testily. "We won't find her in the warehouse, he insists. How the hell does he know that?"

Palms up, Ronnie shrugged. "I don't know, but it looks like he was right. It was quiet in there. *Too* quiet, if you ask me."

"They've moved the women," Malone said in disgust. "Wherever they've taken them is where Bella will have headed. But where would they take them?"

"To the ship, d'you think?"

Malone gave his head a perfunctory shake. "It's still off-loading. They'd have to have gotten the women out right after Bella escaped. Even paid off, indifferent or whatever, the police might have listened to her. The Birds couldn't risk that."

"So where do we look then? The fireworks place?"

Malone nodded, glancing at the sky. It had started raining more than an hour ago, and not a light rain, either. This precipitation slanted down in icy, windblown sheets that made the fog feel tropical by comparison.

Although they hadn't scoured the warehouse, and although he wouldn't have acknowledged it to anyone, Malone sensed a certain hazy truth underlying Chen-Li's assertions. She wasn't here; he could feel it. Better to search the Birds' fireworks factory or the more esoteric House of Mann. Motioning to Ronnie, he ducked out of the alley and around the corner to his cousin's rented Escort.

Esoteric, he thought darkly. Now there was a word to describe Chen-Li. In the end, the old man had told them nothing. Well, nothing except that the photos—including, Malone assumed, the one of Bella given to him by Rudge— were misleading. Wonderful. But what the hell did he mean?

"I can say nothing more," Chen-Li had told him regretfully. "If I'm mistaken, you may use the wrong approach in your search. I will study the matter further while you are gone."

"The man's a bloody loon, if you ask me," Ronnie maintained as Malone pulled away from the curb. "How can pictures be misleading, especially ones as straightforward as those?''

Malone didn't have the answer, and he had no time to ponder it in any event. "Oh, hell.'' He swore, glancing in the rearview mirror. "We've got company.''

"What? Where?''

Ronnie started to turn, but Malone grabbed his arm, preventing him. "Don't,'' he warned. "I want to catch him off guard.''

"Catch who? Tock?''

"Rudge.''

"Ahh.'' Sitting back, Ronnie gripped the edge of his seat. "It's like musical tails around here lately. How did he get behind us?''

"I don't know. Maybe he followed you to Chen-Li's. Or maybe he just got lucky.''

"Stop scowling, Malone. At least with Rudge on the scent, you can be pretty sure the Birds haven't nabbed Bella yet.''

"Unless Tock got her.''

"Well, yes, there is that, but wouldn't Tock be on the Birds' bad side right now? After all, he sold out to Crowe, and we know what happened to him.''

"Exactly, and if it happened to Crowe, it could happen to Bella. Hold on.''

Teeth set, Malone gave the steering wheel a yank and skidded the gritty little Escort sideways. The tires squealed; the back end fishtailed, then spun until the car came to a stop facing in the opposite direction. Nearby motorists leaned on their horns and, red faced, swore at the violators as Malone gunned the engine and the car sped away.

"I don't think we're very popular,'' Ronnie observed in a shaky voice. Prying one hand loose from its grip on the door handle, he dabbed at the beads of sweat on his upper lip. "Please tell me that Rudge didn't match that move.''

Malone squinted into the mirror. "He did, but it put some distance between us. We should be able to lose him in a few blocks.''

"And if we don't? We can't lead him to Bella, and we can't leave Bella to fend for herself with the Birds. When they realize she's looking for them, they'll be there with wings on their feet—no pun intended."

"Yes, I know." Malone controlled his snappish response, glancing back again. He couldn't see Rudge, but then it was only blind luck that he'd spotted him in the first place.

Five more minutes, he decided, jerking the wheel to the left. That's all he could spare for this game of cat and mouse. It was the cat-and-Bird game that really counted.

"Hang on," he told Ronnie, swinging a hard right.

For some reason, Chen-Li's parting words had begun to echo in his head. They rose eerily above the squeal of rain and tires.

Ramrod straight in his chair, the old man had gazed at the photographs of Amanda and Bella. As he did so, he'd remarked in a wise but weary voice, "As individuals, we have within us the capacity for both good and evil. So it is in this instance, I fear, only more, so very much more." He'd lifted solemn eyes to Malone's face. "Find her, Mr. Malone," he'd said with quiet urgency. "Find her and pray. Pray for Belladonna."

Chapter Seventeen

"Where do we go?" Florrie whispered as she and her friend bound another guard hand and foot. "We can't just sashay onto the street in our underwear. And you probably know I'm not a big fan of the police."

"Chen-Li," Bella said suddenly. She handed one of the women a blanket. "He might be able to help you. But you'll have to go to the police after that. The Birds did this. They should pay."

"Yeah, right." Shivering, Florrie looked around. "I heard this shanghai stuff still went on, but I thought it was just a story. Who are these Birds?"

Bella pushed the unruly tangle of hair from her face. "They're more like vultures, I think. I've never seen them. Well, I have, but not clearly. It doesn't matter. Just go to Chen-Li, okay?"

"All fifty of us?"

Were there that many? Bella had stopped counting several cages ago. "No." She peered down an ancillary corridor, saw no one and glanced back at Florrie. "You'll have to go straight to the police. We've tied up four workers, but there are bound to be more."

"Lots more," Florrie declared. "They're probably sloughing off, waiting until they have to bring us food or wine or move us out or..." Her eyes widened and she clutched at Bella's arm. "Listen! Oh, my God, they're coming. Can you hear them?"

Above the rain and wind and running feet, Bella hadn't heard anything, but she did now. Male voices, garbled by the closer sounds, approached from the front of the building.

Her heart skipped a beat. She had to stay calm, even if the the lump in her throat was threatening to choke her.

"Run," she whispered to Florrie, whose panicky eyes scanned the circle of faces around them. Louder, she repeated, "Run!"

They scattered like fleeing deer. Bella didn't know who ran where, but none of them followed her. Somehow she wound up alone in an unexplored part of the building.

The acrid scent of gunpowder assailed her. The darkness pressed in as if to smother her. Corridors sprouted off at bizarre angles—corridors, rooms and funny little wrought-iron stairwells.

She was isolated here—and yet she wasn't entirely alone.

As if summoned, ghosts began to float out of the darkened corners of her mind. There should have been an order to their release, but somehow she knew there wasn't.

She saw Amanda smiling at her, holding out her hand. She saw herself playing with Amanda's silver ring—her mother's only ring, her only piece of jewelry.

She saw a red bicycle lying on the ground. The tires had been slashed, the shiny paint scratched, a rather unnerving sight.

She saw a gray pony with a white mane, and her hand holding a bunch of carrots up to his mouth. Then the carrots vanished, and she saw herself, angry and launching toys at a wall. First a doll, then a puzzle, then a pair of red leather boots.

"Now, now, darling," she heard Amanda soothe. "You can't get everything you want in life. It simply doesn't work that way."

Another memory overlapped—a recollection of her face in a mirror. Her lower lip jutted petulantly, her dark eyes glittered with spite, her hair was loose and disheveled, and there were faint claw marks on her cheeks.

Amanda spoke again. "No, you mustn't hurt the kitten. Bella, come here and pick it up nicely. Yes, that's it. You see? It won't scratch you if you don't try to smother it."

Had she been cruel to animals as a child? Bella was appalled. Maybe she didn't want to remember her past, after all.

A voice similar to, yet different from, Amanda's took over. "How dare you, Robert!" it accused. "You have sex with a whore, then you have the nerve to try and justify it.... Don't you call me two-faced, you snake. Romaine. You promised that it would always be Romaine."

"And Belladonna," Robert said calmly in reply.

"Belladonna comes later, much later. Romaine is the present, and all you want to do is screw it up. You think your whore's worth that much, do you? Well, I don't, and I have just as much say around here as you do. You see me as a silent partner, but only because I let you. When all's said and done, Robert, I run the show. I always have and I always will. I *am* Romaine...."

The darkness of the factory became suffocating. Bella felt dizzy, disoriented. What was Romaine? What did it mean? The woman's accent sounded so similar to Amanda's. The voice itself—she couldn't tell. Was it Amanda talking?

Out of nowhere, Lona's voice came to her, efficient, practical and achingly familiar. Bella's throat burned with emotion. "You are Belladonna, yes? Belladonna Conlan." Then Lona said firmly, "I will call you Bella. There will be no poison in your life, child, as long as I am a part of it...."

The memory faded, and Bella's thoughts shot forward in time. "Just like Romaine," she heard Lona saying sadly. "That's what Amanda told me."

But what did Romaine mean? Bella screamed in silent frustration. What did it represent?

She detected a tiny noise and froze. All memories dispersed.

Were those footsteps she heard? Possibly. She shouldn't be standing still, in any event. Find the Birds, that was her goal.

She hesitated. Was that her goal or was she being a fool? Surely it was foolish to hunt the thing that hunted you—unless, of course, you happened to be more powerful, which she definitely was not. Not powerful, not even whole at the moment. What on earth was she doing?

Malone...

Of its own volition, his name slid through Bella's thoughts. She loved him, but the Birds would kill him for daring to help her. That must never happen. And that was really why she'd really come here—not to overwhelm the Birds but to prevent them from killing Malone in order to get to her.

A grating sound, only faintly perceptible, reached her ears. *Keep moving,* she thought, but which way? Not back to the cages, and certainly not toward the front of the factory.

She decided to circle. A place like this would have any number of exits.

Careful to make no noise, she changed directions and started down a corridor even more dismal than the one she'd been standing in moments before.

The sound came again, a stealthy, scraping noise perhaps fifty feet behind her.

Lack of furtiveness had one advantage. Whoever approached was gaining on her. Bella crept forward for several more nerve-racking seconds, heard the noise again and realized she'd never outdistance the person behind her.

Spying an alcove, she ducked into it, crouching swiftly behind a wooden barrel filled with flammable red rockets. Breath held, muscles protesting at her cramped position, she pulled her jacket tighter, swept the hair from her eyes and waited.

Time might have stopped, that's how long it felt between footsteps. When the next one finally came, it emanated from a point directly to her left.

Knuckles pressed to her mouth, Bella risked a glance around the barrel. *Don't sneeze,* she thought, then promptly wanted to kick herself. Power of suggestion. She'd probably sneeze up a storm now.

Her strained mind flashed intermittent pictures—of Malone waking up in Chen-Li's apartment; of Lona tipping sideways in the hotel lounge; of Hobson Crowe with two circles—or wheels, as she'd interpreted them—painted in lipstick on his cheeks; of two women in black wearing netted hats and sunglasses; of Amanda in the picture case; of herself with Amanda.

She'd been playing with a kitten in one shot. She'd been smug and empty-handed in the other. Only Amanda's expression hadn't changed. There she'd sat in her faded denim pantsuit, with her silver Navaho ring on her finger and Hobby's stable behind her.

The flashing images continued. Disconnected fragments appeared, memories both old and new: a pony, a smashed red bicycle, *The Pirates of Penzance* playing on the stereo. Her mother's dressmaker whispering to her husband, who was the gardener. A gold wedding band being flung to the floor. A thin pink knife, bloodstained and glistening before her eyes, yet visible to her only in the mirror across the room. Amanda pulling on her hand, saying, "We have to go...." Malone pulling on her hand aboard the *Sun Sen,* pulling her away from Charmaine Parret. The funny, tingly feeling she'd had when she'd met Charmaine. Amanda taking her hand, sneaking her out into the night...

The last memory stuck. Bella recalled that Amanda's ring had felt cold against her skin. Amanda's silver ring. Her only piece of jewelry. Denim. The dressmaker coming and going...

What was wrong with these memories? Why didn't the puzzle fit? It seemed to Bella as if some of the pieces came from another puzzle entirely.

She pressed herself deeper into the corner. The barrage in her head had to be stopped. She needed to concentrate on her current predicament.

Malone, she thought, and felt an instant release of tension. *Yes, think of him. Focus on the present.* He'd rescued her. Now it was time for her to return the favor—if she survived, that is.

The footsteps sounded just around the corner. Eyes trained on the shadow that fell across the wall, Bella steeled herself to face whoever loomed behind it.

It was a female shadow; even in the gloom she could see that.

"Bella? Are you there?"

At the halting question, Bella's pent-up breath came rushing out. She leaned her head against the barrel in relief. "Florrie," she breathed. "Thank God."

Florrie heard her and halted. "Bella?"

"Back here." She stood, wincing at her cramped leg muscles. "I thought you were one of the Birds."

"Me, a Bird? Not a chance. Anyway, top guns never do their own dirty work, do they? I bet they wouldn't be caught dead in this grungy old building."

Bella noted a slight movement in her peripheral vision. With it came a cutting chuckle, one that emerged from a female throat.

"You lose, slut," said the English-accented voice behind it. One of the darker shadows shifted. From the edge appeared a steady, black-gloved hand.

Florrie made a strangled sound. "She has a gun!"

"Yes, and it has bullets and everything," the veiled woman mocked. "Hello, Bella. Long time no see. I wish it could have been longer, but that's life."

Bella didn't move. Something about the woman's voice gave her the spookiest feeling she'd ever experienced. "Go," she whispered to the trembling Florrie. Using her elbow, she nudged the former captive in the stomach. "Go," she said again.

Florrie hesitated, then, emitting a garbled sound, turned and fled.

The hand holding the gun took aim, but Bella stepped hastily forward.

"Don't," she ordered sharply. Then, curling her fingers into her palms, she said more gently, "Please let her go. She can't do any more damage than has already been done."

The eerie feeling heightened as the woman's teeth flashed. "Damage done by you, right? Oh yes, I saw the result of your handiwork. I mean, it would have been hard to miss—all those women galloping down Stockton Street in the rain, in their underwear. Naturally, I thought of you right away. After all, who but you knew about our operation—except for maybe Rudge, and he wouldn't have let them out." She rubbed a gloved thumb and forefinger together. "Nothing in it for him."

Bella couldn't control her fear, so she buried it. "I guess greed does make people predictable."

"So do scruples."

Which this woman obviously did not possess. A series of chills chased themselves across Bella's skin.

"No comeback for that, Bella?" the newcomer taunted. "What a shame. You used to be so good at it, too."

A memory desperately tried to surface, yet every time Bella attempted to capture it, it slipped out of reach. Something about this woman, about the taunting edge to her voice. She'd heard it before, but where, when?

The picture of a mirror flashed in her head, followed by a younger version of that taunting voice. "I hate Bella-donna!"

The woman hated her. Why? What had they been to each other? Friends? Cousins? Sisters...?

The last thought forced a shudder from her. *No, not that!* she begged inwardly. *Not a sister.* Hobby's daughter, a cousin—yes, that she could accept.

"Repartee," the woman said now. "I've gotten better at it myself, but Charmaine's still the queen of that social skill." Her teeth glinted again. "Nothing to say to that, either? My, but you are a dull conversationalist, Bella. Or is it that you still don't remember us?"

What could she say? "I don't remember you."

"Neither of us?" The woman sounded surprised, but that wasn't what captured Bella's attention all of a sudden. Something about the shape of the woman's jaw brought her eyes into vivid focus and held them on that part of her face. Her mouth looked frighteningly familiar. Why frighteningly, Bella wasn't sure, but tendrils of fear were definitely running around inside her now.

"Neither of you," she said softly.

The woman thought for a moment. "I don't know if that's good or bad. I thought you'd have figured it all out by now."

"That's amnesia for you." Bella couldn't believe the flippant response that came from her mouth. "It isn't as predictable as greed."

"Still the same nasty tongue, anyway," the woman observed sarcastically. She inclined her head. "Let's get a move on, shall we? Before we're ..."

Bella's ears separated a scratchy sound from the storm outside, which was quite loud at this point. When nothing came of it, she ventured a guarded, "Before we're what?"

A second voice, this one completely disembodied, spoke. "Before we're joined by Charmaine, I should think. Hello, Bella. You look rather different than the night we met on the *Sun Sen*. I hear you're quite good with makeup these days. At least you inherited one good quality from your mother."

Goose bumps spread over Bella's skin like an army of ants. "You knew Amanda?"

To her shock, Charmaine Parret laughed, a full, throaty laugh of genuine amusement. The woman with the gun, Bella noticed, didn't crack a smile.

"Oh, my," Charmaine gasped at last. "I needed that rather badly, I'm afraid."

"I don't think it's funny," the woman said irritably.

"Well, of course, you wouldn't, seeing as it doesn't pertain to you. But forgive me, I'm spoiling your party."

"What party?" Bella and the woman asked in tandem. The echo of their combined voices set Bella's nerves on edge. Who were these women? Why couldn't she remember them?

Charmaine spoke to her companion rather than to Bella. "You surprise me. You're dying to do it. Why don't you just pull off the mask and face her? Do it. Show your big sister what you look like after all these years apart."

MALONE SPOTTED THEM first—a gaggle of females, some clutching blankets, the rest clad primarily in their underwear, running along Stockton Street toward—he didn't know what.

An idea—an unpalatable one he had to admit, but viable—came to him. He jammed on the brakes, almost catapulting Ronnie through the windshield.

"What now?" his cousin demanded.

"Wait here."

Malone vaulted from the car into the rain and intercepted a thin woman with dyed blond hair and badly smudged makeup.

"Please, no," she begged, but he reassured her with a lie.

"I'm a police officer. What's going on here?"

She paused, but took him on faith. "We—we escaped from a place, a hellhole. Back there." She gestured in the direction of the Birds' fireworks factory. "We were held there for days, some of us for weeks. They were going to sell us."

"Abroad," Malone finished for her.

Obviously she mistook his meaning, because she drew back and looked as if she might slap him.

"I meant ship you overseas," he clarified. "Look, did you see a woman who wasn't one of you? Very pretty, dark hair and eyes, tall, slender, probably wearing a brown leather jacket, boots and jeans?"

The woman's head bobbed. "She helped us get out, but we never saw her again after the guards came. I hope they didn't catch her."

Malone released her, raking his fingers through his hair and nodding. "So do I," he said bleakly, then in a tone that boded ill for the Birds, he repeated, "So do I."

"BIG..." BELLA'S HEART gave a sickening thump in her chest, then seemed to stop beating altogether. "You're—my sister? My younger sister?"

In answer, and with the gun aimed squarely at Bella's head, the woman reached up and started to remove her hat and veil. She might have also been planning to step farther into the muzzy pool of light, but a sharp crack like a gunshot stopped her cold.

Her head twisted from side to side. "What was that, Charmaine? Charmaine?" She swore violently and bared her teeth. "Bloody bitch, deserts at the drop of a hat. Charmaine!"

The sound came again, an echoing report that had the woman clutching her chest with splayed fingers. The barrel of her own gun dropped a notch. "What's going... No, wait. Come back here!"

The last order was shouted at Bella, who, seizing the moment, bolted down the nearest corridor. To her shock, the next shot she heard came from directly in front of her.

She skidded to a halt, while behind her, the woman cried to any and all workers in the vicinity, "Get her! She's here. Bella Conlan's in the factory. I want her captured and brought to me."

"Bella !"

Someone hissed at her from the shadows to her right. "Bella, it's me, Florrie."

Bella pressed the heel of her hand to her racing heart. For the second time that day relief all but overwhelmed her. "What are you doing here?" she demanded. "You should have gone to the police."

"I didn't think you'd last that long with her." Florrie held up a string of fireworks and a torn pack of matches. "I found these as I was going for the door. I thought they might sound like a gun. I guess someone around here likes to make things go pop."

"We'll both go pop in a minute if that thunder back there is being made by as many feet as I think it is. Come on."

Grabbing Florrie's hand, she pulled her along the passageway. To her dismay, however, it led to a dead end.

"Wrong turn," Florrie panted. "What do we do now?"

"Go back."

"But they're coming. They heard us. We'll never get past them."

No, they wouldn't, Bella realized. Unless...

Her gaze landed on the firecrackers Florrie still clutched, then on a barrel of explosive volcanoes. Taking no time to think the idea through, Bella broke off half of the fire-cracker string and struck a match.

"What are you—oh, my God!" Florrie gasped. "This place'll go off like my pim—I mean, my boss when his fuse is lit."

"I hope so," Bella said sincerely. She tossed the fire-crackers into two separate barrels, took Florrie by the wrist and tugged. "Let's get out of here, fast."

Florrie offered no protest. In fact, she matched Bella stride for stride, back to the junction.

"There!" a wiry, bearded man yelled. "That's her."

Workers poured like rats out of the woodwork. *Go off,* Bella prayed of the fireworks. *Please, don't be duds.*

The two women switched directions. Florrie raced along behind Bella. "I think they're—"

The rest of her sentence was drowned out by a series of blasts. At first Bella thought it was the workers shooting at them, but when it continued and actually grew louder, she realized it was the fireworks exploding.

"Down here." She pushed Florrie into a narrow passageway.

Florrie glanced back, shouting, "Did you do that? Sounds like an earthquake."

Bella could barely hear her. The corridor echoed like a cavern. Unfortunately, between the explosions and the storm, she could no longer hear their pursuers at all.

They ran full speed along the passage and would have kept going if the entire darkened area ahead of them hadn't suddenly erupted with a blinding flash of light.

After that, Bella wasn't exactly sure what happened.

Out of the corner of her eye, she spied three workers, armed and charging toward them. Except there was no "them" anymore, she realized, dodging both fireworks and men.

"Florrie!" she cried into the glittering darkness. "Flor... Oh, my God!" She ducked swiftly, going down on all fours as a rocket whizzed past her head.

That rocket set off a chain reaction. Fireworks flew in all directions and at all angles. Bella had to dodge, dart and scramble her way through the maze of passages. She only prayed there would be an escape at the end of it all.

Thankfully, through the smoke and sparks, she spied a narrow door marked Exit.

Choking from the toxic smoke, she made a dash for it. Her hands located the knob and twisted.

At first it refused to open, but three hard shoves later it gave way and she was free, back in the soggy alley with a black cloud of smoke mushrooming out around her.

"Stop!" yelled a voice behind her. Bella's heart lurched. She hadn't escaped, after all.

Fireworks continued to bang, sizzle and roar as she ran through the streaming rain for the nearest shelter—a dismal obelisk of a building next to the factory. Like most of the alley entrances, the rear door wasn't locked. Yanking on it, Bella raced inside, her hair and clothes soaked, her ears smarting from the combined boom of fireworks and thunder.

Sheet lightning illuminated the room before her. Except for dust and cobwebs, it was empty. No refuge here. Her frantic eyes located a staircase. She'd have to go up. And pray.

Amazingly, no one followed her in, or if they did, she couldn't hear them.

Lightning flashed crazily as the storm center moved inland. Cobwebs became tangled in her long hair. Rain beat against the sloping roof in a fierce staccato rhythm. She could hear fireworks exploding and beyond that the sound of fire-engine sirens cutting through the wet gloom.

Her boots echoed on the metal stairs. Her head ached from trying to remember things she sensed she didn't really want to know. A parrot on a stick—what did that mean? In her dream it had changed into a skinny pink knife, the knife that had stabbed her father.

Mirrors, silver rings, denim, dressmakers, ponies, bicycles, Romaine, Lona—the images burned in her mind. But above all of them, the imprint of Malone's face stayed with her, touching her deeply. She'd come here alone because she loved him. That love was something she would never forget.

She'd forgotten her sister. How had she done that? Why had she done it? Her younger sister. God help her, she had no recollection of a sibling, no impression of a name, nothing. Unless she'd been called Romaine...but, no, that didn't make sense. Well, it might, but only if she took into account Hobby's cryptic computer message. "Romaine lives," he'd said. But he'd also said that Belladonna was mad, and that, Bella knew, was untrue. She might be many things, but crazy wasn't one of them. Yet.

The staircase wound upward to a second floor filled with crates, barrels and cartons. She could have hidden there, but her instincts urged her to go higher, up the next set of stairs to the door. If she could bolt that door from the other side, and if there were no other entrances, she might be safe for a time, at least long enough to think things through. Maybe a miracle would happen, and she would remember everything about her past.

A violent clap of thunder accompanied Bella as she raced across the upper landing and slammed the door. It did have a bolt—not a strong one, but better than nothing. All she needed now was a place to sit and steady her frazzled nerves. If only she could talk to Malone.

Darkness broken only by a glimmer of light enveloped her. The rain still beat an angry tattoo on the roof, and the fireworks exploded at a fast and furious rate. For some reason, she found that rather comforting. There must be solace in chaos, after all.

Her cold fingers groped for a light switch. She found one, but not before locating several sticky spiderwebs. Unfortunately, when she flipped it on, the bulb was scarcely strong enough to illuminate the center of the room, let alone the corners.

Not that she probably wanted to see the room's contents clearly. The floor was a sea of mannequins, hundreds of them—some with heads, some without, some with heads but no faces, some with faces but no hair. It was ghastly, like a scene out of *Invasion of the Body Snatchers*.

The eyes that stared at her had a weird, vacuous quality about them, and the myriad shadows only heightened that ambience.

Bella sidled cautiously along the wall. She felt dizzy for some reason. Jumbled thoughts and pictures kept colliding in her mind. She heard Malone's voice repeating Lona's last words: *Amanda's not . . .*

She closed her eyes briefly against the brilliant kaleidoscope of color stamped over the blackness. A breath of wind on her cheeks had her glancing upward, but all she saw was a dark shape in the rafters. A sparrow, perhaps, or possibly—she flinched—a bat.

It didn't matter. What mattered was Malone and the shocking discovery she'd made only moments before. She had a sister. Moreover, she had a sister who was a Bird.

Thunder rumbled, shaking the building. More air passed over Bella's face. Ghastly painted eyes stared at her out of shiny faces. Her own eyes closed again. The room spun. "Why can't I remember her?" she whispered out loud.

"Because, Bella," a sarcastic, English-accented voice remarked, "that's how it goes sometimes for people like us."

Bella's eyes flew open. She hadn't heard anyone enter, and the door to her left was still bolted. But there the woman was in her black netted hat and sunglasses, so she'd gotten in somehow.

Her sister moved closer, a wary motion that brought her to within ten feet of where Bella stood plastered to the wall.

"What do you mean, people like us?" she managed to ask. It was hard to be defiant with a gun pointed at your throat.

"Time for the unveiling, Bella," the woman answered mockingly.

She took another step forward, and this time when she reached up to strip off her hat and glasses, there was nothing and no one to stop her. The disguise flew across the floor, landing on a mannequin's outstretched hand. The woman's head rose slowly, until Bella could see every line, curve and angle of her face, every feature in its entirety. Too shocked to respond, she merely stared in mute disbelief.

The woman's smile came slowly, a grim little smile that contained just a hint of malicious mischief. In a high, childish treble, she warbled:

"Mirror, mirror, on the wall,
Belladonna has it all.
But Bella left; she could not reign.
So Donna thus became Romaine...."

Chapter Eighteen

For the life of her, Bella couldn't think of a single thing to say. But that didn't mean she couldn't think at all. A thousand thoughts rushed at her, the most prominent being *Belladonna*.

Just like Romaine, Lona had said. Why hadn't she seen it before? Ro-maine, a combined name. And just as Romaine was a blend, so too was Belladonna.

Dear God, she remembered now, at least that part of it.

It was as if a curtain had parted in her head. "Arabella," she whispered. She could hardly bring herself to utter the name, the one she'd been given at birth. "Arabella and Madonna. Bella and Donna—Belladonna." It was, as Amanda had said, "just like Romaine." "Romaine," she breathed. "From Robert and Charmaine."

"Give the woman a cigar." Her sister applauded sarcastically, then commanded bitingly, "Now open your eyes and look at me. Let me look at you."

Stunned beyond her capacity to endure, Bella complied. One and only one thing registered in her mind: she should have feelings for this woman, overwhelming feelings of love and loss, of sadness and sorrow. But there was nothing, not a single flicker of emotion inside her. This woman—Madonna, as she'd been christened—was a complete stranger to her.

Donna stared back, her expression triumphant. "Do you remember me now?" she demanded.

Bella managed to answer flatly, "Yes."

"That's it? Yes? No 'Glad to see you, Sis, how's your life been going, you're looking great'? Ah, but you'd think you were being conceited if you said that last thing, wouldn't you? Because you think we look alike, don't you?"

"People like us usually do." Bella couldn't, wouldn't, use the definitive term, not like this.

Sheet lightning flickering beyond the grimy upper windows only heightened the weird atmosphere. Although it was impossible, it seemed to Bella that several of the outer mannequins moved, took a step closer, shutting the human pair inside their eerie, clonelike circle.

"We're not the same, dammit!" Donna declared, stomping her foot on the floor. "Arabella and Madonna are two separate people. Belladonna only ever existed in Robert's mind. He thought it up, you know. Romaine, too. He liked cute games, but he was a fool. He was going to give you control."

Appalled, Bella asked, "Of what?"

Donna flapped an angry arm. "All of it. The business, the whole shebang. You, because you were the oldest. Yeah, right, oldest," she muttered. "By two bloody minutes. Plus you were his favorite."

"I was?" Bella didn't remember that.

"Yes, you was." Donna mimicked her cruelly, the way a five-year-old might. "Daddy's favorite, Hobby's favorite, Amanda's favorite. Who got the pony and who got the bicycle? Stupid bicycle. Why didn't he give me a pony, too?"

The answer came to Bella with the next peal of thunder. Dozens of blank, garishly painted faces peered at her as she said, "You were afraid of ponies."

"So what? You were afraid of cats. You got over it when Amanda gave you that kitten to pet."

The kitten in the picture... Yes, she had been afraid, hadn't she? "Be gentle," she said aloud, echoing Amanda's words.

Donna grunted. "Be gentle, be damned. You'd have thought I was dismembering that cat the way she snatched it from me and gave it to you. The silly thing scratched me.

Of course, I was going to give it a taste of its own medicine.''

So that's what that memory was all about. Donna had been abusing the kitten. Amanda had taken it from Donna and given it to Bella. She must have been talking to Donna when she'd said to be gentle.

The air in the third-floor loft felt stuffy, damp from the rain and musty. Too many unreal eyes stared at her. Bella wanted to run from all of it, to escape the hard plastic limbs, the shiny features, the cold, smiling mouths. No movie could have created in her such a strong feeling of revulsion as these mannequins did. None of this felt remotely possible to her at this point—not the storm, not the mannequins, not even Madonna holding a gun on her.

Her sister stared as long and hard as the mannequins. Keeping the gun pointed at Bella's chest, she began to circle. Bella saw her more clearly as she moved from one light patch to the next.

Of course they looked alike; they'd been born identical twins. Mirror images, in fact. The idea of mirrors jarred a little, but Bella temporarily set that thought aside.

While her own hair was long and dark and wavy, Donna's had been dyed a vibrant shade of red. She had it cut short and styled into spikes that reminded Bella of porcupine quills. Her lips were painted with a poppy-colored lipstick; her eyes were vividly outlined in black kohl. She had false eyelashes, false fingernails and, at the moment, a frighteningly false smile on her lips.

"So what's the verdict, sister dear?" Donna asked in a deceptively sweet voice. "Do you like my style? Do you want to copy it?" Her tone and expression hardened. "Do you think you could have done a better job of running the business than me?"

No, no and no, Bella thought. She watched carefully as Donna continued to circle. More memories hammered at her, but she was too afraid of what her sister might do with that gun to acknowledge them.

"Why did you want me dead?" she heard herself ask.

Donna's lips curled. "That's a stupid question. Because you witnessed a murder, why else? Robert's murder, to be precise."

Bella moistened her dry lips. "Did you kill him?"

"Me? Good Lord, is that what you think?"

"I don't think anything. I don't remember."

"But you're starting to, aren't you?"

It seemed to Bella that, with each flash of lightning, the mannequins circled in one direction, while Donna circled in the other.

"I can see it in your face, Bella. You look the same now as you did the day it happened."

Bella tamped down all the fear caused by the illusory, gleaming-faced dummies. "You were there?"

"Naturally." Donna stopped walking to roll her eyes. "God, you really are feebleminded. One little bonk on the head and you go nighty-night for twenty years." She leaned forward, the knuckles of her free hand planted on her hip. "I was right across the room from you."

"You...!" Bella's eyes widened. "I thought it was a mirror across from me."

"Mirror, hah! Did the mirror image have pigtails?"

"No. Why?"

"You always did. Pigtails tied up with pretty ribbons."

"So that was me in the picture case holding the kitten."

"I don't know anything about a picture case, but if the kid in the picture had pigtails, it was you. If it didn't it was me."

"But—I don't understand."

An overbright sheet of lightning created a host of gruesome shadows around them. Even in her shocked state, Bella was positive that one or more of the mannequins moved. So did something in the rafters above them, but she was still far too worried about the gun in Donna's hand to risk a look.

"What's to understand?" Donna demanded. She sounded cranky now. "We saw Robert die. Both of us, but apparently only one of us could accept it. What was the big deal, anyway? Robert screwed around on our mother. He deserved to die. Amanda had no business taking you and running."

Amanda's not... Amanda's not...

The incomplete phrase rang in Bella's head. Were the mannequins laughing at all of this? No, of course not. It had to be a trick of the light that their painted mouths seemed to have stretched into ghastly smiles.

Bella pressed the fingers of her right hand to her throbbing temple. "Amanda took me away," she said, although she still couldn't recall the time frame clearly. There was something else, too, some recent realization that changed things somehow. If only her muddled mind could bring it back to her and organize it. "Mother killed Robert," she said. "But that's impossible. Amanda wasn't a killer. She couldn't have done it."

Donna's laugh wafted through the plastic army and up to the rafters, where something that Bella still didn't care to contemplate moved about with a muffled swish. "Smell the coffee, Bella. Amanda didn't kill Robert. Mother did. For all their similarities, the two were not synonymous."

In Bella's hazy mind, a woman took shape—a striking, blond-haired woman. For a moment, Bella almost panicked. The woman was splitting in two, becoming two people from one. Two women with Mississippi accents.

A thought struck her, but she rejected it. Amanda's body had never been found. Had she survived the accident, recovered, returned...? Returned to what, though? As what? No, that was wrong. The idea of a split personality didn't sit right, somehow. That wasn't what her foggy mind was trying to prod her into recalling.

As if following her confused train of thought, Donna heaved an exasperated sigh. "Oh, all right, I'll spell it out for you. Mother killed Father. Amanda saw her do it. Amanda took you because no one knew you were in the room. On the flip side, Mother knew I was there. She pulled the damned letter opener out of Robert's chest and walked right over to me. I figured, so what? Big deal. He was dead. Now Romaine would be all Mother's and she'd decide which of us would take over. But Amanda had her own plan. She whisked you off to parts unknown. I mean, you have to give her credit, she covered her tracks very well for a yokel. Even Mother couldn't figure out where she'd taken you—which only goes to prove that not all yokels think alike."

"Our mother was a yokel?"

"Yup." Donna crossed her fingers. "They were like that once. Bosom buddies. Amanda was our nanny—until she climbed into the sack with Robert, and that was the end of that. Oh, Mother played along with the charade for a while, but she was scheming the whole time." A pert smile that Bella found more unnerving than her former sneer settled on Donna's poppy-colored lips. "Mother has a mean temper, you see. No flair for the dramatic—that's why she didn't make it on the stage—but a doozy of a temper. Her daddy was Creole, her mother was part German, part Peruvian and, I suspect, part shrew. All parts had bad tempers. It's a trait that gets passed down from generation to generation." Donna's smile widened. An eerie blue light filled the room again as the storm seemed to stall overhead. "One of us was bound to inherit it, Bella." The hand holding the gun rose. "And I have a feeling you know it wasn't you."

BETWEEN THE FEROCITY of the storm and the violent explosions rocking the fireworks factory, Malone had difficulty seeing more than two feet in front of him. Horror swamped him as he stared at the burning building. She couldn't still be in there—could she?

Leaving Ronnie in the car, he blindly forged a path through rain and smoke to one of the side doors. As he ran, he glimpsed men on their knees, gasping for air and swearing between breaths.

"Crazy bitch," one of them exclaimed in a choked voice.

Switching directions, Malone headed for him. He was halfway there when something plowed hard into his shoulder.

"*Oomph!* Oh, hell!"

It was a woman, and he caught her by the arms before she could take off. She wore a black bra, panties and a torn red blouse.

She raised her knee to his groin, but he'd learned that trick years ago and offset it by spinning her around and clamping his forearm across her throat.

"I'm looking for a woman," he said in her ear. "Her name's Bella. I'm told she helped you to escape."

The woman relaxed, stilling her struggles and twisting her head partway around. "You know Bella?"

He frowned. "Do you?"

"I came back to help her. We were running together, but we got separated in the confusion. I'm Florrie."

"Is she still in there?"

Coughing, Florrie pointed to the taller, darker building next door. "Wilma said she saw her run in there. The guards started to follow, but one of the Birds told them to back off. I was just going to see—"

"I'll go." Malone released her abruptly.

"Do you want me to—"

"No. Just get out of here as fast as you can."

He left her staring after him as he flipped up his jacket collar and darted through the streaming rain to the tall black building. A grimy plaque labeled it the House of Mann. The door was locked, but rather than search for one that wasn't, Malone applied his weight to it. Five painful thumps later, the latch gave.

Wind, rain and thunder swept him inside. A repeating flicker of lightning illuminated his surroundings.

Empty. He glanced up. If one of the Birds had waylaid the guards, that must mean she wanted to kill Bella herself.

He started for the stairs, all the while reproaching himself for not picking up a gun somewhere along the line. Thunder rattled the metal railing. He climbed on, bypassing the second floor when his sharp eyes detected a weak sliver of light emanating from under an upper door.

She was alive, he told himself flatly. She had to be. He wished he didn't care quite so much, but he did—and she *was* alive.

Although unaware of it, he must have spoken out loud, because a cool, female voice behind him said, "Oh, she'll be alive, Mr. Malone, at least for a while."

He waited for a beat, steeling himself for the confrontation, then, turning slowly, met the gaze of the woman who'd managed to catch him off guard. He arched one dark brow. "Charmaine Parret, I presume?"

Her mouth curved in a serene smile. Reaching up, she stripped not only the black hat and veil from her head, but also her dark, shoulder-length wig. Shaking her hair to loosen the wheat blond curls, she regarded him calmly. "It's Charmaine Parrette, actually," she replied. "Creole. I changed it to fit." Her gaze challenged him. "I'm Belladonna's mother."

AMANDA'S NOT... Amanda's not...

The words echoed again in Bella's head. Not what? Dead? But she was dead; Bella knew that instinctively. Literally dead.

The answer was staring her in the face; she knew that as well. She simply didn't want to unlock that particular door.

"Arabella." Donna used her full name now, drawing it out in a taunting fashion. When Bella looked at her, her lips stretched into a smile as macabre as those of the mannequins.

She was going to suffocate in here, Bella thought, frantic. Why on earth hadn't she gone about this more logically?

Oh, Malone, she reflected with a deep pang. *If only I'd thought they would have let you live.*

But the glitter in Donna's eyes told her that, had he been with her now, Malone would have been dead already, if not by Donna's hand, then by Charmaine Parret's.

Her head throbbed; thunder crashed; the creature in the rafters rustled, then settled. Bella loved Malone. Did she love Donna? She still could not find a single scrap of feeling for her sister—her twin sister, a person for whom she should have felt an integral connection.

Under scrutiny from scores of mirthful eyes, Bella ventured to ask tentatively, "Who—who is our mother?"

The woman's smile widened. "You're using the present tense, so my fine English instincts tell me you already know."

Bella's heart sank. "Not her," she whispered. "God, please, anyone but her."

"Sorry, Sis," Donna said with a shrug. "But she's it. For what it's worth, she hired Mick Tock to kill you."

Agape, Bella stared. "Is that supposed to make me feel better?"

"Absolutely." With her palm, Donna checked the tips of her spiky hair. "You see, I wanted Rudge to bring you in—you know, bring you to me. But not her, no sirree. Kill And Be Done With It, that's her motto. Like I said, she has no flair for the dramatic."

Bella refused to acknowledge the sensations growing like a toxin inside her. She asked the less daunting of the questions that haunted her. "Where is she now?"

The gun wagged. "Who knows? Around. It doesn't matter. I run the show these days. She sticks to a silent partnership. Except where you're concerned. She would insist on poking her nose into this one. But at least she didn't turn, like Hobby, or sell out, like Tock. Well, they've both paid their dues."

Thunder shook the floor and walls. "Tock's dead, too?" Bella was shocked in spite of herself.

Donna grinned. "Yup. And it wasn't a pretty sight, either."

Bella preferred not to hear the details. "Who killed him?"

But even as she posed the question, she glimpsed a movement among the mannequins. Something scratched and scrabbled high in the shadowy rafters. And with that sound came the answer Bella had suspected all along.

"She did. . . ."

THE MOVEMENT RESOLVED itself into two people. They emerged from the mannequin ranks single file.

Bella's heart leapt into her throat at the sight of Malone's impassive face. He'd guessed, damn him. And now he was being held at gunpoint by a hatless and obviously wigless Charmaine Parret. Ex-best friend of the woman who, for twenty misguided years, Bella had believed to be her mother.

Amanda's not... Well, the mystery of the end of that sentence had been cleared up. Unfortunately, in its wake came a host of other grisly questions and answers.

With Donna's gun trained on her and Charmaine Parret's—she couldn't think of the woman as her mother—response ringing in her ears, Bella didn't dare move. Donna had killed Mick Tock!

"You look shocked, Bella," Charmaine now said, nudging Malone through the maze of mannequins to the cleared space where she and Donna stood. "Why is that, I wonder? Because I'm holding your champion at gunpoint, perhaps? Or are you surprised to learn that your baby sister is, like me, a murderer?"

"I am not her baby sister," Donna declared indignantly. "And so what if I killed Tock? He deserved it—for his treachery and for his greed. It's no different from what you did to Robert."

Charmaine's eyes flicked first to Malone, then to Bella. She was a beautiful woman, Bella noted distantly, but did she look like Amanda? Maybe a little, in the shape of her face and the color of her hair. The Mississippi accent had long since given way to a more-cultured dialect, somewhere between American and British.

"Over there," Charmaine told Malone. Then, to Donna, she said, "Our manner of killing, and for that matter, our reasons for doing it, are worlds apart. You murder, then mutilate, or vice versa, depending on the victim. I simply get the job done. You take pleasure in your handiwork, I do what I must. Rage does not drive me to sever a corpse's fingers."

Bella fought the nausea that climbed into her throat. She felt cold and dizzy. How could a twin of hers be so depraved? Had watching their father die taken its toll on Donna in another way?

Donna glared at Charmaine. "Butt out," she snapped. "How I kill and whom I kill is my business. I am the busi-

ness, I'm Romaine now. Me. The fairest, the best, the
smartest and the strongest. Don't even think about it, Malone," she barked. "You're as big a turncoat as Tock. You
were on Rudge's payroll when all this started." She turned
bitter eyes on Bella, who hadn't moved a muscle for several
minutes now. "What is it about this witch, anyway? Why
does everyone want to help her? Okay, granted, Tock was
in it for himself, but what about Hobby? What made him
turn into a bleeding heart?"

Malone moved silently to Bella's side. She wanted to run
to him, but his eyes and her instincts cautioned her not to.

Her mind went off on a tangent. "Romaine lives"—that's
what Hobby had said. He'd also said Belladonna was
crazy. . . .

Bella shivered. Wind wailed at the walls and eaves. It
seemed to her that the mannequins leaned forward, listening to them.

Another shudder worked its way through her. Was it getting darker in here or just creepier?

Donna's eyes gleamed. Her gaze shifted rapidly between
Charmaine and Bella. "A red bicycle, that's what he gave
me, and red boots to match. A pretty color for a pretty girl,
he said, but I knew he thought that Bella was prettier.
Though how could she be? We looked the same. But if that
was true, then I couldn't be prettier, either, could I?" She
raked her twin with a venomous glare and balled her fist. An
unbecoming flush mottled her cheeks. "I hated Belladonna. I hated being second. I hated you. I still do. I want
you gone. But not quickly, the way Charmaine had it
planned. Oh, no, I want to watch you die. I want to see you
get ugly."

"Look, uh, Donna," Malone began in a reasonable tone.

But Donna was beyond reason, beyond sanity, in Bella's
frightened opinion. And she was waving her gun wildly.

"Shut up, Malone," she snarled, whirling. "All of you,
shut up!"

Somehow Malone managed to edge closer to Bella.
Glancing at her briefly he conveyed a message with his eyes:
Be ready. . . .

Ready for what? They couldn't possibly overpower both women, not without at least one of them getting shot.

Charmaine moved in and out among the plastic bodies, her gaze contemplative as she regarded Donna's red face. "Leave it alone," she advised, passing behind a pale Chinese mannequin. "Bella's here. What she remembers is no longer important. Let me deal with it now."

"No!"

Charmaine's voice grew firm, rose above the grumbling thunder. "Yes."

"I'm in charge, Charmaine, not you." Without warning, Donna grabbed Bella by the arm, yanked her around and jabbed the gun into her ribs. But if Bella recalled one thing about her sister, it was her vanity. Ramming an elbow into Donna's stomach, she knocked her gun arm aside and, spinning, dragged her fingernails sharply across her sister's cheek.

"Aagh!" Donna screeched like a shot crow and clapped a hand to her face. "I'll be scarred!" she shrieked. Lightning emphasized the oozing scratches on her skin. She drew her hand away in horror. "I'm bleeding!"

Malone didn't hesitate. Thrusting Bella aside, he launched himself at Donna's gun arm. But she was quick, and livid at this point. She jerked her hand up and pulled the trigger.

Bella landed on her backside with a painful, *"Oomph."* Three mannequins toppled over beside her, their garish faces smiling in the dim light. Ignoring them, she pushed the hair from her face and scrambled to her feet. Where had the bullet landed? Where had everyone gone?

"Don't move," ordered a deadly calm voice behind her.

Bella obeyed. Trembling, she offered in a semisteady voice, "He'll kill her, Charmaine."

"Or she'll kill him."

No...

Charmaine raised her voice. "Donna? Where are you?"

A shot embedded itself in one of the plastic stomachs, but where it came from, Bella couldn't be sure. All she knew was that the sound distracted Charmaine.

Dropping to the floor, Bella scrambled away on her hands and knees.

More shots whizzed by. She felt cool air on her cheeks—not from a door, but from a point above her. The roof, perhaps. Oh, but there were no ladders in here, and she couldn't leave Malone in any case.

The darkness thickened. Donna's frenzied shouts overrode the lash of wind, rain and thunder.

Breath held, Bella forged a path through the mannequins. Their fingers tangled in her hair; their faces now seemed to be staring down at her. Like lurid, painted angels, she reflected. Oh, God, where in this nightmare of imitation humanity was Malone?

A shot raced past her, then a second, then a third.

"Where's Bella?" Donna shouted.

"I have no idea," Charmaine retorted. "I can't find either of them."

Bella's body went limp with relief. Then she gasped and almost screamed as something touched her hip.

Chapter Nineteen

A hand came down firmly over her mouth. "It's me," Malone hissed.

Bella relaxed again, but only for a moment. When she turned her head, she saw the blood that trickled over the sleeve of his leather jacket.

"You're hurt," she whispered.

He shook his head, eyes darting. "It's nothing, a scratch. Keep quiet."

Ahead of them, mannequins began to topple like dominoes. "Where are you?" Donna shrieked.

Bella stifled a gasp as one of the mannequins crashed right before her startled eyes. This one had only a mouth, no nose or eyes. The mouth was curved in a leering smile, as if painted there by Donna's hand.

"She's crazy," Bella breathed to Malone.

"Tell me about it." He nudged her shoulder. "Okay, go. Head for the door. I think they're on the far side of the room."

Thunder rolled across the sky, causing the building to shudder.

More mannequins toppled, the clawed hand of one actually raking through Bella's hair.

"Stop! Don't move, either of you." Donna materialized directly to Bella's left. "Not a muscle, not even a hair."

Bella lifted her eyes. "Donna, please don't," she whispered.

Eyes glazed, cheeks the color of chalk streaked with crooked lines of red, Donna used both hands to train the gun on Malone.

"Get up," she growled. "The two of you. Twitch one muscle, Sister, and your lover's history. You got that?"

Mutely, Bella nodded.

"Good." With her thumbs, Donna cocked the hammer. "Not that it'll matter one way or the other. Bye-bye, Mr. Butt—insky."

"Donna, no!" Desperation made Bella throw herself at her sister. Malone moved at the same time.

The gun went off as Donna teetered backward on her high heels.

"My God!" she gasped, "You bastard...!" Then she staggered sideways.

The reason for her action was not immediately evident, and Malone gave Bella no opportunity to understand it as another shot flew past them. While Donna made a garbled sound and slowly sank to the floor, he shouted, "Run!" and flung Bella unceremoniously into the outstretched arms of a dummy. To her astonishment, he turned his back on Donna's prostrate form as he did so.

"Get it over with, Rudge," she heard him say calmly.

Bella's head snapped up. "Rudge!"

She spied him slumped against the front wall, his jacket bloodier than Malone's, a cigar clamped, as always, between his teeth, a Magnum resting in his lap.

"Damn bitch Bird," he grunted, slurring his words. "Shot me. Some payment..." His head lolled to one side on the last word.

A double flash of lightning illuminated his face. His complexion looked as waxen as the dummies'; but for the moment he continued to breathe.

As for Donna... Bella glanced fearfully over her shoulder. "Is she...dead?"

Crouching, Malone touched Donna's neck. He nodded grimly. "I'm sorry, Bella."

She bowed her head. "So am I."

He came up beside her, pulling her into the shelter of his arms and glancing around. "Where's Charmaine?"

Bella opened her mouth to say she didn't know, but Charmaine calmly replied, "Right here." There was no apparent anger in her voice.

Lightning flashed in diamond patterns across her face and neck, creating weird shadows beneath her hazel eyes. A gold wedding band glinted dully on her left ring finger. Amanda, Bella realized, pressing herself against Malone's arm, had worn only a silver ring on her right forefinger. No wedding or engagement rings. How could she have missed such obvious detail?

The room had taken on a surreal aspect. Mannequin spectators, some standing, some lying flat on their backs, watched the proceedings with seeming fascination.

The rustling Bella had forgotten about filtered down again from the cobwebbed rafters. The lone light bulb swung on its cord, adding to the grotesque shadows that fell across Charmaine and the mannequins. Bella shivered. With her flawless, unlined features, Charmaine Parret could have been a mannequin herself.

The gun in her hand didn't waver. "I don't relish what I have to do," she said, in that same uninflected tone. "But I suspected such an ending was inevitable from the day that harlot nanny of yours took you away. First she stole my husband, then one of my children. As for the other child—well, I blame a large portion of Donna's affliction on her, as well. Not all of it, mind you. To witness a murder at the tender age of nine would affect the mental balance of anyone, even if that person purported to understand it. Oh, Donna could run the business—run it very well, in fact—but she had a streak of vicious jealousy in her that I never could offset. No, don't move, Mr. Malone," she cautioned. "I don't want to do this, but that isn't to say I'm not going to. The difference between Donna and me is that I prefer a single thrust to the torture that, unfortunately, was her bent."

Malone endeavored to ease Bella behind him, but she refused to let him become Charmaine's primary target.

"You won't get away with it," he said levelly. "It's gone too far this time. You know that, Charmaine."

The woman glanced at Donna's unmoving form, then lifted her eyes to his. "Birds fly," she replied. "I can, too. Don't worry, Bella, this won't hurt. Hobby was lucky, you know, to die as easily as he did at your sister's hands. Fortunately for him, the season being what it is, there were too many people on the piers for her to indulge her whim as she undoubtedly did with Tock—and would surely have done with you and Mr. Malone, as well. She delighted in pain before the fact and mutilation after. As I said, it depended on the circumstances."

Rain pelted the walls and high roof. But it was the eerie howl of the wind that made Bella's skin crawl, as if the mannequins were laughing wildly at the scene unfolding in their midst. She looked at Malone who gave his head an unknowing shake. "Why pain?" she managed to ask.

Dull light and shadow marbled Charmaine's face. "Who knows? Probably because pain isn't pretty. Donna enjoyed seeing other people at their worst. That might stem from the fact that she was a twin. Certainly she was jealous of you."

Malone raised a skeptical brow. "Jealous because Bella was supposed to take over the business?"

"Yes. But more, I think, because Bella was older than her."

"By two minutes," Bella murmured. "She really was crazy."

"Unbalanced," Charmaine corrected. The gun came up a notch. "I, on the other hand, am perfectly balanced. Oh, I'm vain, I won't deny that, and cold as milk from a witch's—well, you know the expression. But my sanity's never been in question."

"What about your maternal instincts?" Malone demanded.

She challenged them with her eyes. "I've never had any, I'm afraid. I'm sorry, Bella. I wish it could have been different. If it's any consolation to you, Amanda was more your mother than I could ever have been." The corners of her mouth tilted. "Goodbye, Belladonna."

The light bulb continued to swing on its cord. Lightning flickered. Fireworks exploded and thunder crashed. For a split second the room turned black—a split second during which Bella and Malone both reacted to the threat before them.

Muttering a prayer, Bella grabbed one of the mannequins' outstretched hands. Yanking hard, she swung it heavily into Charmaine's shoulder. At the same instant, Malone brought his foot up and kicked the gun away.

Off-balance, Charmaine clawed at the air. But all she could do was manage to catch the light bulb as it swung toward her. She collided with Bella, who collided with Malone. Then she lost her balance completely and stumbled forward.

"Be careful!" Bella gasped, trying to maintain her own balance. But Malone held her tightly against him, pressing her face into his shoulder.

"Don't," he said. When she would have looked anyway, he pressed his mouth against her hair and repeated harshly, "Don't."

But she had to see, had to know. Turning slowly, Bella scanned the dim and dusty floor. She spotted Charmaine facedown, lying half on top of Donna, half on a mannequin, unmoving yet unmarked, as far as she could determine.

She dug her fingers into Malone's forearms. "What happened? Is she dead?"

Without answering, he set her aside and walked over to the women. The lightning cast long, macabre shadows over the bodies of her mother and sister. Bella sank to her knees as Malone rolled Charmaine Parret onto her back. There between the woman's ribs she spied a knife—a long, slender pink knife exactly like the one in her nightmares, only deadlier. A letter opener once, it was now a razor-sharp weapon.

"Donna was holding it," he revealed. "It's been modified. She probably used it to cut off Tock's fingers and intended to use it on you in a similar fashion."

Bella blinked, unbelieving. "Malone, look at it. This is the same weapon Robert was killed with. And look! On the top. It's a raven."

He returned to her, drawing her to her feet. "It could be any bird, Bella."

From the rafters, the rustling sound came again. Bella's eyes rose to the darkened hollow, and this time she saw the creature responsible for the noise. A large black raven sat perfectly still on a cross beam, staring down at the bodies of the women below.

Oh, Lord. Squeezing her eyes shut, Bella leaned against Malone's warm, solid body. In the end, even the Birds hadn't been able to escape Chen-Li's raven of death. The shadow had crossed her path, but she'd survived. And so had Malone. A feeling of warmth spread through her as she rested her head against his shoulder. Thank God, so had Malone...

Above them the raven let out a harsh croak and, spreading its wings, flew off into the darkness. A raven that reminded Bella strongly of a crow...

"IT SHOULDN'T HAVE BEEN like that," Bella said sadly several hours later. "My twin sister, my mother and my uncle were the Birds. So was my father at one time." She sighed. "Swift, Parret and Crowe. Romaine—from Robert and Charmaine. I should have realized that as soon as Donna told me that Amanda wasn't my mother. It could only have been Charmaine."

From the circle of Malone's arms, she let her eyes wander around the crowded club—the Dragon's Tail Club in Chinatown, where it seemed to Malone that half the city had gathered to ring in the New Year. It was done, finished as far as the Birds were concerned—but not for Bella, and therefore, not for him.

He released a heavy breath. Damn, but he wished he didn't love her. Or maybe he just wished he didn't love her so much. He would have gone for the Birds with his bare hands if they had harmed her before he reached the House of Mann this afternoon.

The Dragon's Tail was a sea of post-Christmas color. Green, red, gold and silver streamers, glittering stars and twinkling lights made a mockery of the storm outside. Rudge was alive and in the hospital. Would charges be laid against him? Malone doubted it. After all, the bounty hunter had saved their lives by shooting Donna.

Malone let his hand trail through Bella's silky hair. "I should have known that picture Rudge gave me wasn't you. There were differences even when Donna disguised herself as you. She was very hard."

Bella leaned against him, watching the revelry on the dance floor, her back pressed temptingly to his front. "I took a good look at that picture before we turned it over to the police, Malone. Donna looked a lot like me. You couldn't possibly have known. No one could have. I didn't anticipate a twin, so why should you? It's Hobby's message I've been thinking about—well, among other things. I thought it said that Belladonna was mad, but now I realize that Bella came at the end of one line and Donna at the beginning of the next one. He left out the comma."

"Ergo, we read the name as Belladonna rather than as two separate names. A small but important omission."

"Mmm." Nudging him gently in the stomach, Bella glanced into his hooded eyes. "Do you want to dance? It's almost midnight, you know. Your cousin's been out there for an hour already."

Malone's gaze shifted to Ronnie and his cousin, Diana. Diana grinned and waggled her fingers at them.

She'd loaned Bella a long black sliver of a dress that clung to every curve of her slender body. Simple though it was—it had only one sleeve and virtually no back—on her that damned dress was driving him to distraction.

Bella led him to the dance floor, musing, "There were other things, too, Malone, other details that I missed."

"Such as?"

"Amanda wore a faded denim pantsuit, hardly any makeup and only one ring, which wasn't a wedding band. My mother had someone who'd worked for a fashion designer make her clothes, hired a personal cosmetician and

was married. Most married women wear wedding rings."
Wrapping her arms around his neck, she stared up at him.
"I remember more things now, but not all of them. I do remember Donna throwing her toys against the wall because
of the pony Hobby gave me. I also realize that it wasn't a
mirror I saw on the other side of the room the day my father was killed, because the girl I saw didn't have pigtails,
and Donna was right, I always wore my hair in pigtails,
braids or a ponytail."

Malone studied her beautiful, troubled face. "Did Lona
know the truth?"

"I think she knew part of it. She mentioned a letter. I
think Amanda must have written to Lona before she left
England. And I'm not sure, but I have a feeling that the
picture case was the only thing the Alaskan police found
after the crash. They never did, and probably never will,
locate Amanda's body."

Malone glanced away for a moment, then back into her
cloudy eyes. "She *was* your mother, you know. Amanda,
not Charmaine. She saved your life and gave her own in the
process. No mother could have done more."

"I know. And Lona was my grandmother, related by
blood or not. But I still don't understand." Catching his la-
pels, she shook them slightly. "Why don't I have feelings for
Donna and Charmaine? I remember things about them, I
just can't find any feelings. Am I a horrible person, Malone?"

He drew his brows together. "Of course not. You're just
human. You probably never had strong feelings for them.
They don't exactly sound like the most lovable people in the
world."

"Hobby was nice, I think. Well, nicer, anyway. And
Robert, too, although I don't remember much about him
yet."

"You remembered the letter opener that killed him."

Bella swayed against him, head bent. Malone had to grind
his teeth to fight the desire that shot through him. "I
thought it was a knife, a skinny pink knife. It's funny, isn't
it, the things that stand out in your mind? Donna must have

remembered it, too. Obviously, she kept it after our father died. So much tragedy, and all because Robert and Amanda had an affair.''

"People have murdered for less," Malone noted darkly. "Be thankful your mind chose to block the horror out. Donna's just snapped.''

Giving in to temptation, he pulled her closer. He was both pleased and a little unsettled when her arms tightened about his neck. But, no, it would be fine between them—nothing, God forbid, like his parents' marriage. It would be what they made it, and they certainly had plenty of bad examples from which to learn.

"I had a mother and a twin sister for a while this afternoon," Bella reflected. "I think I liked it better when I had only Lona." She raised her eyes to his. "She's being cremated tomorrow, you know.''

"I know.''

"You don't have to come, Malone.''

"Yes, I do.''

"Why?''

He hesitated, then sighed. "Because I love you, Bella Conlan.''

"It's Arabella, actually. And I love you, too. I love you, and I'm going to marry you.''

He stared as if he hadn't heard her correctly. "I beg your pardon?''

"Oh, relax, will you?" She smiled for the first time since the nightmare had ended that afternoon. "We'll go slowly. But it's going to happen sometime, so you might as well accept it. Chen-Li said so, and I believe in him. Did you see that raven or crow or whatever it was flying around in the rafters the whole time we were in the House of Mann today? And what about the carving of the raven on top of the letter opener? Explain that if you can.''

"Coincidence, Bella, nothing more.''

She hit him. "It was destiny. Accept it, Malone. If Chen-Li says we belong together, we belong together. Anyway, in spite of everything, I'm glad we met him. He's quite a character.''

Malone grunted. "Yeah, well, you haven't met a character until you've met my father."

She brightened. "Are you going to introduce us?"

"Maybe."

"When?"

"Next year."

Bella started to object, then caught the humor in his eyes and followed his gaze to the far wall.

"Ten seconds," he said. "Nine, eight . . ."

"Forget the countdown, Malone." She moved suggestively against him. "Let's start the New Year with a bang, hmm? And I don't mean the kind we heard this afternoon." Taking his face between her hands, she reached up and set her mouth on his.

In the very back of his mind, Malone heard Chen-Li's voice whispering softly, "What is in the past is no more. It is to the future that we must look and in the present that we must live. The ravens of death have settled on the Birds. The poison of Belladonna is gone, and with it, I think, your own ghosts. The future lies before you. . . . Happy New Year."

As the clock began to toll, Bella raised her mouth from his and smiled. "It's over," she promised. "The Birds are dead. So is Belladonna. Dead and gone, Malone. Just like Romaine. . . ."

Epilogue

The storm continued, with great sheets of wind-driven rain, loud cracks of thunder and lightning bright enough to illuminate the darkest corners of Chen-Li's apartment.

The old man stood at the window, gazing out on the Birds' warehouse. It neither surprised nor startled him when two sleek, black ravens swooped out of the night to perch on his window ledge. Nor did it surprise him that both birds had expressions on their faces. One of them stared in an openly accusing fashion; the other studied him calmly, as if weighing the merits of his psychic abilities.

The first bird let out a coarse squawk and clawed at the glass. The vengeful sound brought a smile to Chen-Li's lips. Sliding his folded hands into the bell of his sleeves he regarded them in turn and recited softly:

"Mirror, mirror of the soul,
Evil deeds must take their toll.
As you sow, so shall you reap.
I shall, of course, this secret keep."

That said, he turned from the birds and shuffled silently away into the darkness.

BRIDE'S BAY RESORT

UNLOCK THE DOOR TO GREAT ROMANCE AT BRIDE'S BAY RESORT

Join Harlequin's new across-the-lines series, set in an exclusive hotel on an island off the coast of South Carolina.

Seven of your favorite authors will bring you exciting stories about fascinating heroes and heroines discovering love at Bride's Bay Resort.

Look for these fabulous stories coming to a store near you beginning in January 1996.

Harlequin American Romance #613 in January
Matchmaking Baby by Cathy Gillen Thacker

Harlequin Presents #1794 in February
Indiscretions by Robyn Donald

Harlequin Intrigue #362 in March
Love and Lies by Dawn Stewardson

Harlequin Romance #3404 in April
Make Believe Engagement by Day Leclaire

Harlequin Temptation #588 in May
Stranger in the Night by Roseanne Williams

Harlequin Superromance #695 in June
Married to a Stranger by Connie Bennett

Harlequin Historicals #324 in July
Dulcie's Gift by Ruth Langan

Visit Bride's Bay Resort each month wherever Harlequin books are sold.

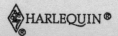

HARLEQUIN ®

BBAYG

Yo amo novelas con corazón!

Starting this March, Harlequin opens up to a whole new world of readers with two new romance lines in SPANISH!

Harlequin Deseo
- passionate, sensual and exciting stories

Harlequin Bianca
- romances that are fun, fresh and very contemporary

With four titles a month, each line will offer the same wonderfully romantic stories that you've come to love—now available in Spanish.

Look for them at selected retail outlets.

Fall in love all over again with

This Time... MARRIAGE

In this collection of original short stories, three brides get a unique chance for a return engagement!

- Being kidnapped from your bridal shower by a one-time love can really put a crimp in your wedding plans! *The Borrowed Bride*— by **Susan Wiggs**, *Romantic Times* Career Achievement Award-winning author.

- After fifteen years a couple reunites for the sake of their child—this time will it end in marriage? *The Forgotten Bride*—by **Janice Kaiser**.

- It's tough to make a good divorce stick—especially when you're thrown together with your ex in a magazine wedding shoot! *The Bygone Bride*— by **Muriel Jensen**.

Don't miss THIS TIME...MARRIAGE, available in April wherever Harlequin books are sold.

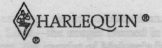

HARLEQUIN ®

BRIDE96